RAVE REVIEWS FOR CINDY HOLBY!

FORGIVE THE WIND

"Wow! What a great addition to this series. Like all the
ot... and
sh... tion

"... ews

"... ews

"... you
e... iews

"... joy-
a... view

"... Civil
V... iews

"... me
i... rs."
...ette

"... look
a... view

"Cindy Holby takes us on an incredible journey of love,
betrayal, and the will to survive."
—The Best Reviews

A NEW RELATIONSHIP

Zane took off his hat and dusted it along the side of his leg.

"I'm sorry for what I said about the letter. I had no right to comment about…er…your life."

"An apology," Mary said to Glory. "He must be civilized, after all."

"Hey," Zane said indignantly. "I didn't have to do this, you know."

"You don't owe me an apology," Mary said, turning to look at him. "I owe you one. I'm afraid I haven't been on my best behavior since I've met you, Mister Brody."

"Zane. Call me Zane."

"Zane."

"We do seem to have gotten off on the wrong foot."

"If I recall, I was off both of mine when we met," Mary said with a smile. Her brown eyes sparkled in the dim light of the car.

"Yes, you were," Zane said with his roguish grin. He propped an arm on the stall.

Lucifer opened one gold-rimmed eye.

Don't you start with me, goat…

"You're used to getting your way, aren't you?" Mary asked.

"I don't know what you're talking about," Zane said.

"With women. You just smile like that and show your dimples and they do what you want."

Whirlwind

CINDY HOLBY

LEISURE BOOKS   NEW YORK CITY

For Justin.

A LEISURE BOOK®

September 2006

Published by

Dorchester Publishing Co., Inc.
200 Madison Avenue
New York, NY 10016

ISBN 0-8439-5308-X

The name "Leisure Books" and the stylized "L" with design are trademarks of Dorchester Publishing Co., Inc.

Printed in the United States of America.

Visit us on the web at www.dorchesterpub.com.

The test of character is not how much we know how to do, but how we behave when we don't know what to do.

—Tom Hilton

Prologue

Chicago, 1857

"How many times do I have to tell you to stay out!" She had seen him quicker than usual and she seemed madder than usual. Maybe business was slow.

"You're right, her face does turn purple when she's mad," the teenage boy commented to the whore he'd been flirting with. The madam of the house stood before him with her bejeweled hands on her satin-covered hips and her ponderous breasts threatening to overflow her tightly wrapped corset. The madam's face turned an interesting shade of violet, a bit darker than the revealing robe she was wearing.

"What did you say?" the madam screeched.

The boy flashed a dimpled grin and turned dancing hazel eyes in her direction as he casually stood and straightened his clean but well-worn clothes.

"I said I was leaving," he said. "But I'll be back," he added with a wink for the young whore who still lounged on the chaise. She giggled at his antics.

"Not until you've got some money in your pocket, you worthless piece of trash," the madam said, following his path to the door with her eyes.

"I'm betting I can get it for free," he said with another flash of his dimples.

"Not in my house," the madam exclaimed, and for emphasis she stomped after him and slammed the door behind him.

The boy stepped out into the bright sunshine of a late summer afternoon and perused the passers by in the street. His stomach rumbled in hunger as he thought about his options. He had gone into the whorehouse more to beg a meal from one of the tenderhearted girls who worked there than for any other reason, but he usually found he was up for a poke if the opportunity presented itself. He could generally get one for free if he used his charm. He was quite good at it, or so they told him, even if he was only fifteen years old.

He'd better move to a better section of town if he wanted some quick money. It was approaching the dinner hour, and he had found that was the best time to score some easy coin. He ducked into an alley by one of the finer restaurants in town to keep the proprietors from running him off and waited for the right opportunity to present itself.

"Hey, mister, you want me to watch your horse?" he asked a gentleman who dismounted in front of the restaurant. The cut of his clothes was fine without being fancy and the man's poise spoke of money and position.

Not the boy's usual target, but he had to be bold if he was going to eat tonight. He was getting desperate.

The man paused by the hitching rail and looked the boy over.

"How old are you, son?" the man asked.

"Fifteen, sir."

"Where are your folks?"

"Dead, sir," the boy answered. Why was the fellow asking him all these questions? He wasn't the law, was he? Another look at his fancy duds made him think not.

"Where you from?" the man continued.

The fellow seemed inclined to talk awhile, and since he really didn't have anything else to do, except maybe, hopefully, eat, the boy scratched at the fine whiskers that had just begun to make an appearance on his chin. "Most recently Chicago . . . sir," he added with a flash of his dimples. It hadn't taken the boy long to learn that charm and manners would usually get him what he wanted.

"And where are you going?" the man asked with a wry smile of his own. He leaned casually against the rail as if he had all the time in the world.

The boy looked into the sharp blue eyes of the man and realized that this man would not be easily charmed by his fine manners.

"I'm not really sure, sir. Somewhere, I hope." If nothing else, the years he had spent with his grandfather had taught him how to be direct when he needed to.

The man smiled as if he kept a great secret, and the boy was suddenly curious to know more about this dignified stranger.

"What guarantee do I have that you'll watch my horse and not steal it instead?"

"Well, for one thing, they hang horse thieves," the boy said, flashing his dimpled smile.

"That's only if they catch them. This is a pretty fast horse; you could be gone before I got through the door."

The boy looked at the animal and saw that it was a fine piece of horseflesh. The saddle was of the best leather and would fetch a pretty penny. It was also well worn, as if the man spent a lot of time in it. It took a while to get a saddle broken in like that. This man worked hard at what he did, and from the looks of him, prospered.

"Because I'll give you my word," the boy said, suddenly wanting this man to like him for some strange reason. "And when I'm hired to do a job, I do it to the best of my ability."

The man looked at him and smiled his secret smile. "How about this?" the man said. "You watch my horse, and if you're still here when I get back, I'll pay you."

"How much will you pay me?" the boy asked.

"You'll have to wait and find out," the man said. "Do we have a deal?" The blue eyes held his gaze for a moment.

The boy looked up and down the street, weighing his options. What if he hung around here for a couple of hours and didn't make any money? He should be moving on to a sure thing. Most of the time, he talked his marks out of a few coins and then went on his way to the next one, but this man was different. He seemed . . . interested.

The boy stuck out his hand. "Deal," he said as the older man shook it and went into the restaurant.

* * *

The evening stretched on. The boy's stomach growled. How much longer would he have to wait? How long did it take to eat a meal, drink a cup of coffee and have some pie?

Pie . . . Memories of the scent of fresh-baked pie sitting on the ledge of the one window in a sod hut filled his mind. His mother, heavy with child again after years of hoping, smiled at him from the door as he helped his father with the planting of a garden. He could still feel his father's hand as he ran it through his hair and told him it was time to eat. He could still see the smile on his mother's face as she laughed at their coming, her two men with their wide, dimpled grins and dancing eyes, as she always said. His mother was beautiful and refined and taught him his manners and how to read and write and quoted Shakespeare, while his father taught him the value of hard work. Someday he'd have a home like that with a pretty wife baking him pie . . .

"So you're still here," the man said.

"Yes, sir." The boy stood and tried not to appear too anxious, but the growl of his stomach gave him away.

The man arched an eyebrow at the sound and pulled a roll of bills from his pocket. The boy swallowed hard. He had seen rolls of money like that before. But that had been in a different place and time. He also knew that he had never seen it handled so casually.

"I'm going to give you a choice," the man said as he peeled off the paper money. "You can take this money and have yourself a good time with it, or"—the blue eyes looked at him intently—"you can get yourself a hot meal, a bed and a ticket on the stage to Laramie, Wyoming."

"What's in Laramie?" the boy asked.

"A job on my ranch. If you want it. The work will be hard, but there's a place for you to sleep out of the weather, and the meals are fine. You could have a home there if you wanted. It's all up to you, son."

"How do I find your ranch?" the boy asked. "If I decide to go," he added.

"It's the Lynch ranch," the man said. "Anyone in town can point you in the right direction."

The boy chewed on his lip as he weighed his options. "I think I'll give it a try," he said.

The man smiled and nodded, as if he'd known that would be his decision all the time. "What's your name, son?" he asked.

"Zane Brody, sir."

"I'm Jason Lynch," he said. "And I think you're going to work out just fine."

Chapter One

Laramie, Wyoming, 1867

Zane Brody, who often considered himself one of the best at what he had just completed, rolled onto his back and stretched his cramped muscles. With a sigh of contentment, he pulled the worn sheets of a well-used bed in what was once a quality whorehouse up to his waist and leaned his back against the rails of the brass headboard.

"Lordy, Missy, I thought we were going to bust straight through the wall," he said as he looked at the stain on the ceiling. It looked as if the roof must have leaked after the last rain. If Maybelle didn't start turning loose of some of her money, the place was going to fall down around her bejeweled ears.

Missy giggled as she usually did. Funny how her giggle wasn't near as cute as it used to be. A few years back he'd considered it one of her more endearing traits. Of course, Missy herself wasn't near as cute as she used to be. Especially in the full light of day. That was as good an excuse as any for cutting out his afternoon visits.

Maybelle's had at one time been a high-toned establishment. But that was back when it had been the only whorehouse within a day's ride of Laramie. Now it had all kinds of competition from the city of tents that had sprung up like weeds on the outskirts of town. The railroad was being built, and all kinds of businesses had come to Laramie to serve the workers who had moved west with the rails of progress.

Zane stretched again as he slid to the edge of the bed and searched for his pants.

"Where you going, sweetie?" Missy asked as she rolled against his back, pressing her ample breasts to his bare skin.

"Time's up," he said as he jerked his pants on.

"That's never stopped you before," Missy said, pouting.

Zane looked over his shoulder and gave her one of his roguish smiles, flashing the deep dimples in his cheeks.

"Jenny made me promise that I'd come back to the ranch for supper," he said as an excuse. "I've got mail for her and Cat."

"Oh, they can wait." Missy flounced back on the bed and picked at the frayed embroidery on her pillowcase.

" 'Love looks not with the eyes, but the mind and is therefore winged cupid painted blind.' " Quoting

Shakespeare usually got him around Missy when he needed to. "You know I love you, sweetheart." Zane also knew how to turn on the charm when necessary. "But Cat and Jenny run the ranch."

"Don't I make you happy?" Missy asked as she pulled the sheet up over her breasts.

"You're the best lay in town," Zane said with his broad grin.

The screech that came from Missy's talented lips filled the rafters of the house. She jumped to her feet.

Zane ducked as a pillow came at his head.

"You two-timing, cheating, whoring son of a bitch!" she screamed. "How many women does it take to keep you happy?"

Zane looked at the usually sweet and docile Missy in amazement. He was sure her shrieks could be heard on the street, and a heavy pounding on the stairs let him know that Maybelle was on her way up.

"Simmer down, sweetheart," he implored as he grabbed his shirt and hat.

"You've been visiting the other houses, haven't you?" Missy stood beside the bed, naked as the day she was born, with a lamp in her hand.

"No!" Zane exclaimed. "I promise, you're the only one." He settled his hat on his head and quickly jerked on his suspenders. "Except for one night, that is—"

The lamp crashed against the wall, nicking his fingertips as it went by. Zane shook his hand in pain.

"How dare you two-time me!" she screamed and hastily searched for another weapon.

Zane spared time for a prayer of thanksgiving that

his gun was downstairs behind the bar as the rules of the house required. There was no doubt in his mind that she would shoot him if given a chance.

"It was Randy's bachelor party," Zane tried to explain, seizing on his fellow cowhand's recent marriage as a convenient excuse.

"Zane Brody, you're lower than a snake's belly in a wagon rut!"

The door flew open as the generous curves of Maybelle crashed into the room, followed by Bill, her bouncer.

"Howdy, Zane," Bill said with his easygoing smile.

"Howdy, Bill." Zane ducked behind Maybelle's wide girth as Missy stomped the floor. "Did we wake you?"

"It was time to eat anyway," Bill assured him. "What's got her in such a tizzy?"

"He's been two-timing me!" Missy answered for Zane, loud enough for everyone in the vicinity to hear.

"You'd better leave now," Maybelle said to Zane, trying unsuccessfully to calm Missy.

Downstairs a few minutes later, Zane could hear Missy still venting her anger when Bill handed him his gun from behind the bar. Zane grinned sheepishly at the confused faces in the lounge and went out into the dusk that had crept over the streets of Laramie.

"I guess you survived," a voice said from behind him.

"Did you think you were going to have to come in and rescue me, Sheriff?" Zane asked playfully as his friend Jake Anderson stepped up beside him.

"Nope. I was planning on watching her tear you apart."

"I thought you were supposed to keep the peace," Zane said as they walked down the street.

"She wasn't bothering *me* none," Jake replied dryly.

"Glad to know you're watching out for me, buddy," Zane laughed.

"The last place I ever want to be is between you and a woman. Especially when that woman wants to skin you alive," Jake said. "Besides, I've got some trouble of my own."

"Trouble?"

"There was a knife fight down at tent city, and one of the railroad workers was hurt pretty bad," Jake explained.

"So why didn't you take him to Doc's?" Zane asked.

"I did. But Doc couldn't help him."

"Why not?" Zane asked, surprise filling his eyes.

"Doc's dead. I found him sitting at his desk with his eyes wide open, deader than a doornail."

"Dang," Zane said.

Chapter Two

Doc was dead. Zane had to shake his head again in wonder as he rode home. He had gone with Jake to Doc's office and seen the crotchety old man sitting at his desk with his eyes wide open, just the way the sheriff had described.

Doc had always done things in his own way and time. It looked as if he had just sat down and died without giving it another thought. No pain, no suffering, no one crying over the loss.

That would be the way Zane would go if he had any choice in the matter. Of course, it would be nice to know that he would be missed.

His friends would miss him, wouldn't they? They had spent a lot of years together. He had arrived at the Lynch ranch all those years ago within days of Jake and Caleb, all three of them trying to hide their loneliness as a grizzled old cowhand taught them their jobs. Then Ty had shown up, then Chase and Jamie, and they had all lived together and worked together and played together before they had all gotten foolish and fallen in love. All except Zane. He had seen what being in love had done to his father. Losing his mother had killed him in a roundabout way, when you got right down to it. Of course, Zane hadn't been there; he only knew what his grandparents had told him. But he had always been smart. He had figured out the rest. If nothing else, the years had taught him that it was best for the soul just to enjoy the benefits of a woman without any of the attachments.

And if his friends didn't miss him when he was gone, then he sure had wasted a lot of time with them. Though when he got right down to thinking about it, that was all he had ever done. Waste time, waste money, waste his life away. He was, after all, his father's son, and the fact that his father had not only ruined his mother's life, but also his own had been pounded into Zane's head.

Zane rode past the schoolhouse. A fresh coat of paint had been added in hopes of impressing the new teacher, if they ever found one. Too bad his buddy Randy had up and married the old one. Not that Zane would have bothered to look twice at her. She was as skinny as a fence post and didn't have a curve on her. But she was a nice match for Randy, and they had gone back to Missouri to work her family farm. The courtship had been slow, even with the teacher living at the big house on the ranch, but it had finally paid off for Randy.

Getting married was something Zane never gave a

thought to. Maybe because when he had just been a boy he had seen what it could do to people.

He was content as a bachelor. He was comfortable and didn't want for anything.

So why did he feel so . . . restless?

Why was he so lonely?

"Dang," Zane said to the silver moon up above. Maybe he should just turn around and head back to town for some more entertainment.

But he knew he'd feel just as empty afterward as he felt right now. Besides, he had mail for the ranch in his pocket—a letter for Zeb from his mother back in North Carolina, another for Ty from his brother and something for Cat from some fancy school back in New York City. Probably something about the new schoolteacher. Zane riffled through the letters in his pocket. There was one for Jenny also. He would have laid odds that it was from a horse breeder in New York about a mare she wanted to buy.

You would think that just once, in all the years since he had come to Laramie, there would be a letter for him.

After all, his grandparents had to know he was still alive. He sent them a letter every Christmas.

What should he expect? He had been warned when he walked out the door. But he had left anyway. Was he better off now?

He liked to think so.

Maybe if he told himself that enough, he'd believe it.

Zane turned down the drive toward the big house and let his horse fall into a gentle canter. He knew the animal was anxious for its own stall and the gentle hands of the former slave Zeb to give him a good rub-down. Zeb's wife, Cleo, stood on the porch with their baby Hector in her arms.

"What's the news from town, Mister Zane?" Cleo asked.

"Doc's dead," Zane announced as he stepped up on the wide front porch.

"Sho 'nuff?" Cleo asked. "How?" She stuck a finger in Hector's mouth to keep him from crying while Zane told the story.

"You best tell Miz Cat," she said when he was done with his news. "She's gonna be fit to be tied, not knowing who's gonna deliver her baby."

"She's got time," Zane said. "She's just cranky because she's stuck in that bed."

"Wouldn't you be too?"

"Not if I had you waiting on me hand and foot," Zane said with a flash of his dimples.

"Lawdy, Mister Zane, you best not let Zeb hear you talking like that," Cleo laughed as she followed Zane into the house.

"That reminds me," Zane said as he pulled out the mail. "Looks like Zeb got a letter from his mama."

"Thank you," Cleo said and stuffed the letter inside her shirt, away from the grasping hands of Hector.

Zane bounded up the stairs, whistling as he went. He knew he'd be the center of attention for a while, since he had the news of Doc's death and everyone would want to know the details. It really was a pity about the man. His gruff exterior had hidden a grand heart, and he would be sorely missed by the community.

Too bad old Doc had never taken time to have a family. Zane wondered if Doc had ever been lonely.

Upstairs, Zane knocked on Cat's door and pushed it open. The voices of Cat, her husband, Ty, and Jenny had carried into the hallway, so he felt no hesitation just walking into the group. After all, they were all practically family, even if he did draw pay.

"You look fit to bust," Jenny said as he came into Cat's bedroom. After Jason's death, Cat and Ty had moved into the master bedroom, which was the largest in the house. A desk and some chairs had been carried up so Cat could continue her part of running the ranch while confined to her bed. After several miscarriages, she'd been ordered to stay off her feet for the duration of her pregnancy. The three of them were going over some papers when Zane walked in. "What's the latest?" Ty asked.

"Doc's dead." Zane let his words sink in.

"What?" they asked in unison. "How?"

"Looks like he died in his sleep, although his eyes were open when Jake found him," Zane informed them.

"Dang," Ty said. "I wonder what killed him."

"His heart probably just stopped beating," Cat said. "But now we don't have a doctor." Her hand went protectively to the small mound of her stomach.

"We've got plenty of time to find a new one before the baby gets here," Ty assured her.

Zane saw the fear in his clear blue eyes as Ty looked over at Jenny, who was a little further along than his wife.

"And we've got plenty of experience between all of us with delivering babies," Jenny assured Cat.

"Says the woman who's not supposed to have any

more," Cat said wryly. Her green-gold eyes were wide with fear, but she was obviously trying not to show it.

"Those were Doc's orders," Jenny said, caressing her bulge. "But easier said than done. We'll be fine, barring any disasters." She looked at Zane. "Have they made the funeral arrangements?"

"Jake and the minister are taking care of it. Doc didn't have any family."

"Bless his heart," Cat said. "I guess we kept him too busy to have one."

"He made his own choices," Jenny said. "I guess we'll never really know why now." She turned to Zane. "Did you get the mail?"

"Yep," he said. "Got it right here." Zane passed on the letters. He hung around as the missives were open, knowing that any news would be shared.

"Looks like we've found a teacher," Cat announced. "Her name is Mary Dunleavy. She's been teaching for a few years in New York City and she wants to come west."

"A city girl?" Zane asked skeptically. "I bet she won't last long out here," he scoffed.

"We'll find out," Cat said. "If we can post the letter on Monday, we can have her here in plenty of time before the school year starts."

"Send her some traveling money," Ty said.

"And hurry," Jenny added. "I'm ready to get Chance and Fox back in school."

Everyone laughed. School had only been out for a few weeks and the two six-year-olds were already driving everyone crazy with their wild adventures.

Jenny's husband, Chase, had taken them out to the lake where he was working on a house for the family. He was sure that a day of dragging and stacking huge rocks would wear the boys out in no time.

"Dang, Jenny, you sound like you're sorry you've got children," Zane said.

"You're just sorry because you're always tripping over them," Jenny replied tartly as she studied her letter.

"It *is* getting a bit crowded around here," Zane said with his wry grin.

"So why don't you take a trip?" Jenny suggested.

"Where?"

"How about New York, to pick up a horse?"

"What?"

"I'm the proud owner of a thoroughbred mare with a bloodline that goes all the way back to England. Her name is Diamond Glory, and she's sitting in a stable back in New York waiting for someone to come get her."

"And you want me to go?"

"Why not?" Jenny asked. "You've been complaining for years that you always get left behind while the rest of us are off having adventures. Here's your chance to go."

Zane scratched his chin as he considered Jenny's proposal. A trip to New York.

"Are you going to pay my expenses?"

"The finest hotels," Jenny said.

"And meals," Zane added.

"Meals, transportation, hotels. I'll pay for everything but your whores."

"Dang, Jenny, what kind of man do you think I am?"

Jenny rolled her sapphire blue eyes, while Ty was overcome by a fit of coughing.

"I'm pretty sure I can get it for free back East," Zane declared.

"I think I'm going to be sick," Cat said from her bed.

"Do you want me to pick up the schoolteacher while I'm there?" Zane asked.

"You stay away from her, Zane Brody," Cat said. "Far, far away."

Chapter Three

Mary Dunleavy slowly wandered through Central Park, ignoring the hustle and bustle around her. She let her mind drift back to the past as her feet followed the same path they had taken many times.

Two years ago today . . .

Two years since her life, once so full of hope and joy, had taken a sudden downward turn.

She gently touched the gold ring that hung from a delicate chain around her neck.

Two years since her husband, Michael Dunleavy, had died in a fire after saving a mother and child who had been trapped on an upper floor of a burning building. Michael Dunleavy, a handsome Union soldier, had swept her off her feet after seeing her strolling through the park one fine day. She had met him at the end of April, they had married in May, and he was dead by the beginning of July. Married and widowed, all before her nineteenth birthday.

Michael, with the laughing blue eyes and the boyish laugh, was gone, leaving her to wander alone the paths where they had fallen in love and planned their future.

A future without him. Mary realized she was still clutching the letter from Wyoming in her other hand and stuffed it in her reticule.

The city that had captivated her when she had come from Denver to be with her brother a little over two years ago now held no charm. She should have moved on with her life a long time ago, but it was hard to let go.

It wasn't as if she had never lost anyone. Her parents had died when she was just a baby. Her first memories were of an orphanage and her brother. Then their uncle and aunt had come for them and taken them to Denver, where they settled into a happy life. When they reached adulthood, her brother Marcus had come to New York to study medicine and she had joined him in the city soon after their uncle had died. She had already earned her teaching certificate and had quickly found a job in one of the city schools.

She had loved her life then. The war that had divided the country had just ended, and the future seemed golden. She had all of her life before her in a city that was full of excitement. It had been a joy just to watch the city awaken each day.

There was always something happening. She loved just watching the glamour of the society folk, who put on their best clothes and rode through the park in elegant carriages that cost more than a schoolteacher would make in a lifetime.

Then there were the harmless flirtations with handsome young men who walked by and tipped their hats, changing their route so they could walk by again.

Michael had done that very thing. And on the third pass he had stopped her by taking her hand and declared that he would die if she did not tell him her name.

It was right on this very path that it had happened. A path that she had walked a thousand times in the past two years. A path that led nowhere.

Mary took a deep breath. Michael would not want her to mourn her life away. He would want her to live. He would want her to love. All she had done for the past two years was read numerous books and miss him.

It's time . . .

She took the letter from her bag and read the essential parts again. A lovely school, the building practically brand-new, children from ranches and farms outside of Laramie, Wyoming. An invitation to stay in one of the rooms on the ranch of the woman who had built the school to honor her dead father. A steady income, a place to live, a new beginning.

We are very happy that you have accepted our offer and look forward to your arrival as soon as possible. Please telegraph and let us know when you will arrive, and accept this draft to cover your expenses. . . . Sincerely . . .

Mary's breath left her body in a whoosh and the letter fluttered to the ground as she was forcibly lifted from her feet. Her dark blue skirts flew up around her as the rush of a team and carriage filled her deep brown eyes with surprise and shock. A pair of strong arms held her securely against a solid body as the carriage passed by. She had nearly walked into its path.

"That must have been a very interesting letter."

Mary looked down at the letter, which had been trampled into the mud from a recent rain.

"Oh, my," she exclaimed. The arms released her, and her rescuer retrieved the letter from the ground, holding the muddy page gingerly between his fingers.

"I hope you've got it memorized," he said with a dimpled smile.

"Oh, no!" Mary exclaimed. "Where's the draft?"

"The what?"

"The bank draft! There was a bank draft with the letter."

Her rescuer surveyed the ground. "I hope it didn't mean life or death, because it's not here," he said, his hazel eyes twinkling with suppressed laughter.

Mary looked at the man in frustration. For some reason, he seemed to think her situation was amusing.

Desperately she jammed her hand in her reticule, hoping and praying that the draft was safe inside. Her fingers closed around the paper, and she released a sigh of relief.

"It's here," she said.

"Looks like you've been saved once again," he said, his dimples flashing. "This must be your lucky day."

"Has anyone ever told you that you are extremely annoying?" she asked indignantly.

"Well, yes, as a matter of fact I've been told that on numerous occasions . . . ma'am."

Mary looked up into the twinkling hazel eyes. The "ma'am" had been added, almost as if he were trying to hide something.

His medium brown hair was straight as a stick and seemed to be newly washed, as it was a bit damp on the ends. The stranger looked and smelled fresh and clean. He must have just had a bath and a shave. His clothes were nice too, not expensive but of good quality and well-fitted over his muscular physique. He seemed rather sure of himself as he stood in the park with his feet set wide and his arms crossed, her letter still dangling from his fingertips.

He noticed her perusal and pushed back his hat, revealing sun streaks in his hair as he flashed his dimples and a nice set of teeth at her. She noticed his hands. They were clean but hardened by work. One nail was purple, as if it had been smashed against something.

"Are you from the city?" she asked. She had to say something. He was just looking at her as if he were ready to share a great secret.

"No, ma'am, I'm just passing through." He gave her an appreciative look with his twinkling eyes. "Would you care to show me . . . around?"

"I think not," Mary refused, snapping her reticule shut. The nerve of this . . . man. She grabbed her letter from him and turned on her heel, wishing for the first time in a long while that she were back in Denver on the farm. If this had happened there, she would have pushed him down in the mud of the pigpen to wipe that self-satisfied smile off his face. If Marcus had been here, he would have set the man straight, she thought to herself as she stormed down the path toward the street.

" 'These words are razors to my wounded heart,' " he said to her retreating form.

He was quoting Shakespeare in the park? He knew lines from *Titus Andronicus*? Had he perhaps escaped from the local sanatorium?

Mary kept going.

"You're welcome," he shouted after her.

Mary stopped in her tracks and whirled around with her hands on her hips.

"For what?" she asked indignantly.

"Saving your life," he said. He took off his hat and bowed, grinning the entire time.

"Oohhh." Mary stomped her foot and took off, her skirts flaring out behind her.

She just knew he was laughing at her.

With a smile on his face, Zane watched the young woman stalk off.

That is one nice backside . . .

She was a bit smaller than he liked up top, but she was very pretty with her dark brown eyes and her dark, wavy hair all pinned up under that cute little straw hat with the red bow and yellow and white flowers on the side. She had smelled really nice too, fresh and clean, not covered up with perfume to mask the odor of an unwashed body.

"Dang," he said to himself. "I should have got her name." As if she would have told him. Zane grinned as the top of her hat disappeared into the crowd of pedestrians. If he'd set his mind to it, he could have found a way to get her name.

Not that it mattered. He was in town for just a few days. After the long trip, first by stage and then by rail, he was anxious to be out and about.

He had gone to a bathhouse and enjoyed a steamy bath, shave and haircut. After that, he had bought himself a new suit right off the rack. He was ready for a good time in the big city.

I hope I don't run into anybody I know.

What were the chances of that happening? He'd been gone for years. He hadn't even been shaving yet when he'd left New York.

He wondered if the old place had changed any since the last time he'd seen it.

He would just walk by the house and see what he could see.

He remembered some of the houses as he walked down Fifth Avenue. They had seemed bigger in his memories, but he had only been eight years old the first time he had seen them. He had also been terrified. But why shouldn't he have been? His mother had only been dead a few months when the men hired by his grandfather had come to Missouri and taken him away from his father. His father never should have told his in-laws she was dead or where he and his son were. His mother's parents had hated his father. He was beneath her breeding and social standing. But his mother had loved him and run away with him.

Just like he had run away the first chance he got.

The fence was still there. It was still as high as he remembered. Of course, scaling it had never been a problem for him.

Zane stood across the street from the house and let

his mind drift back to the last time he had stood within the walls of what he had always considered a prison. He had been accustomed to being able to see for miles and miles across endless plains. His grandparents wouldn't even allow the draperies to be opened to let in the sunlight. He was driven to a private school in a closed carriage each day, then brought home and locked behind the gates as if he were a prisoner.

How he had hated this place. No wonder his mother had run away. Tyranny was not a replacement for love. His autocratic grandfather held complete control over every minute detail of the lives within his domain. But he hadn't been able to control a traffic jam that caused his mother's escort to be late picking her up. He hadn't been able to control a chance meeting in the street between Zane's mother and father that led to secret assignations and the eventual elopement.

Nor had he been able to keep their son from shinnying down a drainpipe and walking to the seedy side of town just to prove that his grandfather did not have total control over his life.

When his escapade was discovered, the old man compared him to his father, who had long been dead from the grief of losing his family.

"Your father was a womanizer!" his grandfather had ranted. *"He just wanted her for her money. He was a bastard, you know, just like you are."*

Zane knew his parents had been married. Not that it mattered to his grandfather. The wedding had been accomplished without his permission; therefore he did not recognize it.

"I showed him. I cut her off without a dime."

And his parents had scraped out a living on a small homestead in Missouri. If his father had wanted her for her money, he had a strange way of showing it. His father had built a life for his family until his mother and baby sister had died in childbirth.

"You reap what you sow, boy. You're just like him, sneaking off to be with whores. Your mother should have been a whore instead of my daughter."

It was then that Zane had realized his father had struck out on his own when only a few years older than he was, and he'd had a wife to support. Why shouldn't Zane be able to do the same thing?

He had left that night and headed west, supporting himself with his wits and never-ending charm, something else he had inherited from his father. He wasn't afraid of work. His early childhood had been spent helping his father as much as he could on their tiny homestead, while his mother had given him an education at home. Then he had attended the private school in the city. He was educated, he was smart, and he knew the value of hard work. He had survived, but he had only found a home when he landed at the Lynch Ranch.

And he had never told a soul about his life except to say that he was born in Missouri and was an orphan. Both of which were true.

He hid some things from his friends. He hid his education. He hid the fine manners that he had been taught. They would lead to questions he didn't want to answer, things he didn't want to explain. And he never mentioned the fact that he was the only living heir to a fortune that his grandfather would rather burn than give to him.

Yet he sent his grandparents a letter every Christmas, telling them he was alive and well. He figured he owed that much to his grandmother, who had been kind to him. She loved him as much as was possible for her to do. Zane had realized long ago that all the love had been squeezed out of her by her husband's hateful ways.

She probably never even saw his letters. His grandfather probably ripped them to shreds without opening them.

A movement at an upstairs window caught his attention at the same time that a carriage pulled up in front of the house. An older man carrying a black bag went through the gate and knocked at the front door. Zane didn't recognize the butler who opened the door. He wasn't surprised. Help didn't last long in that house. Servants would rather starve than put up with his grandfather's miserly ways.

Someone must be sick. I hope it's the old bastard. I hope he's suffering and pissing all over himself.

Zane moved on down the street with the elegantly dressed pedestrians who were out for an afternoon stroll.

The flowers on her hat were daisies.

Now what made him think of that?

Chapter Four

"Are you sure this is what you want?"

Mary looked at her older brother. She was so proud of him. Dr. Marcus Brown had impressed his professors while going to school and training in the hospitals of New York City. His ability had been enhanced by his experiences treating some of the wounded soldiers who were fortunate enough and rich enough to be brought to the city, bringing him cases that most doctors would never see in a lifetime. The war was a harsh teacher, but he had learned from it, and most of his patients had gone on to live full lives.

He was a genius in Mary's mind. An absolute saint. He was all the family she had. And he was very worried about her.

"I'm sure," Mary told him. "It's time, Marcus. It's past time. Michael wouldn't want me to spend the rest of my life in mourning. I loved him with my whole heart. I miss him terribly. I'll never forget him."

Her brother's strong arms folded around her, and her head found its familiar place on his shoulder.

"I want you to be happy, Mary."

"I want me to be happy, too." She leaned back to look up into his wise brown eyes. "And I want you to be happy. You need to quit worrying so much about me and start concentrating on yourself."

"You mean settle down and find a wife?"

"Yes, I do. It's not as if you don't have any prospects."

"You mean I have to pick just one?"

Mary playfully cuffed his arm. "Yes," she laughed. "And you can only have one."

"How about if I become a Mormon?"

"Marcus," Mary said in exasperation. "Are you thinking of moving to Utah?"

"Well, not exactly."

Mary looked at his handsome face, puzzlement written on hers.

"I was thinking of going with you to Laramie."

"What?" Her face lit up at the thought. Was he saying what she thought he was saying? Could he? Would he go with her? "What about your practice and your patients?"

"Mary, I'm mostly diagnosing rich ladies' delicate conditions. I want to practice real medicine. I want to go someplace where I'm really needed, like our father was trying to do."

Mary's heart swelled at the prospect. "I always thought you were wasting your talents here."

"I'm not so sure about that," Marcus said modestly.

"Please," Mary protested. "You're a wonderful doctor and you know it."

Marcus turned away, embarrassed at her compliments.

"Besides, Jenny lives near Laramie," he said, directing their talk away from his talents. Marcus had become friends with Jenny and her brother Jamie during the time they spent together in the orphanage in St. Joe, Missouri. "I'd love to surprise her."

"I forgot about that," Mary said. "I don't really remember her much, except that she was very pretty. I remember Jamie better because of his scars."

"It was so sad that he died," Marcus said.

"Good people die all the time," Mary replied softly.

His arms came around her again.

"I know. I'm sorry that Michael died. I'm sorry you had to go through that. I wish that Michael had lived and the two of you were giving me nieces and nephews right now."

Mary squeezed back the tears.

"I'll give you nieces and nephews someday," she said. "I promise."

"You'll probably have every cowboy and soldier in Wyoming camped on your doorstep," Marcus said. "Then you'll get to choose."

"But what about you? From what I hear, there are a lot more single men out West than single women."

"I won't have a problem at all," Marcus declared. "According to my sister, I'm a great catch."

Mary rolled her eyes and dissolved into a fit of giggles. She was overjoyed that Marcus was going with her.

"I guess we should pack," she said finally. "The train leaves first thing Monday morning."

"I'm sure looking forward to the trip," Marcus said. "It's been a while since I've traveled anywhere."

"Speaking of travelers, I ran into the most insufferable man in the park today."

"Really? What happened?"

"Well, he sort of saved my life," Mary began. "I was about to step in front of a carriage, and he picked me up just in time."

"He picked you up?"

"He grabbed me around the waist and swung me around."

"Oh," Marcus said, picturing it in his mind. "So what made him insufferable?"

"He seemed to think the situation was funny. It was almost as if he was laughing the entire time. He didn't have the look of a New Yorker, so I asked him if he was from here. He said no, and then he had the audacity to ask me to show him around the city."

"You would have just been returning a kindness, wouldn't you?"

"It was the way he said it," Mary explained. "Like it was a joke and he wanted to see me, instead of the city. I just wanted to slap him."

"So he got to you?" Marcus's brown eyes were merry as he looked at his sister.

"I wanted to choke him."

Marcus laughed. "Luckily for him, we're leaving. You'll never see him again."

"Thank goodness. If I saw that smirk again, I'd probably scream."

Marcus shook his head as his sister went to her room to pack. She had noticed a man. She might think she didn't like him, but he knew better. She had said the same thing about Michael the day he had approached her in the park. Maybe it was too bad that they were leaving. It would be good for Mary to spend time with a young man and find her heart again.

Zane was feeling sick. He hadn't felt this bad since he'd come down with chicken pox a few years back. And mercifully, he'd been unconscious through most of that experience.

He kicked away the sheets he had wrestled with the entire night and stumbled to the washstand. The image looking back at him from the mirror resembled a nightmare figure from the horrible dreams of the past night.

He was burning up. He was shivering. And he was supposed to be on his way north of the city to pick up the mare.

He splashed water on his face and over his hair, combing the wild strays into a semblance of order. A sudden cramp nearly doubled him over, so he quickly found his clothes and threw them on, missing a few buttons on his shirt and only managing to tuck it halfway in.

Zane considered the chamber pot for a moment and then stumbled down the stairs to the outhouse.

Oh, how it burned. Fear tingled up his spine as he gasped in pain, hoping that no one would hear him. He looked down in fright, sure that he would see lesions or swelling, but everything looked the same. It just didn't feel the same. It hurt like hell.

He had always been careful about the women he slept with. That was why he always went back to Missy.

But how careful is Missy? Does she check her customers?

And there was the night that he, Randy and Dan had gone down to the tents.

I swear, God, let this pass and I'll never go back. I'll be a saint from now on.

He straightened his clothes and stepped back into the light of day, blinking his feverish eyes. He needed to get a move on. He had a job to perform and he was bound to do it.

Zane slowly walked down the street to the livery stable. His head felt as if it were ready to roll off his shoulders and go bouncing away. He had reserved a horse to ride to the horse farm where Diamond Glory was waiting. He wished now he had rented a buggy and driver so he could sleep. It was Jenny's money, however, and he wasn't going to waste it.

Zane wondered how long it would take him to get to the horse farm. Not long, he hoped. Right now, he felt he might be dead before the day was over.

He deserved it, he guessed, for wishing ill fortune on his grandfather. At least he wasn't pissing all over himself.

Yet.

Chapter Five

"You don't look so good, son."

Zane glared at the man in disgust. He had a vague recollection of following the road up the Hudson River, but somehow he had missed the turn to the farm. After stopping at a tavern and getting a cool drink of water, along with another thorough face splashing, followed by a painful stop behind a tree to relieve himself, he realized that he had better ask for directions. At this rate he'd be lucky to make it back to the city by dark, and he had to get the mare to the station in time to settle her onto the train before the morning departure.

"I don't *feel* so good either," he said. "How far to Wentworth's stables?"

"You should be there within the hour," the man assured him and pointed out the direction.

Zane felt as if death would be preferable to another

hour in the saddle, and then there would still be the long ride back to the city. His mind registered that the countryside he was riding through was beautiful, with its neat white fences that alternated with stone walls, and pretty clapboard houses that had been around for a hundred years or more, but he couldn't appreciate scenic views at this time. He was sure he'd regret the missed opportunity later. What were the chances that he would ever be back this way again?

What were the chances that he would survive this trip?

Before the hour was up, he managed to find the stables, where Wentworth was impatiently waiting for him.

"You were supposed to be here before noon," the man remarked.

Zane nearly fell as he dismounted, too weak even to give the man a look. He had always admired the way that Jake could stop a man with just his looks. But it was a talent that Zane had never mastered. It was hard to look mean when your eyes were always dancing and you had big dimples in your cheeks. It was impossible when you busted out laughing every time you tried to practice the technique.

"Are you sick or something?"

"Something like that," Zane managed to get out. "Got any water?"

"Help yourself," Wentworth said, pointing to a well.

Zane found a dipper in the bucket. He was extremely thirsty, but settled for splashing it over his face and neck. If he drank it, it would have to come out eventually, and the thought was just too painful.

"Where's the mare?"

"Right this way."

Zane followed the man into one of a series of long, low barns. A leggy black mare was brought out of a stall, dancing restlessly in the corridor of the barn. Her coat shone in the dim light, and a long forelock covered a white patch on her forehead. The bleating sound of a goat assaulted Zane's ears. What was a goat doing in a horse barn? he wondered. Maybe he was so sick, he'd imagined the sound.

"Diamond Glory," the breeder announced. He went through a list of her forebears while Zane ran his hands over her. The mare tossed her head impatiently, but she was sound, and that was all he cared about.

Zane produced the envelope of cash that Jenny had given him, and in return he was given a packet of papers.

"Good luck," the breeder said.

Zane took the lead and started out the door, only to be bought up short when the mare refused to move. He turned in exasperation and looked at the breeder.

"What's the secret to getting her to move?" he asked. The last thing he wanted to deal with was a moody mare.

The breeder chuckled and waved to the stable boy. The boy opened the door to a nearby stall, and a white goat charged down the aisle.

"She don't go nowhere without Lucifer."

"What?" Zane asked.

"Lucifer. That's her pet. You want her to go with you; you got to take Lucifer too."

Zane looked down at the goat, which had stationed himself right in front of the mare. The goat stared up at him with gold-rimmed eyes. A set of horns curled out of the top of his narrow head, and a beard grew from his chin.

"Did Jenny know about this?" Zane asked.

"She never asked. She wanted to buy the mare. I'm throwing in the goat for free."

Zane stood with the lead in his hand, wondering if he could just wish himself into an easy death right on the spot. He was feeling worse by the minute, and the city wasn't getting any closer, nor was daylight going to wait for him.

"So how do I get the goat to move?"

"Just tell him what to do and he'll do it," the breeder said.

Zane just knew everyone on the horse farm was going to have a good laugh over him at supper tonight. Chances were that someday he'd have a good laugh about it also. But not today.

"Come on, goat," he sighed.

"Lucifer."

"Come on, Lucifer."

The goat looked him over again and then trotted out of the stable on his cloven hooves. The mare followed along, jerking on her lead as Zane moved with her. The goat stopped by Zane's mount and turned to look at him with his gold-rimmed eyes.

"This is some fever," Zane mumbled as he mounted his horse.

"Should I put a rope on him?" he asked the stable boy, who was watching him with a big grin on his face.

"Naw, he'd just eat it," the boy said, struggling to cover his laughter.

"Come on, Lucifer," Zane said to the goat and touched his heels to his horse.

"Ma-a-a-a," Lucifer said and fell in behind him, Diamond Glory contentedly by his side.

Zane heard howls of laughter as the quartet turned off the drive onto the road.

Zane finally had to stop because the pain of holding it in was worse than the pain of letting it out. Or so he thought. The burning was so bad that he had to grab on to a tree limb to keep from falling over.

To make matters worse, Lucifer wandered off into the woods, which made the mare anxious, which spooked his horse. His mount slipped its tie, and Zane had to chase down both horses. He trailed after his mount, which had to follow Diamond Glory since she was tied to the saddle. The mare was following Lucifer, who had found a nice kitchen garden behind a house in a small clearing.

Zane came onto the scene just as a woman appeared with a broom. She took a swing at Lucifer, who ducked and trotted off with a mouth full of greens.

"Devil's get!" she yelled. She saw Zane standing on the edge of the yard with the horses and turned her attention to him. "Is this your animal?"

"No, ma'am," Zane said. "I mean, yes, ma'am." He grabbed the reins. "I mean he goes with the horse."

"Get him off my property before he winds up in my stew pot," the woman yelled.

"Come on, Lucifer," Zane said.

"Ma-a-a-a." Lucifer stood in the middle of the lawn,

munching his greens and eyeing a line of freshly hung laundry.

"Come here, Lucifer, or I'll kill you myself," Zane said in what he hoped was an encouraging voice. Diamond Glory looked anxiously over her shoulder. Apparently, she was worried about her friend.

"Ma-a-a-a," Lucifer said and trotted toward Zane.

"Dang," Zane said in relief. He painfully mounted his horse and turned back the way he had come.

"Aren't you going to pay for the damage?" the woman called after him.

Zane kept going. All she'd lost was a handful of greens, and he wasn't about to get scammed over a goat. Besides, he had a feeling that if he stopped, he'd never get going again. He was cramping and couldn't decide if it was because of his fever or from lack of food. He was terribly thirsty but he didn't dare drink anything because of the end result.

Zane didn't think things could get much worse. But that was before it rained. A summer storm blew up and drenched him before he even knew the sky had clouded up. Lucifer ducked under some overhanging tree branches to stay dry, and Diamond Glory tried to follow, dragging Zane's mount with her.

And he had to go again. At least the rain was cooling him off, but he knew it wasn't going to help in the long run.

Zane made sure the horses were tied securely this time. Both of them. Then he went to a tree off the road and prepared himself for the pain while keeping one eye on Lucifer.

"At least I know why they named you Lucifer, you sorry sack of. . . . ahhh." The pain sent him searching for a tree limb to hold on to, but the limbs were all out of reach so he pounded his fist against the trunk, which just caused a different kind of pain.

Zane leaned his forehead against the tree while he relieved himself and wondered how his life had gone downhill so fast.

God . . . I don't want to die . . . not like this . . . not because of this . . .

You reap what you sow . . .

Why did his grandfather have to come back and haunt him now?

The next thing he saw was stars as he slammed into the tree and fell sideways with his privates exposed to the world.

"Ma-a-a-a," Lucifer bleated.

Zane opened his eyes to find himself staring at the curved horns on the top of the goat's head.

"I am going to kill you," he said when he could speak again.

He rolled over onto his hands and knees and staggered to his feet. He rubbed his backside after he tucked everything back in place.

How was he supposed to sit a saddle when his spine throbbed all the way up to the top of his head?

"Lucifer, I'm taking this mare to Wyoming. You can stay here and rot, for all I care."

Zane lashed the mare's lead tight to the saddle so that her head was right by his knee. She was coming with him, with or without the goat. He settled into the seat, gingerly, and touched his heels to his mount.

Glory protested, but she had no choice except to follow his mount, which was determined to get back to his nice dry stable. Lucifer was following anyway. Zane wouldn't give the goat the satisfaction of turning to check on him.

He must have dozed in the saddle, because the next thing he knew, the lights of the city were before him. He hadn't even noticed that it was growing dark. At least the rain had stopped.

"Ma-a-a-a," Lucifer bleated as they approached the livery stable.

"Get used to it," Zane replied. His words were slurred, but the prospect of a warm bed kept him going.

"Where am I supposed to put this goat?" the livery man asked when he rode in.

"With the mare," Zane said as he slid from the saddle.

"You didn't say anything this morning about stabling a goat," the man protested.

Zane handed him a wad of bills. "Will this make up for it?"

He didn't look happy, but he agreed, and Zane stumbled down the street to his hotel.

"What do you mean you gave my room away?" he asked incredulously when he was stopped at the desk.

"I thought you'd run out on your tab," the desk clerk explained. "So I packed up your stuff to sell and rented the room."

Am I in hell?

"Give me another room."

"I can't, they're all taken."

"Where's my stuff?"

The clerk handed him his valise from the baggage

room as Zane settled his bill. "Any suggestions as to where I'm supposed to spend the night?"

The clerk shrugged his shoulders.

Zane went out on the street and looked around. His fevered brain figured he had two choices. He could hail a cab and show up on his grandfather's doorstep and hope that he'd be let in. Or he could go back to the stable and bed down in the stall with Diamond Glory.

Zane headed for the stable.

Chapter Six

If only he could sleep. Zane found a blanket and settled down in the stall next to the mare, confident that the livery owner would wake him in plenty of time to make the train, if only to demand payment for the privilege of sleeping in the stall.

Lucifer had other plans for him, however. He considered Zane to be a sleeping banquet, and every time Zane managed to doze off, the goat began chewing on his hat, belt or buttons.

"I think I'll boil you alive," Zane promised the goat as he shooed him away.

"Ma-a-a-a," Lucifer replied from the safety of Glory's side.

The cramping became worse during the night, along with the burning. But now nothing was coming out. Of course, nothing had gone in either, but that didn't make the pain any less.

He wondered if he'd live to see Wyoming.

Mercifully, the soft light of dawn filtered through the stable window at last, and Zane wearily packed up his belongings and led Glory, with Lucifer trotting alongside, to the train. He made the mare as comfortable as possible in the stock car, locked Lucifer in the stall with her and then found an empty corner for himself. Using his valise as a pillow, he curled up in a horse blanket and went to sleep.

"No regrets?" Mary asked Marcus as the train passed over the river from New Jersey into the rolling farmlands of Pennsylvania.

"No regrets," Marcus said.

He had taken out his savings and spent most of the money on medical supplies that he would need to set up a practice in Laramie, where he could be close to Mary. He was anxious to see where Jenny lived. He had gotten a few letters from her, and her return address was Laramie. It would be great fun to show up on her doorstep and surprise her.

He had realized while making his hasty arrangements to leave that even after all these years, he really had no ties in New York City. There was no one he would truly miss.

Yet he would have missed Mary terribly if she had gone west without him. She was his sister. Except for her, he was all alone in the world.

"Excuse me, Dr. Brown." A porter had approached their seats. "Would you mind taking a look at a sick passenger?"

"Yes, I'll be happy to help," Marcus said. He retrieved his black leather bag, which had identified him as a doctor as soon as he boarded the train, and followed the porter out.

"He's in one of the stock cars. At first I thought he was a vagrant, but then I found his ticket while I was going through his clothes," the porter explained.

"What's wrong with him?"

"He has a fever," the man said. "Never even woke up."

"Even when you were rifling his pockets?" Marcus asked.

"Just trying to protect the other passengers," the man said.

Marcus wondered if the porter had made off with any of the sick man's money while searching him. Perhaps not. He had been concerned enough about the patient's welfare to look for a doctor.

Marcus found his patient lying on the floor in a stock car next to a stall that held a beautiful black thoroughbred and a white goat. The pairing was so odd that Marcus had to look again to make sure that he had seen right.

"Ma-a-a-a," the goat offered calmly, looking up at him with gold-rimmed eyes.

Definitely a goat.

Marcus knelt on the floor and pulled the blanket away from his patient's chest. It was soaked through with perspiration, as was the man's clothing. He was burning up.

"I need some water and something to bathe him with," Marcus said. "And go back and get my sister. I'm going to need some help."

Marcus looked the man over. His teeth and gums

were fine, and he looked well fed and basically clean, although it had probably been a few days since he'd had a bath. The only signs of previous ill health were a few faded scars on his forehead, probably from having chicken pox at some time in his life.

"So what's wrong with you?" Marcus asked the man. He put on his stethoscope and listened to the man's heart and lungs. "What's given you a fever? You're going to have to talk to me so I can figure out the problem."

Mary came into the car with a bundle of towels. The porter followed her with two buckets of water.

Apparently, he felt guilty for assuming the worst about the patient.

"Is there anything else?" the porter asked.

"A cot and more blankets would be good," Marcus said.

The porter nodded and went to hunt up a cot in one of the sleeping cars.

"What's wrong with him?" Mary asked when he was gone.

"He's got a high fever, but I don't know what's causing it."

Mary took off her short traveling coat and rolled up her sleeves as she knelt next to Marcus.

"Oh, my goodness," Mary said as she looked at the feverish face. The sun-streaked hair was sopping wet and sticking up in all directions and the rakish grin was missing, but she still recognized the handsome face. "I know this man."

"You do?"

"He's the man from the park. The one who saved me from being hit by a carriage."

"The insufferable one?"

Mary looked up at Marcus and found a devilish smile on his face.

"Yes," she said. "And soon to be the dead one if you don't do something to help him."

"It looks like he's going to get his wish," Marcus said.

Mary gave him a puzzled look.

"You're going to get to know him," he explained.

Mary shook her head in disgust at her brother's innuendo.

"I don't suppose you got his name?" Marcus asked.

"No, I didn't. I guess it would be easier to wake him up if we knew it," she said.

"It wouldn't hurt," Marcus agreed. "Help me get some of his clothes off so we can bathe him and I can look for a wound."

Marcus lifted the patient up from behind, and Mary unbuttoned his shirt. Her first impression of the man had been correct. The frame was covered with muscles, well defined even in his state of unconsciousness.

"Looks like he's not afraid of hard work," Marcus observed as he checked the patient's torso for wounds. The skin was perfect except for some more faint scars from chicken pox. The filtered daylight also showed that he was covered with a sheen of sweat. Marcus lowered the man back to the blanket and examined his abdomen.

"Any clues?" Mary asked.

Marcus shook his head. "Hold him up so I can look at his back."

Marcus lifted the patient and leaned him toward Mary. She caught his shoulders and held him upright while Marcus ran his hands over the sick man's back.

"He doesn't have any bruising that I can see," Marcus said. "Whatever it is, it's internal."

"Maybe it's pneumonia," Mary said.

"No, his lungs are clear and his heart is strong."

"Along with the rest of him," Mary grunted. "He weighs a ton."

"You can put him down."

"So what do we do now?" Mary asked when they had made the patient comfortable again on the blanket.

"We've got to get his fever down. Cool water will work best."

Mary wrung out a towel in the bucket and wiped down the patient's face.

"We should try to get some water in him, too," Marcus said. "He'll die of dehydration if we don't. Keep bathing him while I go check my supplies for something to take care of that fever."

Marcus left for the car that held his supplies. Mary wrung out the towel she was using and dipped it in the water again.

The rhythmic *clackety-clack* of the rails was a soothing backdrop of sound as she moved the towel over the man's chest and neck.

"So what brought you to New York City?" she asked his still face. "And why are you traveling with a horse and a goat?" She looked over her shoulder at the two animals, who were watching the proceedings with interest through the slats of the stall door. "I have to admit that's quite a mare, but I can't say much for the goat."

A pair of liquid brown eyes and a pair of gold-rimmed ones looked at her sternly as if to rebuke the insult to the goat. Mary shook her head and turned back to the patient. She found a set of bright hazel eyes looking up at her from beneath dark lashes.

"Did I pay you?" he said hoarsely.

"What?"

"Have I paid you yet?"

"No," Mary said, totally confused. "Pay me for what?"

"Your services." His head tossed. "I didn't catch your name."

"Mary," she said as she tried to understand what he was talking about.

"A girl as pretty as you must have cost me a fortune, but I'm sure you were worth it."

Mary's brown eyes flew wide in shock as understanding struck her.

"Ooohhh," she steamed. Even in his feverish state, he was insufferable. She flung the wet towel in his face.

He tossed his head and swatted at the towel, then groaned. He curled up on his side into a fetal position and moaned.

"It hurts. Oh, God, it hurts. Make it stop."

Compassion filled Mary as she witnessed his suffering. He didn't know what he was saying. He was dreaming. She picked up the towel, dipped it in the cool water and wiped his forehead.

"Everything will be fine," she said soothingly. "My brother is a doctor and he's going to take care of you."

"Doctor?" he mumbled. "Don't let my cock fall off."

The words were slurred and she missed them.

"What?" Mary leaned closer, hoping he would give her some information about his fever.

"Dang pox."

"Oh, my." Mary sat back on her heels and looked down in shock.

"Did he say anything?" Marcus asked as he came back with a vial in his hand.

"More than I want to know," Mary said. "I think he's got the clap."

Marcus had to take a moment to let the words sink in. He looked at the feverish face, and then at his sister, who was staring at the patient as if he was highly contagious.

"I guess I'd better take a look," Marcus said.

"Oh, my." Mary turned her head. "You can tell just by looking?"

"Yes. There's usually a discharge—"

Mary held up one hand while the other covered her mouth. "I don't want to know the details," she said as she tried to swallow her bile. "Just get it over with."

Mary went to the stall and ran her hand down the satiny neck of the thoroughbred. Both animals looked beyond her at Marcus, who was in the process of unbuttoning the patient's pants. Marcus spread the opening in the trousers and the drawers underneath and began his examination.

"What!"

Zane moved pretty fast for someone burning up with fever.

His hands covered his privates as he scooted away from his attacker and stumbled to his feet. He leaned against the wall of the car and willed his eyes to stay open.

"What are you doing?" he demanded. His feverish brain fought to bring things into focus. He was in the stock car, he remembered that. The horse was here, thank you, God, and so was that dang goat. The woman standing by the stall looked vaguely familiar. He never forgot a pretty face, especially one that pretty. So who was the man who had just a moment ago been. . . . fondling him?

"I'm Dr. Brown," the stranger said, extending his hand. "This is my sister Mary. We're traveling on this train, and the porter asked me to look at you when he couldn't get you to wake up."

Zane looked at the man. A doctor. He looked kind of young to be a doctor, but they all had to have been young at one time or another.

"Why were you touching me?" Zane asked, still unsure of what was going on.

The young doctor made a strange face, and the woman turned to look at the horse. Her shoulders were shaking, and Zane had the feeling that she was laughing.

"We thought you might have the clap," the doctor said.

Zane looked down and raised his hands to take a peek at his privates. "Can you tell just by looking?" he asked, his face screwed up with worry.

"Yes. There's a discharge. Have you had any?"

Zane shook his head. He couldn't recall anything like that.

"To tell you the truth, Doc, there hasn't been anything coming out. And it still burns."

"Why don't you let me have a look to make sure?" Dr. Brown said.

Zane looked past him at the woman, who seemed to be deep in conversation with Glory.

"All right," he said. He might as well get it over with. Dreading it was always the worse part.

Zane rolled his eyes to the ceiling as the doctor bent over him and looked closely at his penis.

"I'm going to touch you," he said.

God, I swear I'll never go back to those tents.

"Ma-a-a-a," Lucifer put in from the stall.

Do you think you could take care of that goat while you're at it, Lord?

The porter came in, carrying a cot and a blanket. He took one look at the pair in the corner, dropped the cot on the floor and walked out.

Mary studied the ceiling over the stall.

"I don't think you have anything to worry about," the doctor finally said.

Zane had not realized that he was holding his breath until he let it out with a big sigh.

"So what's wrong with me?" he asked as he buttoned his pants.

"I think you have an infection in your kidneys. We need to flush it out and get your fever down."

"Flush it out?" That sounded painful.

The doctor picked up a vial. "This is a purgative called calomel. It will clean out your system. You also need to drink lots of water. Keep drinking until you can urinate without feeling any pain."

"That's it?" Zane asked in relief. He had heard stories about cauterizing the inside of a man's shaft with a red-hot piece of iron. If all he had to do was take some medicine and drink some water, he would do it gladly.

He didn't have a disease.

Thank you, Lord.

"Thank you." Zane walked slowly toward the stall. "I'd better check on Glory."

"Is that her name?" the woman asked.

Mary. The doctor had said his sister's name was Mary.

"Diamond Glory," Zane said. "And the goat is Lucifer. He's named after his father. You know, the one down below, stoking the furnaces."

A smile graced her lips. "And what is your name?" she asked as he slipped into the stall.

"Zane Brody." Zane ran a hand through his hair and gave her one of his roguish grins. "I promise I clean up pretty good," he said.

"I know."

Zane checked the feed and water before he gave her a puzzled look.

"We met in the park."

"I saved your life." His dimples flashed with a grin as he recognized her. "And you didn't even say thank you."

Mary blushed. "I was a bit taken aback, sir," she said.

"I've been known to do that to women," Zane said as he leaned against the stall. He was as weak as a kitten but so relieved that he didn't have the clap, he felt like celebrating.

"Has anyone ever told you that you're insufferable?"

"Yes, I believe you did in the park," he said teasingly.

"Ooohhhh." Her brown eyes flashed as she turned away from the stall.

Zane stole a look at her backside as she bent to pick

up her coat. He raised his eyes to find her brother staring at him.

"I've mixed a draught for you," the doctor said.

"I reckon it's time to take my medicine," Zane said as he came out of the stall.

"Get some sleep and I'll come back to check on you later," the doctor said.

"Thanks, Doc," Zane said as he fixed his cot. "I feel better already."

Marcus took Mary's arm as they left the car.

"He's going to feel worse before too long," Marcus said. "I think I mixed the potion a little strong," he confessed.

"Good," Mary said. "He needs to spend some time on his knees."

"Praying for forgiveness?" Marcus asked.

"That would do for a start."

Chapter Seven

After a painful night, Zane had to admit he felt better. Especially since he knew he wasn't in danger of losing any valuable body parts. The train was scheduled to make a stop to take on water and firewood, and Zane felt it would be a great opportunity to get rid of his other problem.

Lucifer the goat.

He would simply take Glory off for some exercise, tie up the goat and then get back on the train. Surely a goat couldn't eat through a rope in the time it would take him to get Glory on the train.

Of course, he would have to convince Glory to get on the train without her dearest friend.

Zane gave the goat a satisfied look as he stripped down to his drawers and gave himself a thorough washing.

Lucifer just looked back at him with his gold-rimmed eyes.

"Don't you ever blink?" Zane asked the goat as he doused himself with a bucket of water.

"Ma-a-a-a," Lucifer replied.

Zane found some clean clothes in his valise and after combing his hair into order and dusting off his hat, which Lucifer had chewed on, he felt downright cheerful. All he needed now was a good meal and a fine woman.

But you promised you wouldn't do that again, remember?

Zane looked around the stock car as he wondered if his conscience had taken human form and decided to talk to him.

"Ma-a-a-a," Lucifer commented.

Straight from the devil.

Zane opened the stall to get Glory ready for her walk. He kicked Lucifer out of the way as he put on Glory's lead. The goat headed straight for Zane's valise, so he stopped what he was doing and shooed him back into the stall.

"Devil's git," he said, recalling the words of the woman from the New York countryside. "That's a good description, you stupid goat."

"Ma-a-a-a," Lucifer bleated.

Zane felt the train slowing down just as a mighty blast came from its whistle. Glory twisted her ears toward the sound as Lucifer ducked under her neck.

"That's right, goat. This is your stop," Zane said with a grin.

He pulled the door of the car open as the train

puffed along the tracks. Zane saw a water tower in the distance and what looked like a few buildings that could be part of a town. He figured they must be in Ohio or Indiana by now, but he couldn't remember how long he'd been on the train since he'd been asleep so much of the time.

He was leaning out the door for a better look when—

That damn goat!

Zane's arms grabbed for air as he sailed out of the train and rolled down a small incline away from the tracks. He slid to a stop with a mouth full of dirt and a deep gash in his right palm from a rock he had scraped on his way down. His spine throbbed all the way up to his head, and the sky was spinning as he flopped over on his back to catch his breath. His brain registered the fact that the train was coming to a stop.

He was grateful for that. There was no way he could have gotten up to catch a moving train.

Zane sat up and saw the goat's head peering around the door of the car.

"You sorry sack of—"

"Are you all right?"

It was the doctor running toward him. Behind him, Zane saw Mary with her skirts bunched up in her hands to keep her from tripping as she ran.

"We saw you fall," Marcus said as he stopped in front of Zane.

"I didn't fall, I was pushed," Zane said.

"Oh, my," Mary said. She covered her mouth with her hand.

"You're bleeding," Marcus said.

Zane looked at his hand. "I guess I am."

"Better let me look at that," Marcus said.

"It's going to have to wait, Doc. I've got to let Glory stretch her legs."

"I'll walk her," Mary volunteered.

"I don't know," Zane said. "She might be a handful for a city girl like you."

Mary opened her mouth to say something, and then snapped it shut.

"I think she's capable of leading a horse around," Marcus said as he wrapped Zane's hand with his handkerchief. He kept his eyes on his task.

"At least I've got enough sense not to be a target for a goat," Mary said saucily as she turned back toward the train.

"Did I say something wrong?" Zane asked as he watched the twitch of her skirts.

"Mary doesn't like to be told what to do," Marcus said. "She's independent."

"Kind of different for a city girl," Zane observed.

"We're originally from Denver," Marcus informed him. "We grew up on a farm."

"Oh," Zane said. "I just figured you were both from the city." His hand was starting to throb.

"I think you're going to need some stitches," Marcus said as he pulled the handkerchief away after blotting the blood. "We'd better go get this cleaned up."

"When I'm done with that goat, it's going to need more than stitches," Zane said.

"I take it you two don't get along."

"I get along fine," Zane said. "It's the goat that has problems." Zane looked toward the train. "She's going to need help getting the ramp down for Glory," he said.

"She'll never ask for it."

Zane laughed. "You know, I have a few women friends who are just like that."

"Must have something to do with the air in the West," Marcus said as they walked toward the train.

"Either that or the water."

Dang if Mary didn't have the ramp in place when they got there. Of course, she could have gotten help from some of the workmen who were hanging around the train, looking at her as if she were a goddess worthy of their adoration.

Zane watched in amazement as Glory calmly walked down the ramp next to Mary. Dang if that mare hadn't fought him nearly every step of the way, always worrying over that stupid goat, who was watching from the stock car. Why was she being so agreeable with Mary?

Mary walked Glory down the tracks while the workers went about the task of replenishing water and loading wood.

"My bag is in our car," Marcus said.

"I'll let you take care of my hand as soon as we get rolling again," Zane said. "Let me make sure that your sister doesn't have any problems getting that mare back on."

"All right," Marcus said. "I'm going to stretch my legs."

Zane watched him go toward a small mercantile next to the station.

Strange how the doc didn't seem to be much older than he was. But he had to be. After all, he was a doctor. That took years of schooling and training.

He sure did look young though. He didn't look a day over thirty.

And the sister . . .

Zane looked down the tracks and watched the gentle sway of Mary's hips beneath her dark blue skirt. She was wearing the hat again. The one with the daisies that she had worn the day he met her in the park.

For some reason, she seemed to be terminally put out with him. And all he had done was save her life. You would think that service would call for some civility on her part.

She sure did have a nice behind . . .

"Ma-a-a-a," Lucifer commented from the car. His gold-rimmed eyes were watching Mary and Glory walk the tracks.

"Well, come on out and join her," Zane said.

The goat ducked back into the car.

"Lucifer." Zane ran up the ramp into the car. "You're going to love it here, I promise."

The goat ran into the stall and ducked under the feed bin attached to the wall.

Zane followed, confident that he had the goat trapped.

"Come on, goat," he said and tilted his head as if he were listening. "Hear that? There's a bunch of nannies out there just waiting for a goat like you."

Lucifer looked at him with his gold-rimmed eyes.

"Glory's looking for you," Zane said encouragingly as he slowly stepped toward the goat.

"Ma-a-a-a," Lucifer bleated.

Suddenly the goat charged, his head down and his

horns aiming right for Zane's groin. Zane dove out of the way and rolled up against the wall of the stall.

"Don't even think about it," Zane threatened as he looked around for the goat.

Lucifer stood in the dark corner of the car, staring at Zane. In his mouth he held Zane's valise by the handle, as if he were a bellhop.

"Put that down, you sorry goat."

A pair of gold-rimmed eyes stared at him.

"If I was wearing my gun you'd be dead right now."

"Mmmmmm," Lucifer replied as if he knew for a fact the gun was in the valise.

Now how would the goat know that?

A long blast of the whistle let the passengers know that the train was preparing to leave.

"Dang it," Zane said and dove for the goat. He landed in the straw, and Lucifer hopped over him, banging the valise against Zane's head.

Zane rolled over, throwing handfuls of straw as he came to his knees. His hand was bleeding through the handkerchief, and he didn't have all day to wrestle with the goat. He was determined to get the animal off the train.

Lucifer was back in the stall, the valise handle still in his mouth.

"You are not smarter than me," Zane said. "You will get off this train."

The whistle blasted again, followed by the clip-clop of Glory's hooves on the ramp.

Zane made another dive and this time caught a hind leg.

Lucifer dropped the valise as Zane pulled him down on the floor.

"Ma-a-a-a," Lucifer bleated as Zane wrestled for control. Straw flew in every direction as Zane pulled on Lucifer's leg while the goat tried to scramble to his feet. Lucifer got in a few good kicks, but Zane was determined to hang on.

"Whatever are you doing to that poor goat?" It was Mary, and the look on her face was one of pity.

For the goat.

Zane released his hold.

"Coming to an understanding." Zane dusted himself off as Lucifer ran to the comfort of Glory. The mare put her nose down and nuzzled the goat's back.

Zane rescued his valise from the floor.

"I'd better get that ramp up," he said and moved past Mary, who was giving him the look that some of his teachers had laid on him when he acted up in school.

Dang, she could make Jake *uncomfortable with that icy gaze.*

Mary rolled her eyes as she led Glory into her stall.

"You're still bleeding," she said.

Zane resisted the urge to mimic her. "I know," he said dryly.

"You'd better have Marcus sew you up."

"I plan on it."

He slammed the doors shut just as the train moved out.

Mary paused by the door that led to the long string of cars. "Are you coming?" she asked.

"Yes, ma'am," Zane said and fell in behind her.

Why did he feel like he was on his way to the headmaster's office?

Chapter Eight

The first person he saw was the porter who had walked in during Marcus's examination. Zane gave him a cheeky grin as the man turned his head away. He didn't care what the fellow thought.

All that mattered was that he didn't have the clap.

And the view of Mary's backside swaying before him in her neat and prim navy suit was driving him to distraction. Too bad she seemed permanently annoyed with him. Why couldn't she just be sweet and adore him like all the other women in the past?

Maybe they just adore the money you pay them—have you ever thought of that?

The sight of passengers feasting on box lunches they had purchased during the layover reminded Zane of how long it had been since he'd had a square meal. His stomach issued a loud, jealous grumble as he followed along after Mary.

"Oh, my," she said without turning her head.

Zane screwed up his face and silently mimicked her *Oh, my* as they made their way through the car. A boy of around eight saw him do it and made a grotesque face at him, pulling his lower lids down with his fingers and sticking out his tongue.

"It's amazing how impressionable young children are," Mary said as they stepped between cars. "And how old are you?"

She must have eyes in the back of her head.

"I'm twenty-five. Why?"

"Marcus is twenty-seven."

Only twenty-seven and a doctor? Dang.

"Is there a dining car on this train?" Zane asked, quickly changing the subject. She was getting to be as irritating as Lucifer.

"There is, but it's expensive," she said.

"I've got money," he replied. "Enough for a decent meal."

There. There wasn't any risk of her wanting him for his money.

"Mommy, isn't that the man who fell off the train?" A little girl asked as they walked through the next car.

"Hush, darling," the mother said.

Zane tipped his hat, which was starting to look a little the worse for wear with Lucifer snacking on it and his fall off the train.

He also couldn't help noticing that Mary had covered her mouth with her hand. She was laughing at him.

"Where is your brother?" Zane asked.

"The next car."

"Could you hurry up? I'm either going to starve to death or bleed to death shortly."

"Do you require assistance?" Mary asked. "I'd hate to think that you might slip and fall off the train . . . again."

"I told you, it was that dang goat," Zane said, a little too loudly.

"Oh, my," Mary said as several heads turned to look at them.

Zane rolled his eyes toward the ceiling.

Marcus was in the next car, obviously waiting for Zane to show up because he had his supplies ready and waiting on the seat, including a bottle of whiskey.

"I could use a drink," Zane said, reaching for the bottle.

"It's for medicinal purposes," Marcus said, grabbing the bottle.

Mary looked smug as she sat down.

"Marcus uses it to clean the wound," she explained. "That means it—"

"I know the value of cleanliness," Zane spouted as he sat down. "Just get it over with so I can eat."

Marcus unwrapped the handkerchief from Zane's hand and examined the wound.

"That's a pretty good slice," he said. "The edges are jagged, so I'm going to have to trim them in order to get a good seam."

"You're going to have to *what?*" Zane felt all the blood in his body rush toward his stomach. It was probably a good thing it was empty. He felt as if he would heave its contents all over the train.

"Are you all right?" Mary asked. "You look a bit green."

Marcus picked up a tiny pair of scissors. "Trim the edges."

"Dang!"

"My, my," Mary said, for once not gagging at the sight of a wound. "I would have thought a rough-and-tough cowboy like you could handle something as minor as this."

Zane stuck out his palm. "Just do it, Doc."

Marcus poured whiskey on the wound and Mary caught the overflow in the bloody handkerchief.

"Here," Marcus said, handing Zane the bottle.

He didn't want to take a drink. She looked so dang haughty sitting there next to him, just waiting for him to cry out as her brother set to work.

Dang, that hurt. Zane's arm tensed.

"You're going to have to relax," Marcus said as he trimmed the wound. Mary looked out the window during the procedure. She always had a weak stomach when injury was involved.

"*You* relax, Doc."

"Take a drink."

This procedure was right up there with pissing nails, which was what his kidney infection had felt like on its worst day. Zane took a swig from the bottle, and kept his eyes on Mary throughout the trimming. She smiled at him when she realized that he was staring at her. It was a forced smile that didn't show in her eyes.

Zane sincerely wished that Lucifer would toss her on her precious backside.

The stitching wasn't as bad as the trimming. Zane

took another swig, one eye on Mary as he did so. She was helping Marcus, handing him the proper tools when he asked for them.

"Are you a nurse?" he asked.

"I teach school."

"It figures," Zane said.

"What do you mean by that?"

"Nothing." Zane took another swig.

"Too much of that on an empty stomach will go straight to your head," Mary cautioned.

"Good. Then I won't be wasting any time."

Marcus paused to look up at the two combatants.

"Your sister thinks I'm incorrigible," Zane said with his cheeky grin.

"I believe the word I used was infuriating," Mary retorted.

"Actually it was insufferable," Zane corrected her.

"They all seem to fit."

"It's a miracle I've survived all these years without your instruction." Zane took another swig.

"Hmph," Mary said. "From what I've seen, it *is* a miracle."

"At least I don't go stepping out in front of carriages while reading letters. What was that anyway, a missive from some poor boy begging you to love him forever?"

Mary's jaw slammed shut. "Excuse me," she said and heavily stepped on Zane's boots as she rose from her seat.

"I guess I hit a sore spot with that one," Zane observed as she moved quickly down the aisle toward the next car.

"Mary lost her husband two years ago." Marcus's

kind brown eyes were steady as he looked at Zane. "They had only been married for a few months."

Struck with shame, Zane looked down the aisle, now empty. "I guess I should apologize. I didn't know."

"There was no reason why you should," Marcus said. He snipped the thread and wrapped Zane's hand. "You need to move this as much as possible to keep your hand from getting stiff and closing up on you. Flex it like this." He demonstrated by opening and closing his own hand. "It could cause problems if you don't."

Zane moved his hand the way Marcus had shown him. "Don't worry, Doc. I'm left-handed, so it shouldn't be too much of a problem."

"Be careful that she doesn't throw you off the train," Marcus said as Zane rose from his seat to follow Mary.

He walked all the way back through the train before he found her with Glory.

Why does that mare take to her so? It's almost like watching Jenny with her horses . . .

Even Lucifer seemed content. He was lying in the straw with his eyes closed, apparently lulled by the sound of the train.

Zane took off his hat and dusted it along the side of his leg.

"I'm sorry for what I said about the letter. I had no right to comment about . . . er . . . your life."

"An apology," Mary said to Glory. "He must be civilized, after all."

"Hey," Zane said indignantly. "I didn't have to do this, you know."

"You don't owe me an apology," Mary said, turning

to look at him. "I owe you one. I'm afraid I haven't been on my best behavior since I've met you, Mr. Brody."

"Zane. Call me Zane."

"Zane."

"We do seem to have gotten off on the wrong foot."

"If I recall, I was off both of mine when we met," Mary said with a smile. Her brown eyes sparkled in the dim light of the car.

"Yes, you were," Zane said with his roguish grin. He propped an arm on the stall.

Lucifer opened one gold-rimmed eye.

Don't you start with me, goat . . .

"You're used to getting your way, aren't you?" Mary asked.

"I don't know what you're talking about," Zane said.

"With women. You just smile like that and show your dimples and they do what you want."

The grin grew broader and the dimples deeper.

"I swear I don't know what you're talking about."

"Yes, you do." Mary tilted her head as if to see him better. "I bet your mother spoiled you rotten."

"My mother died when I was eight. My father soon after."

"I'm sorry," Mary said. "At least you can remember her. I was just a baby when our parents died."

"So you never got to know them."

"No. Marcus and I lived in an orphanage until I was six, then our uncle came for us. He died a few years ago and I came to New York to be with Marcus. He's all I've got in the world."

"Family is important," Zane said, thinking about his

friends in Wyoming instead of the blood relations in New York City.

"Do you have any family?" Mary asked.

Zane flashed his grin again. "None that I'd claim. Or any that would claim me."

Mary laughed. "You're doing it again," she said.

"What?"

"Are you trying to charm me, Zane?"

"No. But I was thinking about asking if you'd like to have lunch with me."

"Do you think you can make it all the way back to the dining car? After all, you are weak from hunger and blood loss."

"I think if you take my arm, I'll be able to make it," Zane said.

Lucifer jumped to his feet as Mary left the stall.

Zane took a moment to give the goat a self-satisfied smirk as he followed Mary to the next car.

"Ma-a-a-a," Lucifer responded as they left.

Chapter Nine

The dining car was nice. Several advances had been made in rail travel since the end of the war. The walls were hung with crystal sconces and the tables were made of fine wood. The chairs were nicely padded, something that Zane's backside greatly appreciated as he slid into his seat.

Some of the richer patrons gave him a disdainful look as he sat down at a table with Marcus and Mary. He knew he wasn't wearing proper attire for the dining car, but he didn't care. He actually enjoyed thumbing his nose at their stiff necks and correct clothing. They reminded him of his grandfather and the world he had left behind all those years ago.

Money didn't buy happiness. He had learned that lesson pretty quick and fairly young.

"Where are you headed?" Marcus asked when they had given the waiter their order.

"Wyoming," Zane said. "That's where I live. My boss sent me to New York to pick up the mare. Glory is going to add more speed to her breeding stock."

"Your boss is a woman?" Mary asked.

"Yes," Zane said, curious at her reaction. "Both of them."

"Oh, my," Mary said.

"What's wrong with my bosses being women?" Why was it that she seemed to find everything about him irksome? What had he done to her, that irritated her so?

"Nothing," Mary replied with a sly smile on her face. "I think it's wonderful. I just find it interesting that *you* work for *women*."

"Now, what's that supposed to mean?" Zane snapped.

"Why, it doesn't mean anything."

"Yes, it does," he insisted.

"So where does the goat fit in?" Marcus interrupted as he saw another battle about to erupt.

"Oh, I have a lot of plans for that goat," Zane said. "And most of them involve a horrible death."

"You can't hurt that poor goat," Mary exclaimed. "Glory would be heartbroken."

"The first chance I get, that goat is gone," Zane said with a confident and evil smile.

Mary opened her mouth to retort, but Marcus touched her hand before she could say anything.

"We're traveling to Wyoming, too," he said. "You two can argue about the goat the entire trip."

"Where are you headed?" Zane asked.

"Laramie."

Zane's dimples showed as his grin spread across his handsome face.

"Planning on setting up practice there, Doc?"

"I was thinking about it. Actually, we're going because Mary has a teaching job there."

Zane's jaw dropped. "Wait a minute. I thought you said your name is Mary Brown."

"Actually, it's Mary Dunleavy. Brown is my maiden name. I'm a widow."

"Dang," Zane said, his grin spreading across his face. "I know where you're going."

"You do?"

"Same place I am. The Lynch ranch. You were hired by Catherine Kincaid, one of my bosses. I was there when she read your letter accepting the job."

"You mean Cat!" Marcus exclaimed.

"You know her?" Zane asked.

"And Jenny!"

"Yes. How . . . Why. . . . Wait a minute. You're the doctor that saved Chase's arm and helped rescue Ty from the prison camp," Zane said. "Then all of you went chasing after Jenny when she got kidnapped and taken to some whorehouse, where of all things she ran into Amanda and then the place burned down around their ears while Chase threw that bastard Wade Bishop out the window." He couldn't believe he'd gotten it all out with one breath. "I knew I always missed out on the fun stuff," he added with a laugh.

"That's me," Marcus said with a grin. "Not sure how much help I was except for saving Chase's arm. I'm better at taking bullets out than putting them in." He turned to his sister. "You never said anything about Cat."

"The woman who hired me said her name is Catherine, and you always call her Cat," Mary explained. "Besides, I told you it was the Lynch school."

"I don't recognize that name," Marcus said.

"Jason Lynch was Cat's father and Jenny's grandfather. He died a few years ago."

"And now Cat and Jenny are in charge." Marcus shook his head. "I was hoping to run into Jenny, but I never dreamed—"

"Oh, it gets better, Doc," Zane said. "Right before I left town, the doctor in Laramie up and died." Zane snapped his fingers. "Just like that. And Cat's fit to be tied because she's expecting and now there's no doctor. She's had a few miscarriages and is pretty scared about this baby."

"Is she taking care of herself?" Marcus asked, immediately concerned.

"Confined to her room. Which makes her mad because Jenny's out running around."

"Jenny's expecting also?"

"Number three."

"Jenny has three children?"

"This will be four. She adopted Jamie's son, too."

"Jenny, the mother of four children." Marcus shook his head in disbelief.

"I remember Jamie," Mary said. "He was so handsome, even with his scars."

"Mary had a crush on Jamie when she was little," Marcus explained. "We were all in an orphanage together in St. Joe. Our uncle came for us shortly before Chase showed up."

"They had a pretty rough time of it, from the stories

they tell," Zane said. "Jenny was forcibly taken from the orphanage one day while Jamie was away working. By the time she was able to escape, Jamie and Chase had left the orphanage to search for her. For five years neither of them knew whether the other was alive or dead."

"I would have died if someone had taken Marcus away from me," Mary said.

"You were only six," Marcus said. "Just a little girl."

"Still," Mary said, squeezing his hand. "We're family. We need to stay together."

"That's why I decided to go out West with Mary," Marcus said to Zane. "I couldn't stand the thought of her taking off and having an adventure without me."

Zane laughed. "I know the feeling. I was always complaining about everyone having adventures but me, so Jenny sent me off to New York to have one."

"And how is it so far?" Mary asked.

"It's had its good parts and bad. I could definitely live without Lucifer." He flashed his dimples. "On the other hand, the scenery is beautiful." His grin let her know he wasn't talking about the farm land they passed.

"Oh, my."

"Too bad the train ride is almost over."

"We've still got a lot of country to cover by stage-coach though," Marcus said.

"Maybe you do. I'll be riding across half of Nebraska dragging Glory behind me while you take the stage. You'll beat me there by several days."

"Don't forget about Lucifer," Mary said. "He'll be traveling with you."

Zane grinned evilly. "Not for long. That goat is going to be roasted over a fire our first night out."

"You wouldn't!" Mary said in horror.

"I would." Zane said. "I plan on enjoying it, too."

"You couldn't."

"Care to join me for dinner one night?"

"Marcus!" Mary protested. "Do something."

"That all depends on you, Mary. We could ride along with Zane, if he doesn't mind. Or we can take the stage."

"It won't be near as dusty if you ride," Zane said with a grin. "Or as hard on your joints. I'd rather ride a horse than a stage any day of the week."

"It's been a while since I've ridden hard," Marcus said.

"Me too," Mary added.

"Like I said, you're a city girl," Zane teased. Why was making fun of her so dang . . . enjoyable?

"So tell me all about Jenny," Marcus said before Mary could spout off a retort.

"She's mostly happy. She misses Jamie real bad sometimes. We all do. But I know it's worse for her and Chase. It was scary right after Jamie died and Chase went after his killer. We didn't know if he'd come back, and even after he did, it was like he was still gone." Zane touched a finger to his temple. "Chase can get scary sometimes. I don't know if it's because he's part Kiowa or just because he's Chase. And he swears that Jamie's not really gone. He thinks he's still around watching out for us."

"What do you mean?" Mary asked.

"Chase almost died when he went after Jamie's

killer. We never would have known he'd come back except one day Ty was out checking the herd and he saw this red fox. It led him right to where Chase was lying in the snow, about to die from pneumonia. Another time the house was attacked and someone told Amanda to get the boys and get out. Except no one else was there. Chase swears it was Jamie's ghost. Then I was about to die from chicken pox and Jenny took me out in the snow to get my fever down. She said a fox walked up while I was lying there and curled up right next to my head. It was the darndest thing I've ever heard of. But I got better, and every time that fox has turned up, everything's come out fine in the end."

Mary and Marcus both looked doubtful at his story, but Zane didn't care. He'd lived through it and seen it happen. If Jamie was watching out for them, it was fine with him. He figured he could use all the help he could get.

"And Amanda? How is she?" Marcus asked after a moment. He had helped Cole place her in a sanatorium to recover from her addiction to opium after they'd rescued her from Wade Bishop.

"Married to my friend Caleb and stirring up trouble with her newspaper."

"Really?" Marcus asked as Zane related Amanda's story.

Mary watched her brother as Zane told him about people that were only names to her. Marcus's face showed an excitement she had not seen since he'd left Denver to go to medical school.

Marcus, so steady, so dependable. He had always been there for her. She didn't even remember their parents. She had been just two when their wagon train had been attacked by Indians and her parents killed, leaving her mother's brother the only one to care for the two little orphans. Their uncle had tried, but he had no idea how to take care of a baby girl. Especially one who cried all the time. She still had a scar on her thigh from where she had fallen against the stove one day. Her uncle had taken them to the orphanage at St. Joe. Both of them because Marcus wouldn't leave her, even when their uncle had said Marcus could stay with him. He just didn't want *her.*

Marcus could have ignored her in the orphanage. After all, she was just a tiny girl and six years younger than he was. But he didn't. He made time for her every day. He told her what he remembered about their parents. He made sure that she knew he was her brother and he would always watch out for her.

And then their uncle had come back with his pretty young wife and offered to bring Marcus and Mary back home. They were unable to have children of their own, so they gave their niece and nephew all of their love and attention. They sent Marcus to medical school in New York, and Mary had stayed in Denver with them and earned her teaching certificate. Sadly, they both had died in the chicken pox epidemic at the end of the war when there was no medicine to be had anywhere.

Mary had gone to New York to be with Marcus then. She had met Michael Dunleavy and fallen madly in love.

And when he died, Marcus had been there for her. He had held her while she cried for endless nights, and he had supported her when she climbed back into life and started teaching again.

And he was coming with her now, back across the country to start a new life.

What would she do without Marcus?

"I can't wait to see them," Marcus was saying as Zane regaled them with a story about one of Jenny's boys and a skunk.

Zane's laughter was infectious. He really was entertaining, and she was surprised to note that his manners were as refined as those of anyone she had met in the city. She couldn't remember laughing so hard since before Michael died. And she knew it had been a long time for Marcus, too. Their food was eaten, the car had emptied, and still they sat and talked and laughed. Zane was good company. He was good for Marcus. If only he weren't so . . . cocky.

"I have to admit I had a crush on Jenny back when we were kids," Marcus said.

"Better not let Chase hear you say that," Zane said with a flash of his dimples.

There it was again. That quick hint of charm that probably had all the women in Laramie falling at his feet.

"I'm pretty sure he already knows," Marcus said sheepishly. "Jenny was the first girl I ever kissed."

"You kissed her?" Mary asked in amazement. "When?"

"The day we left the orphanage."

"I never knew that."

"It's not something I'd tell you. Actually, this is the first time I've ever told anyone."

"I hope you came out on the better side of it than I did," Zane said.

The two looked at him expectantly.

"I tried to kiss her once and wound up walking funny the rest of the day."

Good for Jenny! I'll give him more of the same if he tries to kiss me . . .

Oh, my!

Why was she even thinking about kissing Zane? She barely knew him, and what she did know about him made her palms itch to slap that grin off his face. He was the most insufferable, conceited, cocky, swaggering man she had ever met.

Never mind the fact that his dimples were cute and his eyes danced in the midday sun that shone through the windows. Never mind that his lower lip moved in the most tantalizing way.

Mary fanned herself with her napkin. It had been too long since she had been with a man. That was the problem, and that was all there was to it. Michael had shown her the path to physical love. Their journey of discovery had been innocent and clumsy and wonderful . . . and over much too soon.

"Mary?" Marcus asked. "Are you all right?"

"Yes? Why?" she asked as she fanned.

"You look a bit flushed." Marcus touched her forehead. "Do you think you're coming down with something?"

"No." She stood quickly, which brought both Marcus and Zane to their feet. "I'm just a bit warm. I'm going for some air. Please keep talking. I'll be fine."

Her words ran together as she quickly moved away

from the table toward the door. Between cars, she found the relief of fresh air. She longed to unbutton her blouse and wipe her face and neck with cool water. If only she had some.

Glory had fresh water. A whole bucketful. Glory wouldn't mind sharing with her. Mary looked back into the dining car and saw her brother and Zane deep in conversation.

"Looks like we'll be riding to Wyoming instead of taking the stage," she said as she moved toward Glory's car, making a mental note to find some appropriate clothing for riding when they reached St. Louis.

Chapter Ten

"Tell me about Mary's husband," Zane asked. The two men were sipping coffee in the dining car and watching the miles of farmland roll past. They would be crossing the Mississippi soon and stopping in St. Louis overnight before they changed trains to make the final leg to North Platte, where the railroad ended. "She seems pretty young to be a widow."

"She met Michael in Central Park right after the war was over. He had been in the Union Army and fought bravely, from what we heard. He pretty much swept Mary off her feet, and as you can see, she's rather stubborn."

"He must have been quite a man to do that."

"He was. He was young, handsome and too kind-hearted for his own good. He ran into a burning house to save a mother and child who were trapped on an upper floor. None of them made it out. Mary blames herself for not stopping him. She was there and saw the entire thing. They were walking home from my place when it happened."

"It would be hard for another man to live up to that legacy," Zane commented as he stirred cinnamon into his coffee. *Why should you even care?*

"I'd hate to think of her being alone the rest of her life," Marcus replied.

"How 'bout you, Doc? How has such an eligible bachelor stayed single all these years?"

Marcus laughed. "I've never had the time, or the inclination, to go courting."

"I bet there have been plenty of offers from those high-society ladies in New York," Zane said with his grin.

"More than I wanted," Marcus said. "But never from the right woman."

"Still pining after Jenny?"

"If only there was another one like her."

"I hope not," Zane said. "Being around Jenny is adventure enough for me."

"I probably should go check on Mary," Marcus said as the conversation wound down.

"I'd better check on my girl, too," Zane said. "Maybe I'll get lucky and find that Lucifer has fallen off the train."

"If you know what's best, you'll leave that goat alone," Marcus warned. "Mary's decided to stick up for him, and if you don't watch out, she'll be booting you off the train."

Zane flashed his dimples. "I think I can handle your sister *and* the goat."

"The goat is nothing compared to my sister," Marcus said.

"If you say so."

Glory didn't mind sharing her water at all. She seemed to welcome the company. The mare's wise brown eyes settled on Mary as she dipped her linen handkerchief in the bucket of water, fresh from their recent stop, and wiped the sweat from her neck and between her breasts.

Wisps of dark hair had escaped her pins, so she removed her hat and with a teasing glance at Lucifer, who was watching her with his gold-rimmed eyes, hung it on a nail high on the wall. Mary wiped the back of her neck and then removed the pins from her hair, shaking it loose until it fell in waves down to her waist.

She moved closer to the door, which Zane had left open a crack to allow a breeze to circulate in the car. Mary leaned against the wall of the stall and watched the countryside roll by in time with the clackety-clack of the rails. She reveled in the moment, allowing the wind created by the train's passage to caress the exposed skin around her neck as she laid open the placket of her blouse. Her hair skipped around her, twisting in the air, and she took a moment to smooth it down behind one ear before her hand went automatically to the ring on the gold chain that hung between her breasts.

Time to start over, Mary. Time to put the past behind you. The time for mourning is over.

She kept her brown eyes toward the west. There was nothing to look for behind her. Nothing there. The precious memories she would always carry with her, but Michael's face had long since faded from her mind, just as the city where they'd loved had faded away in the distant east.

Too little time together to make memories. Too little time to memorize the lines of his face and the way he smiled. Too much time ahead to spend alone.

"Ma-a-a-a," Lucifer announced.

Mary turned with a start, her hair tumbling across her features as she did so.

Zane stood in the middle of the car. Mary straightened her hair and waited for the cocky look, the insufferable grin, the sudden assault of charm.

"You still miss him," he said quietly.

Zane's dancing hazel eyes were serious for once. The look on his face was one of simple concern.

Mary suddenly realized that she was revealing too much. But which did he see more of? Was he looking at the skin she was showing on the outside, or the pain and regret that she kept on the inside? She pulled her blouse together and closed the tiny pearl buttons with nimble fingers.

"You presume too much, sir," she said as she looked down at the scuffed straw on the floor of the car.

"I've been told that before also." His grin was fleeting this time, showing just a glimpse of something else, but the expression was gone too quickly for her to determine what he was feeling . . . or hiding.

A sudden blast of air swirled through the opening and blew her hat up from the nail. It hung in midair for a moment before it floated down, landing on top of Lucifer's horns.

"Ma-a-a-a," the goat bleated.

Zane and Mary looked at the goat and then at each other. They both burst into laughter as Lucifer casually chewed straw while wearing Mary's hat.

"We'd better rescue it before he realizes that it's tasty," Zane said. He grabbed the hat just as Lucifer decided to give it a try. The goat chased Zane's hand with clomping teeth, but Zane was too fast for him.

Zane steadied his hand, stopping just short of placing the hat on Mary's head. Her dark, wavy hair, tumbled by the breeze, cascaded over her shoulders and down her back. Her face and neck were moist, her lips parted over perfect teeth as she smiled at the goat's antics. She had removed her short traveling coat, and Zane realized he could easily span her waist with his hands. Her figure was trim and petite, but her backside still held that delicious curve that had tantalized him from the first time he saw her in the park. That was what had captured his attention when he came into the car and saw her standing by the door. But as his eyes traveled up the length of her, he realized there was more to see than a few sweet curves.

Her husband had swept her off her feet, Marcus had said. Zane didn't blame him. He would have, too, if he knew how. Had he ever done that to a girl? Sure, he had charmed them and cajoled them and even paid them. But had he ever swept a girl off her feet? Had he ever wanted to?

"Your hair is pretty," he said. His fingers brushed a curl that lay on her arm.

Mary blushed from the roots of her hair down into her prim white blouse.

"Oh, my," she said and quickly gathered the lush strands together and started twisting them into a knot. "I must look a mess," she said as she searched the pocket of her skirt for her pins.

Great way to sweep a girl off her feet. Great line, Zane. The boys back home would get a hoot out of that one, you dang fool.

Zane mentally flogged himself while holding on to the hat. Mary nervously apologized for her inappropriate behavior, her words tumbling out a mile a minute as she pinned her hair and found her jacket casually lying over a rail. She was almost running by the time she reached the door.

"Wait!" Zane called after her. "Don't you want your hat?"

"Oh, my," she said. She turned and reached for it. Zane let it go before she had it in her hand and it fell to the floor. They both bent to pick it up, and their heads collided.

Zane saw stars and blinding light but he managed to grab on to Mary before she fell to the floor. His head throbbed, so he knew hers must also, but he couldn't focus his eyes enough to find her.

"Oh, my," she said. There was a tangle of skirts and a flash of petticoats as she escaped, scooping up her hat with one hand while the other was held firmly against the top of her head.

Zane slid down to the floor with his back against the stall, shaking his head to clear the cobwebs that had quickly gathered.

"Ma-a-a-a," Lucifer commented.

"Shut up!" Zane said as he rubbed his forehead.

* * *

Mary slid into the seat next to Marcus. Her head was throbbing, and she couldn't help rubbing the top of it, where she was sure she'd have a bruise accompanied by a giant knot.

At least that verifies that he's hardheaded.

"Are you sure you're not coming down with something?" Marcus asked.

"I'm fine, Marcus. I just hit my head on something."

"Let me look at it."

Mary pushed him away. "Can you stop being a doctor for five minutes?"

"What's got you in such a bad mood?" Marcus asked with a grin.

"I am not in a bad mood. I hit my head. It hurts, but not that much," Mary said as she ducked his searching hand. "I'm hot and I'm tired and I just want to rest."

"Is it your—"

"Don't say it, Marcus," Mary warned. "You might be my brother and my doctor, but *that* is none of your business."

"If I had known you were going to be this difficult to travel with, I would have stayed in New York."

"I am not being difficult!"

"Shhh," Marcus said. "Everyone is looking at you."

"How do you know they're not looking at *you*?"

"I'm not the one shouting."

Mary opened her mouth to protest and then snapped it shut when she saw the light dancing in her brother's warm brown eyes.

"You are antagonizing me on purpose," she said.

"You make it so easy, Mary." Marcus put his arm

around her and pushed her head down on his shoulder. "Now, tell me what's happened to make you so . . . ill." His hand traced a lazy circle through her hair, easing the pain on her scalp.

"Nothing," Mary said. She forced herself to relax as his hand worked its magic. It was amazing what he could do with just a simple touch. There had to be some sort of mystical healing powers inside him. He always knew instinctively what to do for his patients, even when they were being impossible, as she was.

She was so lucky to have him for a brother. What would she ever do without him?

The steady rumble of the train deadened her senses to the other passengers and the countryside flying by the window. Her world closed down except for Marcus and the beating of their hearts.

"I want to take the stage to Laramie," she said with a yawn.

"What did he do?" Marcus's hand stopped circling her hair.

"What did who do?"

"Zane."

"What makes you think he did something?"

"You've been in this . . . tizzy . . . ever since you met him."

"I have not."

"Mary," Marcus sighed.

Mary sat up to look at her brother. His handsome face was full of concern, but his eyes seemed mischievous.

"All right, I admit I have been a bit cranky since I met him, but he didn't do anything. It's just that he's so . . . infuriating."

"If he didn't do anything, then what is it that infuriates you?"

"Everything," Mary said after a moment. "Everything about him. He's just so . . ."

"Cocky?"

"Yes."

"And used to women falling at his feet?"

"More than likely."

"But you haven't."

"Haven't what?"

"Fallen at his feet."

"Marcus. How could you even think that I would . . ." Mary folded her arms across her chest and sat back with a huff.

"I just want to make sure I don't need to go defend your honor."

"My honor is quite intact, thank you. And I am more than capable of defending it myself."

"I don't doubt it for a minute." Marcus laughed as he pulled her back down to his shoulder and resumed the lazy circles.

"Marcus," she said when the world had faded again. "We can travel with Zane if you want."

Chapter Eleven

"Hello, St. Louis," Zane said as the train rolled over the Mississippi River and into the bustling city. He had always enjoyed visiting St. Louis. Happy memories of driving cattle into the city with Jason and his friends filled his mind. Of course, most of the happy memories had been before the war, before life had changed so much and they had all begun separate lives. The city was still pretty much the same as it had been the last time he passed through. It was growing, just like the nation, but the people were the same. And the feel of the city was the same. It was obvious that good times were to be had there. Zane opened the door of the car, after checking on Lucifer's whereabouts, as the engine slowed its pace. He waved a greeting to the busy laborers working in the train yards.

"Lucifer," Zane said to the goat. "I'm going to have a fun night in the big city. But don't you fret none, because I've got plans for you, too. The first night we're on the trail, you and me are going to get real close." Zane rubbed the muscled ridges of his stomach as he looked at the goat with a wide grin. "Real close."

"Ma-a-a-a," Lucifer replied.

Zane's pleasure at threatening the goat was suddenly interrupted as a vision of Mary's pretty face passed before him, her brown eyes filled with disappointment at the thought of Lucifer's demise.

"She'll probably ride with me to Laramie just to make sure I don't roast you on a spit," he said.

"Ma-a-a-a," Lucifer bleated.

"You haven't got the best of me yet," Zane promised. "And neither has she."

Lucifer followed as Zane led Glory down into one of the holding pens at the train yard and made arrangements for her care for the night. The man in charge wasn't happy about the presence of the goat but Jenny's money once again smoothed the way.

"I'd better start writing all these bribes down," Zane said to Glory as he turned her loose in the pen. "You are turning out to be one expensive lady."

And speaking of expensive ladies . . . Zane's mind turned toward a good meal and a night of entertainment.

I thought you weren't going to do that anymore.

But I deserve it.

Zane wasn't in the mood to argue with his conscience. He had been sick while in New York City, and after his aggravation with Lucifer, a night on the town was just what he needed. With his valise in hand, he stepped out onto the busy streets of St. Louis and sucked in a deep breath of city air.

He took one last look at Glory and noticed two men casually leaning on the fence admiring her. Zane wondered where they had come from so quickly, but he couldn't blame them for looking. She was, after all, a pretty lady. The mare stood in the corner of her pen, cautiously watching the activity around her. Lucifer, on the other hand, had his head stuck between the wooden slats watching Zane.

"Ma-a-a-a," he called after Zane as he stepped into the street.

"Tell it to your girlfriend," Zane said. He'd had enough of the goat to last him a lifetime.

"Looks like he misses you," Marcus said as he and Mary happened to pass by.

"That's *his* problem," Zane replied. He tipped his hat to Mary, who was looking everywhere but at him. "Do you two have plans for the evening?" he asked. The fact that Mary continued to ignore him was quickly becoming irksome.

"A bath, a good meal and a nice comfortable bed," Marcus said. "We're checking into the hotel down the street. Would you care to join us for—oof—dinner?"

Zane couldn't help noticing Mary's elbow dig into Marcus's side. A mischievous grin lit up his face. She didn't want to be around him. She didn't want to have anything to do with him. He decided it was time to convince her otherwise. She thought she had been swept off her feet before? She hadn't seen anything yet.

Besides, aggravating her was so much fun.

"I would enjoy that very much," Zane said, showing his dimples. "It would be a real treat to have dinner with such lovely company."

She had to acknowledge his compliment—it would be rude not to. Zane had learned a thing or two about polite society while living with his grandparents. He knew how to play the game.

Dang, if she didn't look downright bored! She was in for it now. Mary Dunleavy had no idea whom she was messing with.

Zane named a nice restaurant where Jason had taken the crew after one of their last cattle drives. Mary thought he was beneath her notice. She thought he was nothing more than a hired hand. Boy, was she in for a surprise.

It was time Mary Dunleavy learned a lesson. The schoolteacher was about to receive an education.

Cat's warning to stay away from the schoolteacher rang in his ears, but it just made his grin grow wider.

"What's so funny?" Marcus asked.

"I'm just happy to be here," Zane replied, grinning deliciously.

Mary kept looking off in the distance, at the sky, at the ground, her brown eyes roaming everywhere but him.

Tonight, you won't be able to keep your eyes, or your hands, off of me.

"Marcus, I'm tired," Mary said. "I just want to stay here and get some sleep."

Marcus managed to place his hand on her forehead before Mary could knock it away. "Are you sure you're not coming down with something?"

Mary rolled her eyes in exasperation. She had come down with something, all right. Something she called Zaneitis. He was the most infuriating, maddening, annoying, irritating, frustrating man she had ever met. And she didn't want to eat dinner with him.

"I'll have something sent up for both of us," Marcus said.

She could see the disappointment in his eyes.

Mary turned from Marcus and went to the window. The gaslights cast a warm glow over the street, which was already bustling with evening traffic. In his reflection in the window she saw Marcus run his fingers through his wavy brown hair.

He was frustrated with her. And why shouldn't he be? She was acting like a shrew. There was absolutely no reason for him to spend an evening in the room with her when the entire city begged to be explored and he only had a few short hours to do it.

How long had it been since she'd seen him excited about anything other than his work? How many years had he spent diligently studying and working to become a doctor, and how many more years had he spent caring for his patients at all hours and in all types of weather? And despite his dedication to his work he still put her first, making sure she was comfortable and happy and not wanting for anything. This evening he had even insisted that she bathe first; he had then used the same water, tepid and soapy, so they wouldn't waste time waiting for another tub to be prepared.

All he wanted was to spend time with Zane, talking about his friends. Yet he would sacrifice a pleasant evening because he was worried about her.

"Just let me get dressed," Mary said, dropping the curtain back in place.

"I'll wait for you downstairs," he replied and brushed a kiss on top of her head.

Sometimes the serious doctor reminded her of a small boy, Mary mused as she heard him clattering down the stairs.

She picked up the jacket of her traveling suit. She had brushed the dark blue fabric of the skirt and short coat and had put on a fresh blouse. If they were going to ride with Zane to Wyoming from North Platte, she would have to buy some clothes for the trip. Nothing she had would do for that kind of traveling.

Dinner with Zane Brody. The man who thought he was God's gift to women. Well, it wasn't as if she hadn't turned a few heads in her day. She was young. She was still pretty. Why, just last year at the New Year's Eve party . . .

The New Year's Eve party. Mary opened her suitcase. Marcus had teased her about wasting space in her bag instead of putting the garment in the trunk they shared.

The bright blue satin gown was at the bottom of her bag and still carefully wrapped in paper to keep it from wrinkling. She shook loose the folds of the gown as she held it up to her trim figure. The neckline was a bit daring, but her shawl could help with that. There were a few wrinkles but not many. It wasn't as if the matrons of New York society would be giving her the once-over as she made her appearance.

Zane Brody thought he was God's gift to women? Well, he was about to find out that this woman wasn't interested. Not one bit.

*   *   *

The weather was perfect. The night air was cool for early summer, and the absence of the moon allowed the stars to twinkle brilliantly above the glow of the gaslights. The fresh smell of the breeze from the west let all who felt it know there would be clouds later on, but no one would complain about that. Rain was a welcome gift.

A young girl, pretty in spite of her crooked teeth, sold flowers on a street corner, and Zane couldn't resist picking up a bouquet of violets. He also couldn't resist flirting with the girl, who giggled appreciatively behind her hand. She could have been easily swept off her feet if he'd felt so inclined.

He had other prey on his mind tonight.

It was a short walk to the restaurant, and the scent of the violets along with the cool caress of the night air added a sense of gaiety to the evening. Still more enticing was the sight of a delicious backside gently swaying beneath the skirts of a blue satin dress that shimmered in the soft blaze of the lamps.

Dang. That was Mary and Marcus in front of him. Where had she found that dress?

They stopped at the entrance of the restaurant. Marcus was looking at his pocket watch while Mary stood under the light with her profile turned toward Zane.

He stopped in his tracks as he watched Mary look up at Marcus, affection plainly written on her face. Her skin seemed almost radiant in the lamplight. As she smiled, her teeth glistened like Zane's grandmother's pearls. Her dark hair was arranged in what seemed a careless twist on top of her head. A few curls hung down around her ears and tickled her shoulders, which were covered with a luminous shawl that seemed to match the gown.

Suddenly his stomach dipped down into the vicinity of his boots. Zane's throat tightened, and he loosened his collar and tie a bit.

Dang, she was pretty.

His hand was sweaty around the lacy paper that covered the bouquet of violets, and he didn't quite know what to do with them. The resolution to that problem was standing right in front of him.

" 'But soft! What light through yonder window breaks?' " Zane said as he walked up to Mary and Marcus.

"I beg your pardon?" Mary said.

"Pretty flowers for a pretty lady," Zane added hastily and handed Mary the bouquet.

"Oh, my," Mary said as she took the bouquet. "Thank you." She held them to her nose to inhale the fragrance and gave Zane a shy smile.

She likes flowers. I'll give her fields of flowers.

It is the east and Mary is the sun.

Now where did that come from?

"Shall we go in?" Zane extended his arm to Mary. Her eyebrow arched in surprise at his manners.

Ha! Bet you weren't expecting that!

The restaurant served fine food without being snobbish, and Zane couldn't help noticing that heads turned when Mary came into the room. Of course, her dress was a bit elaborate for the place, but most of the glances were of appreciation, not disapproval.

Mary must have noticed the glances, too. She kept

a tight hold on her shawl. Zane wondered what she was hiding underneath it. If memory served him right, not much.

Corsets were miraculous things, Zane decided when the three of them sat down at the table and Mary loosened her shawl to reveal a creamy expanse of breast. There was enough there to fill a man's . . .

Zane rubbed his palms together as if they itched.

"Watch the stitches," Marcus warned too late. Zane shook his hand to relieve the pain that shot up his right arm. What he wouldn't give for a nice cool drink. As if on cue, a waiter appeared. After ordering, they settled into polite conversation.

For the life of him, Zane could not figure out what he was doing there. He had a vague recollection that dinner had been his idea, but the sight of Mary in her bright blue satin with the lamplight glowing on her skin, her dark curls teasing her shoulders and the rosy color in her cheeks, was driving him to distraction. He gulped down the glass of wine that mysteriously appeared in front of him.

"Shouldn't you pace yourself?" Mary said, her dark eyes dancing like flames.

Zane attempted to loosen his collar.

"Are you feeling all right?" Marcus asked. "You look like your fever may have come back."

"I'm fine," Zane said.

"Marcus, can you quit being a doctor for five minutes?" Mary said. "You're always asking people how they feel."

"Sorry."

"No, really, I'm fine," Zane said.

Mary patted his hand. "We know," she said as if reassuring a child.

The look of pure satisfaction on her face hit Zane like a bucket of cold water.

She's turned the tables on me. She's trying to sweep me off my feet.

And she was doing a pretty good job of it.

A delicious grin split his face.

"What's so amusing?" Mary asked.

"Just a thought," Zane said as he refilled his glass.

"Care to share it?" Mary asked, sipping her wine.

"I might be persuaded to . . . later." His dimples showed as dark slashes in his cheeks as his eyes dropped to her neckline.

Mary sputtered over her glass and cast a glance at Marcus for help as she gathered her shawl around her shoulders. He had missed the innuendos while the meal was being served, and now his attention seemed to be focused on the other side of the room.

"That looks like Ben," he said.

"Ben?" Mary asked.

"We went through medical school together," Marcus explained. "Excuse me a moment."

"He seems to have a lot of friends," Zane commented as he and Mary watched the reunion across the crowded restaurant.

"He always has," Mary said, nervously clutching her shawl. She suddenly felt very alone and very vulnerable.

"What about you, Mary? Do you have many . . . friends?" His hazel eyes danced mischievously beneath his dark lashes.

"I have Marcus," she said. "He's all I need." She was being vague and she knew it. She toyed with her food. She had friends, or maybe acquaintances would be a better word. There wasn't anyone or anything that had torn at her heart when she left New York City, except for her memories of Michael, and even those had faded into the recesses of her mind as if they belonged to someone else.

"You, on the other hand, seem to have more friends than Marcus and me combined," she said, taking the offensive once again.

"Having good friends is one of life's blessings," Zane said without the usual teasing in his voice. He turned his attention to his meal, hiding his face from her.

"But?" Mary asked. She had caught a hint of longing in his tone. Did he feel as if he were missing out on something?

"But what?" Zane asked, raising his head and grinning widely.

He used that cocky grin like a weapon, using it to keep the rest of the world from getting too close.

"You sounded like there was more to say."

"What would you like me to say, Mary?"

More innuendos. What she wouldn't give for a bucket of ice to dump on his head. Or better yet, down the front of his trousers.

"Do you ever stop?" she asked.

"Stop what?"

"Hiding."

Zane took a moment to blink and carefully lay down his utensils. "What are you talking about?"

"You hide behind your . . . charm." Mary said.

"You think I'm charming?" he asked, flashing his dimples.

"I think you're hiding something." *Ha! I've got you backed into a corner now. See if you can charm your way out of this one.*

"Everyone is hiding something, Mary," he said smoothly. "What are *you* hiding?"

"I asked first."

"Did you learn that from one of your students?"

Mary's hand tightened on the stem of her wineglass. How did he do that? She thought that she had him pinned down and he swiftly and sweetly backed her up against a wall again. She'd put him back on the defensive with another question.

"Where did you say you were from?"

"Changing the subject?"

"No, just wondering about how you grew up."

"I was born in Missouri. About a day's ride from here."

"And what happened after your parents died?"

"My grandparents raised me," he said. "When I was old enough, I got a job."

He was hiding something, all right. Something about his past.

"Sorry I left you for so long," Marcus apologized, interrupting the impasse. "Mary, would you mind if Zane escorted you back to the hotel?"

Trapped. She could say no and ruin Marcus's evening. Saying yes would mean fighting more of this battle with Zane, and she wasn't sure if she could win it. She had already used all her weapons, a mistake she now realized as she saw his eyes dancing mischievously behind his dark lashes.

"I'd be happy to see your sister safely home," Zane said, quickly answering for her.

"Thanks, Mary," Marcus said, dropping a kiss on top of her head.

Would he have even noticed if she said no?

Chapter Twelve

At least he had the weather figured out. That was more than he could say about the woman on his arm. Clouds had arrived while they were eating and were scattered across the sky, giving the stars a chance to play hide-and-seek as the breeze moved their cover eastward.

Zane and Mary walked along the boardwalk toward her hotel. Her skirt rustled against his pants leg as she clutched her shawl close. The cool breeze ruffled her bouquet of violets. A sudden gust raised her skirts, and she placed her other hand against it to hold it down.

Their hands brushed against each other and Zane wrapped his fingers over hers, holding her palm against the bandage on his right hand.

His reasons for doing so tumbled through both their minds.

Should I pull away from him?

What the heck—her hand feels so good in mine.
What would it hurt just to kiss him?
Dang, she's pretty.

Mary shyly looked at his profile, highlighted by the lamplight. He was too good-looking for his own good, and he knew it. She could tell by the way he carried himself. Even the slight pockmarks added an endearing quality to the perfection of his profile.

He knew she was watching him.

They came to an alley off the boardwalk. Zane pulled Mary into the shelter of darkness, and she suddenly found herself trapped between two solid walls, one made of brick and the other of warm flesh and pounding blood.

"Are you ready to know my secrets, Mary?" His sturdy build surrounded her as his cinnamon-scented breath caressed her cheek.

"You presume too much, Zane," she said breathlessly.

"Do I?" His hands casually drifted up her arms, sliding beneath the cool satin of her shawl. Goose bumps broke out on her arms, prickling the smoothness of her skin.

"You do," she said, her eyes dark in the dim light of the alley. "You presume that I'm interested in you."

"Aren't you?" His left hand settled on her shoulder while his index finger traced the line of her jaw. "After all, you're always asking questions about me." His head tilted sideways and his hazel eyes glittered as the lamplight was reflected in them.

"I'm not a bit interested," Mary said, casting her eyes downward, veiling her own secrets.

His breath was warm against her cheek.

"Not one bit," she sighed, realizing that a kiss was

inevitable. She really didn't want to fight it. If only he weren't so . . .

"Mary—"

"Ma-a-a-a."

Zane's head flew up in surprise. "Lucifer?"

"Ma-a-a-a," they heard again, and both their heads turned toward the sound.

Zane stepped out toward the boardwalk and was amazed to see Lucifer trotting down the middle of the thoroughfare, dragging a long trail of rope that was knotted around his neck. The goat saw Zane and ran straight to him, butting his horns against a sturdy hip.

"Glory," Zane said, realization overcoming his astonishment. "Someone is messing with Glory." He took off toward the stable.

"Ma-a-a-a," Lucifer complained to Mary. She touched the goat on the forehead and gathered up her skirts to follow Zane.

Glory's screams of frustration added wings to Zane's boots as he flew down the street amidst the curious stares of pedestrians. He turned a corner and saw the mare sitting on her haunches in the middle of the street. A rope was looped around her neck, and two riders were attempting to drag her off, one by yanking on the rope and the other by hitting her withers with a crop.

Zane quickly recognized the two riders as the men who had been admiring her earlier. He wondered whether the man he had paid to care for her had been in league with them as he vaulted onto a hitching rail, took two running steps and then launched his body through the air. He struck the lead rider straight in the midsection and they tumbled into the street, falling right in front of Glory, who quickly decided she had had enough adventure for the evening. She twisted away while Zane and her kidnapper rolled beneath the hooves of the other two horses.

The man wielding the crop dismounted and used it on both combatants as they rolled in the street. Zane used the advantage of his bulk and righteous anger to come out on top, which quickly became a disadvantage as the crop beat against his back and head. He let go of the first man long enough to ward off a blow and wound up with a boot in his chest that flipped him onto his back on the boardwalk, knocking the breath from his body.

The figure of a man loomed over him, his features lost as the lamplight glowed behind him, but his intent was clear. Zane tried to draw a breath as he prepared himself for the next assault.

"Ma-a-a-a," Lucifer bleated. The goat attacked with head down, butting the horse thief's backside.

Zane scrambled away just as the shrill sound of whistles filled the air. The police were on their way. The attackers decided it was time for a retreat, and the sounds of their hoofbeats were fading away just as the policemen arrived on the scene on foot.

"Ma-a-a-a," Lucifer gently butted his horns against Zane's thigh.

Zane rubbed the goat's head between the knobs of his horns.

"Thanks," he mumbled, wondering if he should actually apologize to the goat. He decided not to as he climbed to his feet and beat the dust off his clothes. After all, the goat hadn't apologized to him for butting him off the train.

Or had he?

Mary was holding on to Glory's halter with one hand as she gestured wildly with the other, explaining the incident to one of the policemen. Two of the others decided that Zane needed help and came to his aid, after he found his feet.

"Is this horse your property?" asked the one who seemed to be in charge.

"I've got her papers at my hotel," Zane said as he quickly ran his hands over the trembling mare. He was satisfied that she was unhurt, except maybe for her pride. Mary rubbed Glory's forehead and whispered in her ear while Zane checked her.

"Is she all right?" Mary asked, concern for the mare plainly written on her face.

"I think so," Zane said. He gave his attention to the police once he was satisfied that Glory was all right, but since the would-be thieves were gone and he couldn't identify them, there wasn't a lot the officers could do. His bandage had come loose in the fracas and Zane tugged on the end of it as he talked to the police.

"Your hand," Mary said when the officers were finally gone. She grabbed it and turned the palm up to check the stitches.

"It's fine," Zane said as he gave his palm a good look.

"We should replace the bandage at least," she declared.

"I don't want to leave her," Zane said as he rubbed Glory's arched neck.

"I guess you're planning on spending the night with her?"

Zane smoothed back a lock of Mary's hair that had

come loose in her run to help him. "Are you jealous?" he asked, his voice strangely quiet but the mischief still dancing in his eyes.

Mary aimed a swift kick at his shins.

"Ow!" Zane rubbed the front of his leg.

"Ma-a-a-a," Lucifer put in with his mouth full of Mary's violets.

Zane refused to let Glory out of his sight. They walked the mare to his hotel, or rather, Zane limped and Mary walked to his hotel. They made a strange sight, with Mary in her elaborate dress and Lucifer following along, trailing violets, greenery and lace.

Zane retrieved his valise and checked out of his room, knowing that it would be many days before he would enjoy the comfort of a bed. They moved on to Mary's hotel, where he waited while she went up to get Marcus's bag so she could tend to his hand.

"Have you got anything for my leg?" Zane asked when she was satisfied with his hand.

"Did you hurt your leg?"

"Don't you remember? I got kicked by a mule," Zane teased.

Mary laughed. "You deserved it."

"That's nice."

"What?"

"You laughing at me instead of looking at me like I'm an unruly student and you want to sit me in the corner after giving me a thorough switching."

"That's because most of the time you deserve it."

"You think I deserve another switching after the beating I got tonight with the crop?"

"No, I think what you did tonight was very brave and heroic."

Zane flashed his dimples. "I didn't do anything. I've got a couple of friends that could have dropped those guys with just a look."

"Sounds like they'd be handy to have around."

"They are."

"It was brave of you to go after those thieves." Mary looked into his eyes. "They could have been armed, for all you knew."

"Now I'm thinking that what I did was stupid."

"I'm pretty sure Glory doesn't think so. And I don't think so either."

"I just did what I had to do, and it wasn't anything more or less than anyone else would have done. They were stealing Jenny's horse. In the West there's nothing lower than a horse thief."

"So you were just doing your job?"

"Yes, ma'am," Zane said. He didn't like talking about the fight even if it was scoring him points with Mary. He knew that any one of his friends would have had the bandits tied up and sitting on the boardwalk in a heartbeat. He wasn't a hero, he was just lucky that things had happened the way they had. Lucifer had probably done more to affect the outcome of the struggle than he had.

"I'd better get this lady to bed," he said, patting Glory's rump. "Care to join us?"

He took a step backward out of range of Mary's foot. His dimples flashed along with his wide grin. " 'This bud of love, by summer's ripening breath may prove a beauteous flower when next we meet.' "

Mary put her hands on her hips and shook her head at his audacity, but she was smiling as she did so. "'Good night, good night. As sweet repose and rest come to thy heart as that within my breast,'" she responded, quoting *Romeo and Juliet*. Why and how had he learned Shakespeare? "Good night, Zane."

"Good night, Mary. Sweet dreams."

She watched as he moved down the street.

"Come on, goat," he said. "I've decided not to roast you over a spit."

"Ma-a-a-a," Lucifer replied as he trotted along behind him.

"At least not the first night out," Zane added.

Chapter Thirteen

He should have wished himself sweet dreams. After a restless night, Zane wearily rose from his bed in Glory's stall and blearily greeted the miserable excuse for a day.

He had tossed and turned all night. His dreams were filled with visions of a more-than-willing Missy beneath him, who suddenly turned into Mary. That sweet dream was interrupted by another dream in which Glory screamed wildly. But when he fought his way back he found the mare resting peacefully. After he finally fell back asleep, Zane dreamed that Lucifer was laughing at him. It all made for an extremely restless night.

And it looked as if the day was going to be as miserable as the night before it. Zane felt tired and cranky, and he ached from the morning erection that greeted him.

"You are definitely cramping my style," he said to Glory as he dumped feed into her bin. "I should have spent last night in the arms of a beautiful woman instead of with you and Lucifer."

Glory whickered in protest.

"Not that you aren't beautiful. You're just not my type." Zane ran his fingers through the mare's forelock. "Although your eyes are the right color."

Zane looked into the brown eyes of the mare. Since when had he preferred brown eyes over any other color? Missy's eyes were a cornflower blue, and most of the other times he didn't even pay attention. It wasn't as if he really looked at them anyway. There were other parts of a woman's body that usually held his attention.

"I'm ready to get home," he confided to Glory.

Home seemed very far away and he knew the trip would be a long one. Especially if he woke up in this condition every morning.

He should have found himself a good whore last night instead of flirting with Mary. But if he had, chances were that he'd be sitting down at the police station right now trying to figure out how to tell Jenny that her mare had been stolen. He'd be afraid to show his face at the ranch again if that had happened.

In reality, he knew Jenny would have forgiven him eventually, but he also took his responsibilities seriously. Jenny had entrusted him with this job, and he was going to get it done. And he wasn't going to let horse thieves, goats or pretty schoolteachers get in his way.

"Let's get on the train," Zane said to Glory and Lucifer. A few more days of easy traveling and then they would be on the trail.

With Mary.

His jeans sure did feel tight.

Westward the train moved, through the pouring rain that brought with it unseasonably cold air for early summer. Thunder pounded and lightning flashed across the sky, sending the wildlife and the settlers of the Northern plains to seek shelter. It was a miserable day for man or beast.

Inside the stock car, Zane and his charges snoozed, lulled into slumber by the steady rhythm of the rain and the gentle swaying of the train.

Once again his dreams were vague and disjointed. The sound of the thunder became the laughter of strange painted faces, and the flash of the lightning became brands of fire that seared his skin.

And through the haze of his dream came the sound of Lucifer's bizarre laughter. Zane tossed restlessly on his blanket in the straw only to jerk himself awake, haunted by the strange images.

The rain pounded, Glory and Lucifer dozed in the stall, and the train chugged its way westward.

The atmosphere was much the same in the passenger cars. Children whined with boredom at the dreary, monotonous landscape. Tourists who had hoped to see herds of buffalo and tribes of wild Indians sighed in frustration at the money they had apparently wasted on the trip.

The other passengers settled down to sleep, but none were able to rest. The cars were smelly and stuffy with the windows closed to keep out the rain and the cold.

As day turned to night, Mary dozed on Marcus's

shoulder, fighting her own dreams. She saw herself wandering aimlessly across endless plains, searching for something.

The loneliness of her dreams was terrifying and brought her swimming to the surface of consciousness, gasping for breath. She kept a tight hold on Marcus's arm as she dozed, trying to reassure herself that she was not alone, that her dear brother was near and would not leave her.

An abrupt blast of the whistle brought Zane staggering to his feet. He looked around in a daze at his surroundings, as his mind desperately sought for something familiar to grab on to.

He was on a train.

Glory and Lucifer looked at him, both seeming to be as confused as he felt. Zane ran his fingers through his hair, more to calm his mind than to restore order to the unruly strands. In the next moment, he went flying to the floor, landing with a whoosh as the train came to a sudden, screeching stop.

The whistle blasted again and then the sound of gunfire erupted.

The train was under attack!

Zane rolled to his knees and quickly checked to make sure Glory was still standing before he went crawling toward his valise. His gun and holster were packed away; he'd felt he had no need of them while traveling by train.

He strapped his belt on, checked the load of his forty-five and crawled toward the door. He didn't have to look to know that the train was being attacked by Indians. The sounds of their battle cries made the source of the fighting all too clear.

Zane slid the door open a crack and scanned the area around the train. The locomotive had stopped dead in what seemed to be the middle of nowhere. The rain had ended sometime in the night, but the ground was still soggy and the Indian ponies chewed up the sod as their riders raced back and forth, firing at the train. He figured it was early morning, as the sun was still low on the eastern horizon.

"What in the hell?" he said as he watched the attack. A million questions tumbled through his mind as he tried to figure out what he should do. Why were the Indians attacking? How had they stopped the train? Was Mary all right? What about Marcus? He would protect her, wouldn't he? What should he do if the attackers came after Glory?

His first responsibility was to Glory. A mare like her would be a great prize for men who valued horses as much as white men valued money.

They were Sioux and Lakota. Zane recognized the signs and the markings. Chase had taught Zane how to tell the differences between the tribes and what to expect from each one.

Why in the world were the Sioux attacking a train?

A few of the warriors had fallen. Someone, somewhere, was fighting back. Zane wondered if anyone on the train had been injured. Even though the train was full of people, most of them were unarmed. How long could they hold up against a full-scale attack such as this? There were thirty riders or more that he could see.

Why had the train stopped? Why didn't it just move

away from the attack? The Indian ponies couldn't keep up with a train going full bore down the track. Of course, once the engine was stopped, it would take a while to get it started again. The engineer would have to build up steam.

The warriors were boarding the passenger cars. It was only a matter of time until they found Glory. What could Zane do against thirty armed men? If only he had a rifle—but his was stored with his rig in North Platte, waiting for his arrival. He had to do something. He shoved the bar across the door and looked around for a miracle.

The roof. From the roof he would be able to see the entire area, have a bit of cover and take out anyone who made an attempt on Glory.

At least until his ammunition ran out. Lucifer and Glory watched as he moved a bale of straw to the center of the car and disappeared through the hatch on the roof. Zane took a moment to lean in and talk to the animals.

"Shh, girl," he said soothingly to Glory. "And I suggest you stay quiet, too, unless you want to be the main course in a feast tonight," he cautioned Lucifer.

Zane snaked to the edge of the roof and once again scanned the area. The engineer and the coalmen were standing by the engine with their hands raised. There were two Lakota on horseback guarding them, along with what looked like a white woman in a raggedy calico dress. She must have come with the Sioux, and her reason for being there was another mysterious piece of the puzzle that had greeted him this morning.

Screams came from the passenger cars. They

sounded more fearful than desperate, however. He didn't hear any shots being fired and got the idea that a massacre was not the intent of the attackers. If it were, the engineer and coalmen would be dead.

Unless the attackers were saving them for something special.

The Indians didn't seem a bit concerned about the stock car. He didn't have a clue how many were inside the train, but the majority seemed to be outside, patiently waiting for something.

Mary.

Was she all right? What about Marcus?

What was going on?

Zane rolled over on his back and looked up at the morning sky. The air was cold, unseasonably, so and the sky was clear and cloudless, washed clean by the rain.

The Indians had no idea he was on top of the car. He could lie low and easily remain unnoticed.

But he had to know if Mary was all right.

Zane holstered his forty-five and crawled to the edge of the car. A quick look let him know that he was still unobserved, so he rose to a crouch and leapt to the next car.

He'd be lucky if he didn't break his neck.

Mary had awoken with a start. Marcus was gone, and his absence had shocked her into awareness quicker than the gunshots that sounded outside the train.

Gunshots! Why were there gunshots?

Mary stood and realized that the rest of the passengers were just as confused as she was. The train had stopped! Women started screaming, and men rushed to the side of the car that faced north.

"We're under attack!" someone said.

"Are those real Indians?" a child asked.

"Everyone take cover!" someone else exclaimed.

Now Mary was becoming frightened.

"Marcus?" she called, hoping he would hear her above the cacophony of panic-stricken voices.

Miraculously, he appeared at her side.

"What's happening?" Mary asked, her voice trembling.

"Indians are attacking the train," he said calmly as he pulled her down to the floor. "You need to take cover."

"Not without you." The screams were louder, and so was the gunfire. Someone was firing back.

"Get under the seat, Mary." They flinched as a bullet whizzed by. "Watch your head," he said as he pushed her under the bench.

"Marcus, where are you going?" The heartbreaking sobs of a woman filled the air along with the cries of an infant.

"Mary, I have to see to the wounded." His handsome face was earnest, full of resolve. She knew that look. She had seen it more times than she could count.

"Let me help you," she pleaded, clutching at his hand. Fear bubbled up inside, fear of the loneliness that threatened to consume her. She looked at Marcus with terrified brown eyes, but her mind saw Michael as he looked up at the burning house and saw the woman holding a baby and crying for help from the upstairs window.

"I have to get them out, Mary."

"Don't leave me, Michael. It's too dangerous, the fire is too big. Don't leave me, Michael."

"Don't leave me, Marcus."

"Stay here, Mary. Stay safe." He held his bag in his hand. He was going to help the wounded. He was going to do his job, this was his calling, his life.

Someone bumped into him as he stood to leave, and a heavyset man dove under the seat opposite Mary as Marcus took off down the aisle. She rose to follow her brother, but was trapped by the man wedged into the opening between the seats.

"Marcus!" she cried out, but he didn't answer. Injured people needed him more than she did. Or so he thought.

What was happening? She couldn't see anything past the fat man, who was soaking wet with sweat and noisily breathing in her ear. Mary gagged at the smell of him, covering her mouth with her gloved hand. The smell of fear was horrendous.

She couldn't see anything. She heard screams and shots and the yells of the men, but no one gave her answers.

Where was Marcus?

"They're on the train!" someone shouted.

"God save us!" a woman prayed.

The noise quieted as the Indians entered the car.

"Dock-tor."

The word was recognizable even though it was unfamiliar to the man who spoke it.

A collective gasp went through the car.

Mary shoved with all her might against the ponderous backside that was blocking her escape. The man shifted, and she squeezed through the narrow opening.

"Dock-tor?"

Mary made it to her feet and found herself looking at the painted chest of a Sioux warrior. He held a rifle in his hand, and his bright eyes quickly scanned the people gazing at him with fear and loathing. There were two more behind him, both looking as if they were ready to kill at the slightest provocation.

The fat man on the floor pointed toward the next car.

"He went that way," he said with a trembling voice.

The warrior looked at the shaking hand. He shoved Mary out of his path, and she landed on a bench. The warrior moved on with the other two behind, cautiously watching their backs as they went into the next car.

"You idiot!" Mary exclaimed as she regained her feet. She followed up with a swift kick to the heaving gut of the betrayer. "That's my brother they're looking for."

The man painfully climbed to his feet. "I've always believed that it is best to sacrifice one to save many," he said indignantly as he straightened his clothing.

"Coward!" Mary gave him another kick, this time to the shins, before she followed the Indians.

They had found Marcus. They were watching him as he tended one of the porters who had been wounded in the attack. The aisles were crowded with passengers straining to see the wounded man, the doctor and the Indians, who were all gathered at the other end of the car. Mary climbed on a bench so she could see what was happening.

"You must come," the lead Indian said.

"I can't," Marcus calmly explained. He never took his eyes off his patient. "This man might die if I leave him."

"Come now," the Indian said. He placed a firm hand on Marcus's shoulder.

"Marcus, no!" Mary yelled.

"Mary?" Marcus said. "Let her through, please."

Why did he always sound so calm, no matter what was happening? Mary shoved against the bodies that blocked her passage. She had just gotten to her brother when the door at the front of the car opened and an older woman in a raggedy calico dress came in. Mary dismissed her as one of the passengers until she realized that she was wearing moccasins that laced up her calves beneath the too-short and uneven hem of her dress. Her hair was untidy and tied with a rawhide thong, and the skin of her face was darkened by the sun. When the warriors pointed to Marcus and spoke in their native language, she turned to him.

"Please, you must come with us," the woman said. Her speech was slow, as if she were taking time to think about her words.

"Mary," Marcus said. "Hold this." He grabbed her hand and placed it firmly against a wound in the porter's arm. "Don't let up until the bleeding slows down." He stood and wiped his hands on his handkerchief. "Why must I come with you?" he asked the woman. "And why have these warriors stopped the train?"

"My husband," she said. "His spirit is gone, yet his body breathes."

"How was he hurt?" Marcus asked.

Mary looked up at her brother, fear once again consuming her. He wasn't actually thinking of going with the woman, was he?

"His head. His head was struck. He sleeps but does not waken."

"A coma. How long?"

"One moon."

"A month?"

"Yes. A month."

"No!" Mary cried.

"You must come."

"What happens if he doesn't?" Mary asked.

The warriors with the woman understood the question. The lead one grabbed a passenger and pulled her close, his arm around her neck, pulling her up on her toes.

"Please," Mary managed to gasp out, her eyes wide with fear as she looked at Marcus.

"My husband is also this man's father," the woman said in explanation. "He values his father's life over any of these."

"Marcus, you can't go," Mary protested. "You don't know what they'll do to you."

"I must," Marcus said. "People will die if I don't."

"I'm going, too," Mary insisted.

"No!" Marcus said firmly. "Find Zane." Marcus looked at the roof above them. "Stay with him and go to Wyoming. I'll find you there when this is over."

"Are you insane?" Mary asked incredulously. She stood up, forgetting about the porter. Blood gushed from the man's wound as she abandoned him, choosing her brother over a random stranger that Marcus had chosen to help.

And now he would risk his life for another random stranger. An Indian. God only knew what would happen to Marcus if he was unable to help the man.

Marcus knelt to help the porter.

"We must go," the woman said.

Marcus found a pair of willing hands and instructed his helper on the care of the porter before he turned to his sister.

"Mary—stay with Zane. I'll find you in Wyoming, I promise." He placed her arm in the hand of a burly man standing nearby. "Don't let her off this train," he instructed him. "No matter what she does." He picked up his bag and turned to the waiting Indians. "Let's go."

"No!" Mary screamed, fighting the hands that held her.

Marcus followed the Indians out of the train. Mary and the other passengers watched through the window as he was instantly surrounded by the waiting group of braves. He swung up on a painted horse behind the woman in the raggedy dress, and they were off, leaving silently, wordlessly.

Mary struggled against the strong hands that held her. There was no release. Her mind swam. Marcus couldn't leave her alone. He was her brother. She had to help him.

"There, there, child," a woman said as she patted her arm.

Mary looked out the window, watching as the group

disappeared over the horizon. She marked the direction in her mind before she fell down in a faint.

Zane had moved over the roof of the train, jumping from car to car after checking to make sure he hadn't been spotted. The war party had been concentrating on the happenings inside the train, and he'd managed to move up to the passenger cars without any problem.

When he'd seen Marcus come out of one of the passenger cars with a woman and three braves, Zane had been confused.

Why was Marcus leaving with the Sioux? Was he their prisoner? He'd seemed willing enough as he'd swung up behind the woman and ridden away with the rest of them. They had gathered their wounded to take with them and left nothing behind but a spotted horse whose leg was tangled in his reins.

The horse neighed after the warriors, asking them to wait, to come back, to save him from this lonely, frightening place. They ignored him and kept on riding until they disappeared over a small rise.

Zane jumped from the roof to the platform connecting the cars, and was even more surprised to see Mary in a dead faint. She was lying on a bench, and a woman was alternating between chafing Mary's hands and fanning her face.

"Is she all right?" he asked.

"She fainted after they took her brother away," the woman explained.

"Why did they take him?"

"They needed a doctor."

It made as much sense as everything else that had happened so far.

Satisfied that Mary would be all right, Zane jumped from the car and ran toward the engine.

"Why did you stop?" he asked the engineer, who was busy with his coalmen, trying to build up steam.

"There was a woman lying on the tracks," he said. "I purt near killed her trying to stop in time. If I'd known she was with them Indians, I would have run her over." He spat in disgust. "How are things back there?"

"Some folks are wounded, I think, and the Indians took Dr. Brown with them."

"Imagine that."

"Need any help?" Zane asked.

"You could help stoke the fire."

Zane climbed into the engine to help just as the conductor came running up. From what Zane could hear, there were only a few wounded and no one had been killed.

Zane's primary concern was how to help Marcus. What could he do? He had no supplies and wasn't very good at tracking. The best thing to do would be ride on to the next town and send word to the closest fort.

Poor Mary.

Mary cautiously opened one eye. Just as she'd hoped, everyone had left her in peace. She had hardly dared to breathe, not even when Zane came in. She knew there was no way he would let her escape. If he even suspected what she had in mind, he'd tie her up and throw her in a trunk. And probably enjoy every minute of it.

She opened the other eye and was gratified to see

that everyone was distracted with the wounded and comparing versions of the morning's attack. In a few seconds, she was off the bench and on her way out the door. She jumped to the ground and ran down the track to the stock cars at the back of the train. She needed a fast horse, and there just happened to be one on the train.

And if Zane tried to stop her, well, she'd deal with that when it happened. It would help if she had a weapon of some sort. There was a shovel in the stock car. It would do.

The door was locked. All of them. How to get inside? Mary hastily looked around. She knew she didn't have much time. She had no idea how long it would take to get the train started, but it wouldn't be long.

How had Zane gotten out?

Mary looked up. The roof. He'd probably been crawling around on the roof of the train the entire time. That was how he'd shown up so fast after Marcus had been taken.

Mary hiked up her skirts and climbed the ladder on the end of the car to the roof. She found the trapdoor still open and quickly dropped to the floor inside.

"Ma-a-a-a," Lucifer greeted her.

"Sorry, Lucifer, you can't go with us this time," Mary said to the goat.

She wrapped the lead around Glory's halter and led the mare out of the stall. She pulled the door open and took a quick glance up and down the tracks. Except for some people around the engine, there was no one in sight.

She saw a spotted horse with its reins tangled

around one leg. Maybe she should take that horse instead. But what if it was lame? Better not risk it.

Glory was a taller horse than Mary was used to riding, and without a stirrup she had no way to mount. She scrambled around until she found a bucket and used it to climb onto Glory's muscular back.

Glory looked around in surprise as Mary untangled her skirts.

"Let's go, girl," she said and kicked her heels into the mare's side.

Glory tossed her head and with a giant leap hit the ground running, with Mary bent over her neck, holding on for dear life.

"Looks like one of them got your horse," the conductor said to Zane.

Zane threw a chunk of wood into the furnace, wiped the sweat from his eyes and looked in the direction the man was pointing.

His jaw dropped as he saw Glory galloping off in the same direction the Indians had taken. It wasn't an Indian on her back, however—it was Mary. Her well-curved backside gave her away, along with the red flowers on her hat.

"Dang it all," he yelled as he jumped from the car and ran down the track. Zane wasn't a bit surprised when Lucifer jumped nimbly from the car and took off after the horse and rider.

"Mary!" Zane yelled toward the horizon.

She was gone like the wind. Lucifer couldn't keep up and returned at a trot with Mary's hat in his mouth.

"Ma-a-a-a," he said, dropping the hat at Zane's feet.

Chapter Fourteen

Well, if that just don't beat all.

How was he supposed to explain this to Jenny and Cat?

Zane realized there was no explaining it. He'd just have to go after Mary and Glory. And when he caught up with that spitfire of a schoolteacher, he was going to wring her neck.

With soothing tones, Zane approached the spotted horse with the tangled reins. The horse didn't shy, he actually seemed grateful when Zane released his leg from the reins and ran expert hands over him to make sure he was sound. Zane was relieved to find no sign of injury.

"Are you going to hang her when you catch her?" the conductor asked.

Zane grinned and shook his head. "I'll think about it. I guess a few swats on her backside wouldn't hurt."

"You're going to have to catch her first."

"I'm not worried. Glory is fast, but she'll run herself out before too long. I'll probably meet them heading back this way."

"We can't wait for you."

"I know," Zane sighed. "Would you mind delivering a letter for me?"

"I'll do what I can," the conductor said.

With a stub of a pencil the conductor handed him, Zane wrote a short note.

The Indians took Dr. Brown.
His sister took Jenny's horse.
If I don't come back, you can fire me.
Your friend,
Zane.
P.S. Cat's schoolteacher is Dr. Brown's sister.

He addressed it to Jake.

"I need you to make sure the sheriff of Laramie gets it. He'll know where to send it."

"I'll make sure it gets there."

"Can you send our bags on too? Dr. Brown's and mine?"

"We'll take care of it, son."

"I wish I had a rifle."

"I wish you did, too."

So much for that. Zane had hoped that the conductor would volunteer one from the train. He figured he was lucky for the canteen the man offered. He grabbed his blanket from the car and swung up on the spotted horse.

"Ma-a-a-a," Lucifer bleated.

"Do you mind taking care of my goat?" Zane asked.

"There's not a chance in hell, boy. I seen what that goat did to you, knocking you off the train, and I figure he likes you."

"He's got a strange way of showing it," Zane said. He looked at the train regretfully. The last thing he wanted to do was take off for the middle of nowhere after some foolish woman and a horse that was better suited for a fancy stable than the wilds of the badlands.

"Let's go, Lucifer," he said. "I hope you're a better tracker than I am."

Lucifer trotted after him, with Mary's hat in his mouth.

The sound of the train fading into the distance as Zane rode north was the loneliest sound he had ever heard. At least the tracks of the war party were visible. Glory's too, easy to pick out since she was shod. The rain-soaked earth left a clear trail of churned-up mud flung by horses' hooves.

How long could Glory run flat out? Would she stop? Did Mary have sense enough to stop her when she tired and let her blow? Did she know enough to rub her down to keep her from getting chilled? Or would they just keep racing across the plains until the thoroughbred's heart exploded in her chest. And what would they do about water?

How long would a schoolteacher have to work to pay for a horse such as Glory?

He knew Jenny wouldn't say a word about the theft of her horse. She would do the same if there was a chance it would bring her own brother back.

Zane might have done it, too, if it had been one of his friends who'd been taken. Marcus was Mary's brother and the only relation she had in the world. No wonder she'd done whatever was necessary to go after him.

For the first time in his life, Zane found himself thinking about the baby sister who had died along with his mother. He had always missed his mother, but he had never given the baby girl much thought beyond blaming her for his mother's death. What would have happened if she had survived? What would it have been like to grow up with a sister to take care of? What would it be like to have someone depend on you and need you the way Mary needed Marcus? And Marcus doted on her.

Which brought his thoughts around again to the question that had been bugging him for ages: What would it be like to share the kind of love that he saw every day on the faces of his friends?

Was it worth the fear they experienced when something happened to the one they loved?

Hadn't his own father grieved himself to death after the death of his mother?

Yet all his friends seemed happy. Blissfully, foolishly happy.

He understood why Mary had taken Glory. Love was a powerful force.

But that thought didn't take the heavy weight of his responsibility away. His job was to deliver the mare safely to the Lynch ranch. And since he'd gotten involved, he felt obligated to deliver the schoolteacher, too. The doctor was an added bonus, since the town needed one and he was Jenny's friend.

There was no way he could show his face to his friends again if he failed in this mission.

"How fast is she, Lucifer?" Zane asked the goat.

"Ma-a-a-a," Lucifer said.

Zane looked at the goat. He was still carrying that dumb hat.

"At least you've got something to eat," he said. Zane realized he had slept through an entire day without eating; that was why his stomach was rumbling. And without a rifle he would be hard-pressed to find something to eat. Forty-fives were better suited to shooting at big targets like men than small ones like rabbits.

If only Jake were with him. Or Chase. Even Ty. Someone who was better suited to this hunt than he was. Someone who could track and shoot and look death in the eye and spit at it.

Someone who could tell him what he should do.

Someone with real experience at being a hero.

He was probably going to wind up dead. Marcus and Mary, too.

And Glory.

And Lucifer.

Dang it all.

Where are you, Marcus?

Mary knew she was in trouble. She had always been the impetuous one while Marcus was the steady, dependable one. But now he was gone, leaving her to do foolish things like chase after him on a high-strung thoroughbred through the middle of the Badlands.

No wonder she needed him.

At first she had thought she wouldn't have any

trouble catching up. And once she caught up to the war party, she would demand that they take her along, too. The plan had seemed pretty simple when she had first thought of it. Take Glory, find Marcus and stay with him.

She had thought that somehow she could protect her brother from whatever fate the Indians had in store for him.

Now she realized she was just a foolish girl on a foolish mission. But she wasn't about to give up. She would find Marcus and stay with him, no matter what it took.

They had run like the wind for a while, with Glory's long legs eating up the distance as if it were nothing. But suddenly the horse had slowed to a walk; now she seemed indignant when Mary tried to urge her back into a run.

"I guess you're built for speed, not distance," Mary said to the mare.

She hoped they were going in the right direction. The tracks seemed pretty obvious, and she followed them carefully.

How far ahead of her could Marcus be?

The air was surprisingly cool for midday in June. She now realized she should have grabbed a blanket before her hasty escape, but she hadn't had time to think things through.

What if she didn't find the war party today and had to spend the night out here alone, without a weapon, or a blanket, or food, or even a fire?

"You really should have thought this through, Mary," she said out loud. But when had she ever done that? Even her marriage to Michael had been done in haste because she was swept up in the moment. Not that she regretted the decision; it was just that she was suddenly realizing how impetuous she was. She should think things through.

But hadn't she given careful thought to coming out West? Hadn't she mulled it over for days before she accepted the position? Or had she just been jumping at the chance to escape her past and start over again?

"Start using your head, Mary," she said. "This isn't a disaster . . . yet."

Glory tossed her head in agreement.

The warriors couldn't be that far ahead of her, could they? They might be just over the ridge, just out of her line of sight.

"Come on, Glory, I know you can move a little bit faster." She dug her heels into the fine-toned flanks of the mare. Glory moved into a canter. It would have to do for now.

Marcus, where are you?

They would need water soon—Glory more than she. There hadn't been any since they'd left the train. And the sun was starting to burn her nose. She had lost her hat somewhere along the way. Not that it provided much protection. It was more decoration than anything else.

What about the Indian horses? Surely they would need to drink also. She was still following their trail.

Mary looked at the ground, churned up from the passage of many hooves. Then she realized that the entire area was churned-up earth as far as she could see in every direction.

When had she lost the trail?

Panic filled her. What should she do? Where had they gone?

Foolish girl.

Marcus, where are you?

There was a rise ahead. And beyond it she saw a shadowy movement that reminded her of the sea on a stormy day. Glory slowed as she approached the rise and tossed her head, fighting the hands that guided her.

"Easy, girl," Mary said as the horse circled instead of going forward as she commanded.

Glory stopped, dead set against going any further.

"What am I supposed to do now?" Mary asked the mare.

Glory stood with ears pricked forward, listening to the angry sounds beyond the rise.

What was that inhuman sound? Mary slid from Glory's back and immediately regretted doing so when she realized she had no way to get back on again.

With a firm grip on the halter, she pulled Glory beside her up the rise, the horse balking the entire way.

The sight before her sickened her like nothing ever had before. The rise she was on sheltered a small valley. A valley full of death. The bodies of innumerable buffalo lay before her, their stomachs swelling in the heat of the sun. The sky above the bodies was dark with the wings of buzzards, landing to tear away a piece of flesh and then rising again so another could move in to feast.

The smell was horrible. It reminded her of the fat man on the train. It gagged her, and she retched, losing what little sustenance she had taken the day before.

Mary fell to her knees, letting her hand slide down the lead that was attached to Glory's halter, and looked at the waste that lay before her.

"Oh, God, what am I going to do?" she sobbed and collapsed to the earth in tears with Glory standing guard over her heaving body.

Marcus, where are you?

Chapter Fifteen

Zane turned around for what seemed the hundredth time since he had left the train. Where was that dang goat? Lucifer couldn't keep up, and Zane didn't have time to wait.

He was pretty sure that if he gave the spotted horse his head, the animal would lead them to wherever Marcus was being taken.

But he had to find Mary first.

"Come on, Lucifer," Zane yelled.

"Ma-a-a-a," the goat complained as he broke into a trot to catch up.

Zane rolled his eyes in exasperation. Several hours had passed and he had yet to see any sign of Mary or Glory. Yet he was sure he was on their trail. The tracks he was following were those of a shod horse, and that had to be Glory.

"What am I going to do with you?" Zane asked as Lucifer finally caught up.

The goat looked up at him with his gold-rimmed eyes.

"Dang goat," Zane said as he dismounted. He poured a bit of the precious water from the canteen into his hat and let the goat drink.

"We've got to find some water or we're going to be in trouble," he said as the goat drank greedily. "I wonder how Mary and Glory are faring."

"Ma-a-a-a," Lucifer bleated, raising his dripping chin and looking off to the north.

"Yeah, I miss them too," Zane said. "You know, we're not making very good time."

Zane gathered the goat up in his arms and slung him over the back of the horse, which looked at him with ears pricked in confusion.

"If you want to get home, you're going to have to carry him," he said to the horse.

"Ma-a-a-a," Lucifer responded.

"Quit complaining or you'll go back to walking," Zane said as he swung up behind the goat.

Zane kicked the spotted horse into a canter and kept a firm hand on Lucifer's back to prevent the goat from squirming around. It was an uncomfortable ride, but as least they were finally making some time.

If only he knew where they were going.

Even with Lucifer squirming before him, Zane's mind wandered again. What would he do once he found Mary? *If* he found Mary. The smart thing to do would be to get them back to civilization as soon as possible. They had no business wandering around out here in the middle of nowhere looking for Indians.

Would she go? Could he make her? Did he really want to? How could he expect her to leave when her brother was out there . . . somewhere.

What should he do?

The thought suddenly occurred to him that he'd never had to plan his life beyond the next payday. It had always been the same. Work, eat, sleep, get paid and then run to town and waste it all on a good time. He had some money saved, of course, but most of his income he just frittered away. It was another way of defying his grandfather. A way of saying, See, money isn't as important as you think it is.

And when something out of the ordinary did happen he usually waited for Chase or Ty to make the decisions and tell him what to do. It was easier that way. Someone else assigned the job; he accomplished it. He was proud of himself because he never did back down from a job. He'd show his grandfather that he was responsible.

Zane realized the joke was on himself. His grandfather had no idea how he was living his life.

Well, this time he'd be calling the shots. There was no one else to turn to.

So what are you going to do now?

Take it one step at a time. Find Mary. Find Glory. Make sure they're safe. Then he'd worry about Marcus.

But first he had to find Mary.

The tracks of hoofprints widened. Zane stopped the spotted horse and let Lucifer slide to the ground. He studied the churned-up earth. The warriors were no longer riding single file, he decided. He urged the horse into a trot as the trail grew wider still. Surely there hadn't been that many horses in the war party.

Zane dismounted to take a closer look. It almost looked as if a herd of cattle had run over the ground here. Wait a minute—buffalo. A buffalo herd had passed this way, and the Indians had used the tracks for cover.

But they'd have to come out somewhere on the other side, wouldn't they? Just how big was this herd? Zane looked around and realized that as far as he could see, the ground was torn up by hoof marks.

Mary had to be somewhere in front of him. He swung back up on the spotted horse.

"Come on, Lucifer," he said. "I've got a feeling we're getting close."

"Ma-a-a-a," the goat bleated as he followed along.

Zane made note of the landmarks, not that there were many. Around him were nothing but rolling plains, but in the distance he could see a rocky outcropping, and he marked the way it looked. He might have to circle the tracks to find the Lakota's trail and he wanted to make sure he didn't waste any time getting turned around.

He rode into a hollow and then followed the swell of the ground up the other side. In the distance was another ridge.

Was that a horse standing on it? It was hard to tell, especially since the horizon behind it seemed strange, almost as if it were moving.

Zane kicked the spotted horse into a canter and broke into a grin as he realized it was indeed a horse, a tall black horse. But where was Mary? Why was Glory just standing there?

"Mary!" he shouted.

He saw a movement below Glory. Had Mary fallen? Was she hurt?

He kicked his horse again, this time into a flat-out run, which left Lucifer bawling after him.

"Mary!" Zane vaulted from the horse and gathered her into his arms. "Are you hurt? What happened? Did you fall? Did she throw you? What is that smell?"

Mary rubbed her eyes and pointed.

"Look," she said, her voice nothing but a whisper.

Zane followed the line of her hand and saw the waste that lay before them. The hollow was covered with the bodies of dead buffalo, more than he could count. The buzzards continued their work, oblivious to the human witnesses of their carnage.

"Why?" Mary asked. "Why would the Indians do this?"

"No Indian did this, Mary. This is the work of white men." Zane pulled her to her feet. "We did it."

"What?"

"They wonder back in Washington why the Indians fight us when we claim to be so good to them. They fight us because of this."

"You don't think they'll use this as an excuse to hurt Marcus, do you?"

Mary's brown eyes were moist with tears as she looked up into his face.

"No. I think they had a very good reason for wanting Marcus. I don't think they'd come all this way to get him and then hurt him."

"The woman said her husband was sick and needed a doctor," she said.

"And they got lucky and found one of the best," Zane assured her as he held on to her hands. "They won't hurt him."

"You came after me," Mary said, as if suddenly waking from a trance. Her hair was wild from her ride, and her brown eyes glowed, whether from tears or happiness, he couldn't tell. She was a mess, but the look on her face dazzled him. His first impulse was to spank her delicious backside since she had worried him so, but that was quickly overruled by the desire to kiss her softly parted lips.

Neither response would be appropriate, he told himself sternly.

"No, I came after Glory," Zane said, and he dropped her hands as if he'd been burned. "You stole my horse."

"I thought she was Jenny's horse," Mary retorted. How could he go from being so soft one minute to aggravating the next?

"She is, but she's my responsibility."

"I'm sure, considering the circumstances, that Jenny wouldn't mind my borrowing her."

"What makes you think that?" Zane asked.

"Because I've known her longer than you have."

Dang, she could be smug when she wanted to.

"You said you didn't even remember her," Zane pointed out.

"I said I barely remember her, but from what I remember, I know she wouldn't mind."

"Well, I know her *better* than you do."

"Now, what's that supposed to mean?"

"It means that I've spent more time with her in the years I've known her than you did since you knew her, so I can guess what she'd think better than you can."

"And what would she think, Mister Know-It-All?" Mary asked with hands on her hips. She waited while he tried to remember exactly what he had just said to make sure it made sense.

Zane rolled his eyes in exasperation. "Are you like this with your students?"

"What do you mean, am I like this with my students? And quit trying to change the subject."

"I'm not trying to change the subject. The subject is closed. I know Jenny better than you do."

"You sound like a petulant child, you know," Mary said.

"Funny how I never had that problem until I met you," Zane mumbled under his breath as he turned to check on Glory.

"Ma-a-a-a," Lucifer cried as he ran up to them.

"You brought Lucifer," Mary exclaimed incredulously as she knelt to greet the goat.

"It's not like I had a choice," Zane declared in exasperation. "No one else wanted him. He tried to follow you but couldn't keep up."

"Oh, Lucifer, I'm sorry," Mary said as she put her arms around the goat's neck. "I'm sorry we left you behind."

Zane watched in disgust as she fussed over Lucifer as if he were a child.

"So what are we going to do now?" Mary asked as

she pushed Lucifer away from the buttons on her blouse.

"Find some water, make camp, go home." Zane pulled his mount up close to Glory.

"Without Marcus?"

"Mary. We have no supplies. All I've got is this forty-five. I'm not that good at tracking. This is a big country, and I don't know where to look for Marcus. The best thing for us to do is go home and get some help."

"But that will take too long. It could be weeks before we get back."

"He'll still have a better chance than the two of us wandering around out here for days."

"I don't believe that you can't track thirty horses," Mary said.

Zane threw his arm out to encompass the hollow below. "Where do you suggest I start?"

Mary stomped her foot and turned her back to him.

"Now who is being petulant?" Zane asked, then jumped back as she took a swing at his shin with her foot.

"Where do you really come from?" Mary asked in exasperation.

"I've already told you that."

"I find it hard to believe that a boy raised on the frontier would know what 'petulant' means."

"So you're a bit of a snob also," Zane said. "I didn't realize that the schools in Denver were more hoity-toity than the ones in Missouri. Or maybe you didn't get to be smart until you moved to New York City."

"That's not what I meant."

"So what did you mean? Just because I'm a ranch hand, I can't read a book?"

"I never said that."

"Well, when you figure out what you did say, let me know." Zane swung up on the spotted horse. Daylight was running out, and it was time to make some decisions for the night. "I'm going to find us some water. Then I'm going to make camp. Are you going to do your thinking here or are you coming with me?"

"Ohhhh," Mary growled. "You are the most insufferable man I have ever met."

Zane looked down at her from the back of the horse. "I think we've already established that fact."

Mary crossed her arms and looked off into the distance.

"Suit yourself," Zane said and turned the horse to go.

"I can't get on," Mary said as the spotted horse stepped away.

"What?"

"Glory's too tall. I can't mount without help."

The wide grin came back in a flash, cutting deep dimples in his cheek. "I might be insufferable, but at least I'm not impetuous."

Mary gave him a confused look.

"That means I don't dash off half-cocked."

"I know what it means."

Zane swung down from the spotted horse and stood in front of Mary with the wide grin still on his face. "Are you ready?"

"Yes," Mary said, not really sure what he was going to do. She felt trapped between Glory and his body, much as she had felt in the alley. He was looking at her with that cocky grin of his. He wasn't planning on kissing her . . . was he?

Zane grabbed her around the waist and tossed her onto Glory's back as if she were a sack of feed. Mary had to grab on to the mare's neck to keep from sliding off the other side. "Oh, my," she said as she found her seat.

"Next time, steal a saddle too," he said as he swung back onto his horse.

Mary made a face at his back as she arranged her skirts.

"Watch out, Miss Dunleavy," Zane said. "You know how impressionable children are."

"Ma-a-a-a," Lucifer bleated as he followed along after them.

Chapter Sixteen

Zane decided the best thing to do was to let the spotted horse have its head and see if the animal would lead them to water. He turned the horse to the west to escape the smell of the slaughtered buffalo and then loosened his hold on the reins. He figured there was water nearby if the buffalo had chosen this place to stop and graze.

He briefly wondered if they had sensed their impending doom. The sight of so much death seemed to have had an effect on Mary. Zane supposed he was lucky the sight of the dead buffalo had stopped her, or else he'd still be chasing after her and wondering what she would do when night came. Zane stole a look at Mary, who had finally stopped talking and was riding behind him. He didn't like the look on her face. He was certain that she was plotting something.

As his stomach rumbled, he wished he had a knife.

He could ride down into the hollow and cut off a prime piece of buffalo steak. His mouth was practically watering at the thought. The meat might be a bit gamey but he didn't think it was spoiled yet.

What a waste. Why would anyone just kill all those animals and leave the hides and the meat? There was enough lying there to provide several tribes sustenance through the winter.

His stomach rumbled again and he wondered if he could tear a piece of meat loose with his bare hands.

Zane swallowed back the bile that rose in his throat. How could he think about eating flesh that produced that horrible smell permeating the air?

Yet he had to find some kind of food or they'd be too weak to go on.

Once again he wished that Chase were around. Chase would know what to do.

"Chase isn't here," Zane mumbled to himself.

"What?" Mary said.

"Nothing," Zane replied.

As long as he was wishing for things, he might as well wish for a rope to keep Mary from running off again. And a gag.

The picture that formed in his mind was enough to bring a devilish grin to his face.

The spotted horse stopped and turned his nose into the slight breeze that had picked up. The sun had begun its descent into a strangely pale western sky. It was going to be a cold night.

At least they could have a fire. Zane felt confident about that, although it might be from a source other than wood. There were plenty of buffalo chips around.

But the recent rain might make that difficult. So maybe they wouldn't have a fire.

"Ma-a-a-a," Lucifer bleated and went charging past Zane's horse down the ridge.

"What is it?" Mary asked, pulling up next to Zane. Glory seemed restless, and Mary had trouble keeping her in check.

"Must be water," Zane said, rubbing the neck of his horse. Whomever he had belonged to had trained him well. The horse wouldn't move until his rider allowed it. When Zane urged him forward, he quickly went off after Lucifer, who had seemed to drop off the face of the earth.

"Water!" Zane said when he realized that Lucifer had jumped down into a rift caused by a narrow stream.

"Thank God," Mary added as they rode up to the stream.

The spotted horse seemed to know his way around and found a path that led to a sandy wash. The water was tumbling merrily along and sparkled clean and fresh.

The horses buried their muzzles deep into the water as their riders dismounted and scooped it up with their hands to drink.

"He knows where he is," Zane said, looking at his horse.

"Maybe we're close," Mary said hopefully.

"Maybe the Lakota came here to hunt," Zane said, "and their camp is miles from here. They're always on the move, you know."

"Why?"

"To hunt new game, and so their enemies can't find them."

While Mary considered that information, Zane took a moment to look up and down the creek bed.

"What are you doing?" Mary asked.

"Looking for a hotel," Zane replied. "Stay here." He took a few steps and then turned to look at her. "Mary, please stay put."

"I will." She rubbed her arms as the sun's rays dipped low to drift across the cut in the earth. "I might be impetuous, but I'm not stupid. Night is coming, and the last thing I want is to be out here alone."

Zane flashed his grin at her. "I'm going to see if I can scare us up some firewood.

"A fire would be nice," she said hopefully. "See if you can find a couple of steaks, too."

Zane had to smile as he wandered up the creek bed. At least she still had her sense of humor and wasn't complaining. He was surprised at how well she was taking the situation. Even Jenny wouldn't have done much different.

The sudden realization of what he was thinking pulled Zane up short. He turned to check on Mary before the creek led him around a bend. She waved at him.

All this time he'd been aggravated with her for doing something foolish, but it turned out she was acting just like the women he admired.

He had realized earlier that Jenny would approve of what Mary had done, and he had always considered Jenny brave and strong and self-sufficient. He admired her. He also admired Cat for the courage she'd shown after losing her father and her determination to keep the ranch.

Grace, the woman who cooked for them and took care of them was a beautiful courageous woman and she had the scars to prove it.

Shannon had proven herself, throwing herself in front of a bullet to protect Jake and later facing down the outlaws that had kidnapped her and Grace.

And Amanda. The things that had happened to Amanda were horrendous, but yet she faced each day with a quiet dignity that amazed him.

Hadn't Mary proven herself to be just as brave by going after her brother instead of dissolving into a hysterical mass of tears? She might have been foolish for not planning ahead, but he had to admit she was brave.

Watch out, Zane, next thing you know you'll be falling in love with her.

He shivered. He'd better find tinder for a fire.

Mary had kept her eyes on Zane as he'd disappeared around the bend. At first she'd told herself it was just because his walk was so cocky, but her face flushed when she realized she'd been admiring the muscles of his backside beneath the fit of his pants. She had never seen him with his gun on; it added a certain flair to his swagger, along with the gloves that hung carelessly from his back pocket.

Looking for a hotel. She shook her head recalling his joke. Even out here in the middle of nowhere he was playing his games, using his charm.

"Maybe he can charm us up some dinner," she said

to Glory as she turned to take a good look at their surroundings. They were somewhat sheltered from the weather here along the creek's sandy bank; it seemed to be a good place to make camp. The earth was back under a ledge where the water had worn away the soil, the overhang would keep them dry if it rained.

Mary took inventory of their possessions and realized that all they had were a blanket and a canteen that Zane had left lying by the creek. Mary knelt to fill it and realized that her chores were done.

The horses would probably need to graze, but Mary wasn't sure if they'd run off or not, so she decided to wait for Zane's return. Both horses seemed content, and Lucifer was already browsing among some plants that grew along the banks.

The need to relieve herself became urgent, so Mary walked downstream a bit. She didn't want to be exposed to Zane if he came back.

"Oh, my," she said as she realized that her time of the month was upon her. No wonder she had been so irritable for the past few days.

Sometimes she hated being a woman. Men never had to deal with this.

Mary ripped off a piece of her petticoat and fixed herself up as best she could under the circumstances.

What she wouldn't give for some food. Visions of plates heaped high with sausages and pancakes dripping with syrup filled her mind. She felt as if she could eat a horse.

Or a goat.

Zane had threatened to roast Lucifer over a fire the first night out on the trail. Surely he wouldn't do that now.

"Lucifer!" Mary called out as she ran back to where the animals were waiting.

"Mmm," Lucifer responded as he munched on something.

"If only I were a goat," Mary said.

Lucifer butted his head gently against her hip, and Mary rubbed between his horns.

"You'd better stick close to me tonight unless you want to wind up on a spit," she said.

The goat went under the ledge and folded his legs to rest in the sand. Mary took the blanket from the back of Zane's horse and spread it out under the ledge close to Lucifer. She put the canteen in a safe place and looked around to see what else she could do.

A pit for a fire would be nice, and there were some rocks lying about, so she went to gather them. It kept her mind off her hunger and the cramping that had started with the onset of her flow.

As she arranged the rocks in a circle, she wondered if Marcus was warm. Was he hungry? Was he safe? What had he found upon entering the Lakota camp? Would he be able to help the woman's husband? If not, what would they do to him? Would they take their grief out on Marcus, subjecting him to endless torture?

"Oh, Marcus," Mary cried and wiped at the tears that had snuck up on her.

She couldn't cry. The last thing she wanted was for Zane to think she was weak. She had to convince him to go after Marcus instead of going home.

Mary made herself comfortable next to Lucifer and braided her hair as she waited for Zane to return.

* * *

You're not going to find any firewood, Zane predicted as he walked up the creek bank. Still, he dreaded the prospect of collecting buffalo chips, so he decided to look a little longer. Maybe the rain had washed some dead wood down the creek, he told himself. But the truth of the matter was that he just wasn't ready to go back to Mary. He didn't know what he was going to say when he saw her again.

He couldn't be falling in love with her, could he? How would he even know? Did love mean you wanted to wring a woman's neck one minute and kiss the living daylights out of her the next?

All he knew was that he sure had been twisted up ever since he'd met her. But then, he had met Lucifer at around the same time. Maybe it was the goat that had gotten him all confused.

Once again he wished for the company of his friends. Jake and Ty could tell him what was going on. Or else they'd talk some sense into him and tell him to run away as fast as he could.

But both of them had run toward love, once they'd met the right woman.

Well, actually, they had both done it in a roundabout way, now that he thought about it, but neither one had any regrets that he knew of.

"Neither one of them is saddled with Mary," Zane grumbled aloud.

He decided to give the search for firewood a few more minutes. Daylight was fading fast. The last rays of the sun were hitting against the opposite bank above the creek, and the upper part of his body, where it showed above the ravine cast a long shadow.

He almost tripped over something protruding from the earth. Part of an arrow shaft was sticking out of the ground. Zane pulled it out and felt as if he'd won a prize when he saw that the arrowhead was still attached.

It wasn't much of a tool, but as desperate as he was for help, it was something.

He rounded a bend and was amazed to see a tree branch wedged in between the sides of the ravine.

His luck had changed for the better. The branch hadn't been there long, but long enough for the leaves, still attached, to turn brown. With luck, the wood would be dry enough to burn. It would do for a start, and with the abundant availability of buffalo chips— which he decided he could collect if he had to—they should make it through the night.

Zane pulled on the branch and fell flat on his back when something very much alive practically jumped in his face.

A rabbit! Its long hind legs scrambled for purchase against the muddy side of the bank, and then the critter fell back into the ravine. Zane dove for it with his arrow shaft poised as a weapon and couldn't believe his good fortune when he managed to spear it on the first try. Zane quickly and mercifully snapped its neck, grimacing at the sound.

Satisfied that he had done what he could to make sure they'd survive the night, he turned back downstream toward Mary. He held the rabbit in one hand while he dragged the branch behind him with the other.

All he needed was something in his stomach and he'd stop thinking about foolish things like falling in love. Falling in love got you nothing but heartache. His parents had proved that to him. Life was better without attachments.

I hope Mary likes rabbit.

Chapter Seventeen

The mournful howl of a coyote rent the darkness just as the sun dipped below the horizon in the west. Mary shivered and pulled the blanket tighter around her shoulders. The light of the small fire was reflected in Zane's eyes as he stood and scanned the plains beyond the ravine that sheltered them. The horses stopped their grazing and looked off into the distance, their ears perked toward the coyote's howl. Zane, satisfied that they were alone and that the hobbled horses weren't going anywhere, dropped another buffalo chip onto the fire.

"Where do they come from?" Mary asked.

"Who?"

"The coyotes, the buzzards, the rabbit. I rode all day and didn't see a sign of life until I came upon the buffalo. Where do they all go?"

"They hide. We're noisy, they're quiet. They know

we're coming so they hide." Zane poked at the fire with the broken arrow shaft. "It's the same with the Indians. They probably know we're here and they're watching us to see what we're going to do." Zane instantly regretted making that observation. He wasn't sure what Mary would do if she thought Marcus was close.

"So what would happen if we kept tracking them?"

"They don't want us around, Mary."

She chewed on the comment for a moment, much as she had the tough meat of the rabbit. Another mournful cry sounded far off in the darkness.

Lucifer raised his head from his snooze and snuggled closer to Mary.

"They're telling each other about the feast," Zane said as he turned toward the sound.

"Who do you think did it?" Mary asked.

"The buffalo slaughter?" Zane shrugged. "Easterners, probably. Rich men who got tired of shooting deer on their estates back East and wanted to hunt something more exciting."

"Lying on a ridge and shooting at defenseless animals doesn't seem exciting to me. The buffalo probably didn't even have a chance to move when the hunters started shooting at them."

"They don't want the excitement as much as they want the bragging rights," Zane said. "They want to stand around in their fancy parlors, drinking their brandy and smoking their cigars, and brag about how many buffalo they killed on their trip out West. They probably didn't even load their own guns, they have servants to do that."

Mary's brown eyes were lost in the darkness, but Zane knew she was looking at him, studying him.

"You sound as if you've actually been there."

"Where?"

"Back East, in a fancy parlor, listening to men brag about their prowess."

"Me?" Zane flashed his grin. "Nope, not me. I'm just a dumb cowboy, remember?"

"You're doing it again."

"What?"

"Hiding behind your charm."

"I'm not hiding anything, Mary. What you see is what I am."

Mary wrapped her arms around her legs and rested her chin on her knees. "If you say so, Zane."

"We can't go after him, Mary," Zane said after a while. The horses moved restlessly on the bank above them, and he spoke more to chase away the darkness and the wild things that were creeping about than to convince Mary to give up her foolish quest.

"I know," she said. "It would be foolish. We have no supplies. We don't know where he is. We would probably wind up dead." She looked at Zane. "That doesn't make it any easier to turn back, you know. He's all I've got, and I can't help wondering what's happening to him right now."

"He's fine."

"Do you think just because you say something, that makes it so?"

"I know that the Lakota are an honorable people, and if he agreed to help them, they won't hurt him."

"If they're so honorable, why did they attack the train?"

"Perhaps they were desperate." Zane blew the ash from the end of the arrow shaft. The arrowhead had been handy for skinning the rabbit, but he'd had to take it off the shaft to make use of it. Now the shaft was useless and he wondered if maybe he should have kept the two pieces together. The arrow had been handy for killing the rabbit.

"Is that woman any more desperate to save her husband than I am my brother?"

"I never said you were wrong in your intentions, Mary. I just said we aren't capable of helping Marcus."

"How do you know? You haven't even tried."

Zane flung the shaft into the darkness.

"What do you want me to do? Get us both killed so I can prove that I'm right?'

Mary jumped to her feet and flung the blanket off. "You probably would, just for the satisfaction of it," she said as she huffed off downstream.

"Where are you going?" Zane asked.

"None of your business," she called back.

"Mary?" Zane started after her.

"Do you mind? I need some privacy!"

"Oh," he said. "Oh . . . er . . . sorry. I'm going to check on the horses."

"You do that," Mary called out. "Idiot," she added quietly as she squatted in the darkness.

She was going to be in trouble tomorrow. Luckily she had a lot of muslin in her petticoat to work with, but the privacy she'd need would be hard to come by.

Of all the times for this to happen, now was probably the worst. Her back was killing her from cramping and the hard riding she had done. The thought of getting on a horse again, especially bareback, was enough to make her sick to her stomach.

Mary fixed herself up and washed her hands in the stream. At least they had water, and food, such as it was. Zane seemed to be confident that Marcus wouldn't be hurt. Things could be a lot worse.

It could be raining. Mary looked up into the sky. Millions upon millions of stars twinkled in the heavens, so close that she was sure she could reach her hand up into the brilliance and bring one down to hold within her grasp as if it were a firefly.

A memory of Michael filled her mind. They had been in the park one evening, about a week after their wedding and the first fireflies of summer were dancing along the edges of the woods. Michael had caught one and placed it in her hand as if it were a great treasure.

Mary recalled looking through her fingers at the light that glowed from the tiny insect.

"I wonder where their light comes from," she had asked.

"It comes from the heart," Michael had replied.

She had opened her hand and let the insect fly free until its light was lost among the others that flitted about, blinking on, blinking off in the darkness. It was gone as quickly as it had come, its life just a blink of an eye in the passage of time.

She always felt insignificant when she looked at the stars. There was so much out there. So many things that were unexplained, that she didn't understand, just like the light of the firefly.

Why had Michael been taken from her after surviving the vicissitudes of war? Why had her parents died when she was just a baby, victims of an Indian attack as they made their way west? Why had her brother been taken from her by Indians also, when he was all she had?

Why?

"What's wrong, Mary?" Zane asked later. He was leaning against the embankment with his hat pulled down over his eyes, trying to sleep. He was cold, he was uncomfortable, and he was getting tired of listening to Mary toss and turn.

The sand was soft, she had the benefit of the blanket and she had to be tired, so why didn't she just fall asleep instead of rolling around all night?

"My back hurts," she said. "It's been a while since I've ridden," she added as an excuse.

"Couldn't prove it by me," Zane said. "You jumped off that train like you'd been doing it all your life."

The fire, burned down to embers, cast a soft glow around their campsite. Zane took advantage of the moment and tossed another chip onto the coals.

"Believe me, it was all Glory," Mary said as she sat up. "I was just holding on and praying I wouldn't fall off."

Lucifer climbed wearily to his feet and looked at the two of them with his gold-rimmed eyes.

"Did we interrupt your sleep?" Zane asked the goat with just a hint of sarcasm in his voice.

Mary rubbed the goat's head between his horns. "I was actually afraid you were going to roast him for our dinner," she said.

"I was," Zane said. "Until the rabbit came along."

"Don't listen to him, Lucifer," Mary soothed. "I promise I won't let him hurt you."

"Mmmm," Lucifer grunted as he lay down next to Mary.

She let out a big sigh and laid her head on her knees.

"Where does it hurt?" Zane asked. He moved next to her and ran his hand down her spine.

"Oh, right there," Mary said when he reached the base of her spine. "Just push there . . . harder . . . oh, my," she sighed as his strong hand relieved her discomfort.

Zane moved her braid over her shoulder and then placed his other hand on the back of her neck and used his fingers to rub the sides.

"How is your hand?" Mary asked.

Zane looked at the bandaged right hand that was rubbing Mary's neck. "Fine, I guess. I haven't really thought about it."

"You need to keep it clean," Mary reminded him as she arched her back against his hands.

"Yes, ma'am." Zane leaned around to grin at her. "I take it you mean when I'm done."

"Yes, I do," Mary said with a wry smile. "No need to stop what you're doing," she added with a sigh of contentment.

Zane bit off the retort he was thinking of adding. No need to tell her how bossy she was. He was pretty sure she already knew it. Besides, it was nice sitting here with her in front of the fire, and he liked the way she felt under his hands, even if there were several layers of clothing and a blanket between them. He could feel the knots in her muscles fading away under his touch, and it delighted him to know that he was making her feel better after all the heartache she had fought during the day.

She was brave. He hadn't seen her cry over Marcus, just over the buffalo, and that sight had nearly brought him to tears, too.

She was smart and she was persistent. He guessed she was probably a good teacher, too, never giving up on her students.

Zane recalled some of his teachers at the private school back East. Most of them were men, a few women, none of them as pretty as Mary. None even close.

Wouldn't it get her nose out of joint to know that he had gone to an exclusive private school with some of the richest kids in the city! But it was also fun watching her trying to figure him out. He would never tell her about his former life. Then there'd be all the questions about why he'd left, and how could he just walk off and leave all that money behind?

It was best if nobody knew about that part of his life.

Mary's head flopped against his hand as if she were a rag doll.

"Mary?" he said.

"Mmmm?"

She leaned heavily against him, so he took her weight and lowered her to the ground.

"I'm cold," she murmured.

Tell me about it.

Zane spooned up against her, her back to his front, her legs tucked against the bend of his, his arm wrapped around her, and her head pillowed on his arm.

Lucifer raised his head to look at them and then climbed to his feet, moving around to the other side of Zane.

"What are you doing?" Zane whispered to the goat.

Lucifer dropped to his knees and snuggled up against Zane's back with his head turned toward the fire.

"Thanks," Zane said to the goat.

Mary moved around a bit and pushed the curve of her backside right up against him.

Zane's spine stiffened as he fought against the natural urge that overcame him.

This is not the time, or the place, or even the woman.

Satisfied that he had convinced his more rambunctious parts, he drifted off to sleep.

Chapter Eighteen

"Oh, my," Mary said as full awareness hit her. Something was poking her backside. Something strong and stiff and totally inappropriate.

She scrambled to her feet, clutching the blanket close to her chest.

Zane, suddenly aware that it was full daylight, rolled to his feet in a flash and drew his gun, wondering what had awakened him with such a start.

"Go ahead. Shoot it," Mary said. The look on her face gave him pause. He couldn't quite figure out if she was scared or just annoyed.

"Shoot what?" Zane asked, fully alert now and still looking for the threat.

"That," Mary said, pointing to the front of his pants. She turned on her heel and marched downstream for a moment of privacy.

Zane looked down at the peak that stood out proudly

before him. "You are totally without a conscience, do you know that?" he scolded as he holstered his gun.

"Ma-a-a-a," Lucifer commented from above. Apparently, the goat had risen early and joined the horses in the grass.

"Shut up," Zane said. He moved upstream to relieve himself and convince his nether parts to behave before he went to check on the horses.

The eastern sky greeted him with a red-streaked dawn. The western horizon, however, was full of heavy gray clouds, and the breeze had a touch of warmth that had been missing the day before.

"Looks like rain," he told the horses as he loosened their hobbles. He led them down to the stream to drink and snuck a look at Mary, who was folding the blanket. She probably wouldn't speak to him for the rest of the day.

Zane decided that might not be a bad thing.

"It will keep her from griping at me," he told Glory as the mare drank from the stream.

"Did you say something?" Mary asked.

Zane shook his head. Her students probably couldn't get away with anything. It was almost as if she could hear what you were thinking.

"Nothing," Zane said.

"I beg your pardon?"

"I didn't say anything," he yelled.

"I'm right here. You don't have to shout," Mary said.

Zane rolled his eyes. She'd be lucky if he didn't kill her himself.

Mary knelt by the stream and washed her face, then quickly rebraided her hair. She tied the end of it with the rawhide that had been wrapped around the arrow shaft and then smiled at Zane.

"I'm ready to look for Marcus," she announced.

Zane's jaw dropped as he looked at her in shock. What was wrong with her? Had she not been listening to him? Did she actually think he was going to wander around out here with no supplies and only one Colt .45 for protection?

Patience, Zane, patience. She must not be thinking clearly . . . must be the shock, or grief.

"Mary—" he began.

"I've been thinking about it, Zane. I'll take the other horse, and you can take Glory and go home. The Lakota horse should lead me right to Marcus."

"You are without a doubt the most stubborn, hard-headed, frustrating woman I have ever met," Zane said, his temper finally exploding into a tirade.

Mary placed her hands on her hips and watched while he ranted.

"Are you about done?" she asked when he stopped to draw a breath.

"Am I about done? I've barely gotten started."

"You're wasting time," she said as she took the reins of the spotted horse.

"Give me that."

"No!"

"Mary!"

"Get your hands off me!" she protested when he grabbed her.

"Not till you start acting like you've got some sense."

"What are you going to do, tie me up?" she asked as she struggled against him.

"If only I had some rope," Zane yelled. "Ow! Quit biting me."

"Let go of me."

She landed a kick to his shin and he dropped her. She landed in the sand. She picked up a handful and flung it at him.

"My eyes," Zane cried and covered them with his hands.

"Are you all right?" Mary asked as she scrambled to her feet.

Zane grinned at her. "Yes, I am, but you're not going to be."

"You rat!" she screamed. She kicked out again, and to her horror, her foot landed right in his groin.

"Oh," he squeaked as he dropped to his knees.

She had never seen a look like that before. His face was contorted, yet no sound came forth.

Mary saw her chance and took it. She grabbed the spotted horse and led it to the side of the embankment, where she could hop on from above. Once she was mounted, she kicked her heels into the horse and took off toward the ravine where the buffalo lay. That was where the trail had ended. She was hoping she could find where it began again.

As she rode she wondered if Zane would be all right. She knew that was an extremely vulnerable area for a man, and Marcus had informed her that if she ever was accosted, that was the spot she should aim for.

Don't let my cock fall off.

Those were the words Zane had spoken to her on the train when he was feverish and sure he had the clap.

He deserves it. He probably pokes his thing into every woman he sees . . .

Maybe I should go back.

He's probably just pretending, like he did with his eyes.

Mary kept her eyes to the north. She was sure she'd find the trail again once she got past the dead buffalo.

With any luck, she would find Marcus before the day was out.

His head was still attached, along with other body parts. For a minute there he hadn't been sure. Zane spit out the sand he had sucked in when he fell face down on the ground.

"I might just kill her myself," he decided as he rolled over on his back to give his body another moment to return to normal. Lucifer and Glory both stuck their noses in his face as if they were checking to see if he was still breathing.

A few seconds earlier it would have been doubtful. He shoved the concerned animals away and crawled to his knees.

Luckily, he didn't throw up.

She hadn't even had enough sense to take the canteen and blanket.

"I oughta just leave her out here," Zane muttered as he rolled up the blanket. At least he had it to protect his injured groin. He swung up on Glory and held on to the pommel as his head swam and last night's dinner threatened to make an appearance. Gingerly he tucked the blanket between his legs.

"Come on, Lucifer." They moved up the trail out of the gully. "This time I'm going to knock her out and hog-tie her. I'll rip this blanket to shreds if I have to. Dang, that hurts."

Which way had she gone? Zane looked around, knowing she had a good ten minutes' head start on him. He turned Glory north. That was the direction they'd been heading before they ran into the buffalo. It was the most likely direction for Mary to go.

"I'm going to kill her," he promised Lucifer.

"Ma-a-a-a," Lucifer replied.

"Most likely I'll kill you, too, you stupid goat."

The sun, which had greeted him so brightly not long ago, was now warring with a heavy bank of clouds quickly scudding in from the west. The sky was a strange shade of gray-green that gave fair warning of bad weather headed their way.

"Of all the luck," Zane said as the breeze quickened.

There was going to be a storm, and he could see no shelter nearby.

He'd better find Mary quick.

He needed to protect Glory also. She wasn't bred for this kind of life. She was a thoroughbred, used to living a pampered existence. How would she react when the forces of nature caught up with them?

What if it hailed? Zane recalled the feel of the hailstones against his back when everyone on the ranch had gathered to bury Jason and a sudden storm had swept over the group.

Nature's fury had seemed to drive home the pain they were all feeling at the loss of a great man, the man who had brought them all together.

Far off in the distance he heard thunder rumbling. The storm was going to be a fierce one.

He hoped they'd survive it.

"Tracks!"

Mary couldn't believe it. She had circled around the dead buffalo and found a long line of tracks heading north. They were dry but had been made when the earth was wet. All she had to do was follow them.

Tracking wasn't so hard—Zane just wanted her to think they couldn't do it. Now all she had to do was keep her eyes on the ground and follow where the hoofprints led. She'd be with Marcus in no time.

And even if the tracks ended, the spotted horse knew where he was going and seemed anxious to get there. She let the animal have his head. She would let him lead her to his home and her brother.

At least it wasn't as cold as yesterday. The air seemed muggy, and she noticed clouds building up to the west.

"I'll reach the Lakota village before it rains," Mary told herself.

Marcus would surely be mad at her, but there wasn't nothing he could do about it once she got there. He'd yell at her for a minute, and then he'd hug her and tell her he understood.

I hope Zane is all right.

Mary felt a twinge of guilt about the condition she had left him in. It wasn't as if she'd meant to do it. The night before he'd been so . . .

Sweet.

He really had been sweet to her, even when she'd

been on her worst behavior. Sure, he'd flirted a bit, and teased her, but what had he done that had been so terribly wrong?

And why did he infuriate her so? What was it about him that brought out the worst in her? Every time he smiled that cocky smile and flashed those dimples, she just had an overpowering urge to . . .

Kiss him.

"Oh, my," she said aloud.

She was attracted to him. From the first minute she'd met him, he'd preyed on her mind.

He was brash and conceited and a terrible flirt. But he was also kind and caring and very sweet and considerate. He behaved like a perfect gentleman and then threw in something outrageous just to keep things interesting.

He also had the most beautiful eyes she had ever seen on a man. They seemed to sparkle with life, if you could say that about a man without making him sound like a sissy, and Zane was definitely not a sissy. The parts she had seen were all man. She had even stolen a look at him when Marcus was examining him in the stock car. She had been impressed—not that she had much to compare him to. But his eyes were his best feature. Their expression seemed to say he was hiding a great secret, but if you were good and special enough, he might just share it with you. His smile said the same thing.

Mary wanted to know his secrets. She knew he was hiding something about his past, but he was also hiding something about his present.

"Maybe I should go back . . ."

The spotted horse reared and bucked, and Mary

went tumbling to the ground. Her breath went out in a whoosh as she landed hard on her side, and stars exploded in her head as it struck the ground, hard.

She heard the horse screaming, whether in anger or pain she couldn't tell. Then a distinctive rattle filled her ears. She knew that sound.

The horse took off with a kick of its heels just as Mary rolled to her hands and knees and found herself face to face with a rattlesnake.

Don't move. Don't move. Don't move.

The snake shook its rattle and hissed at her, studying her terrified face with its beady eyes.

Please God. Oh please . . .

How much longer could she stay like this? She didn't dare breathe, and her head hurt from the blow it had received when she fell from the horse. Dark spots danced before her eyes, but she didn't dare blink them away for fear of what the snake would do at the slightest movement.

Thunder rumbled in the distance. The snake hissed at her again and then turned away, slithering off through the scrubby grass.

Mary watched it go and then let out a sigh of relief as she laid her head down on the ground.

Thank you, God.

Chapter Nineteen

"Mary, where are you?" Zane called as his eyes scanned the earth. He had worked his way around the churned-up area, and had found one set of tracks leading away, but there were no fresh hoofprints on top of them. The way the earth was turned up from the rain a few days ago, he knew that another horse passing through would disturb the tracks. All he had to do was look behind him to see what Glory's hooves had done to the trail.

So where was Mary? Had she cut across the area and found another trail? Was she circling, looking for signs? Where had she gone?

He had already lost time by riding over the tracks he'd found in the hope that he had missed something. He knew Glory should be able to catch up with the Lakota horse once they were on open ground, but there was nothing to show that Mary had even been here. He was losing time, and the storm was coming. It seemed as if the prairie had opened up and swallowed Mary whole.

"Ma-a-a-a."

Zane looked at the goat. "I'm open to suggestions," he said.

Lucifer turned and trotted east.

"At least it's away from the weather," Zane said as he turned Glory to follow the goat.

Mary limped back in what she hoped was the direction from which she had come. Along with hitting her head and bruising her ribs in the fall from her horse, now long gone across the prairie, she had managed to turn her ankle also. At this point she was grateful she hadn't wound up poisoned by snake bite.

If only Zane would come looking for her. What if he didn't? She had been so sure of his pursuit this morning, especially after she had felt his morning greeting poking her in the backside. What if he was fed up with her shenanigans? What if he'd simply had enough and had chosen to leave her to her fate?

She deserved it. She'd behaved terribly. Like a spoiled child who held her breath until she got her way and wound up passing out instead.

She'd been absolutely cruel to Zane, and he'd been nothing but kind and patient. He was a saint.

Well, maybe not a saint. He had too much of the devil in him for sainthood.

In spite of the pain that shot up her leg with each step, in spite of the dire circumstances that surrounded her, she smiled.

Zane Brody, part angel, part devil.

Where did he come from? He claimed to be from a homestead in Missouri, orphaned at an early age and then raised by his grandparents.

Maybe his grandparents had been teachers. That made sense. He was obviously well educated.

It wouldn't surprise her a bit if she heard him quoting Shakespeare while lassoing a cow, Mary realized as she hobbled along the trail.

He was an enigma.

A dear, sweet enigma that she'd been horrible to.

She deserved whatever fate dealt her.

Please, God, lead me in the right direction.

The wind was stronger now, hot and muggy. The thunder that had at one time sounded from a distance was now closing in, and lightning flashed across the sky.

Glory fought the hand that held her reins. She didn't want to be here, and she let Zane know it every inch of the way.

Lucifer seemed to be of the same mind. He continually ran ahead and then back to Zane, who was keeping his eyes down, focused on the trail.

Angry raindrops blew against him. Zane took his eyes off the ground to scan the skies. They were piled heavy with dark gray clouds, split wide from time to time by a jagged bolt of lightning.

He was vulnerable. A target. The lightning that flashed above could just as easily come down to the ground. As if to prove it, a bolt came down close enough to make the fine hairs on the back of his neck stand up.

The thunder accompanied it with a resounding boom, and Glory reared, pawing the sky.

There was no shelter. Nothing but endless, rolling prairie. Nothing but dips and swells and numerous gopher holes. Was Mary out in the middle of all this?

"Zane!"

The wind tossed the sound of her voice against his ear. He couldn't tell from which direction it had come.

"Mary!"

"Zane!" She waved her arms as she came up a rise, limping.

Thank you, God.

Lucifer went charging toward her, but Zane couldn't get Glory to follow. She was still fighting him, trembling, nervous, the whites of her eyes showing. Zane swung off and grabbed her halter to drag her after him. He couldn't afford to let go of her.

"Zane!" Mary cried again, ignoring Lucifer as she struggled to run straight to him. She didn't stop when she reached Zane, but charged right into him, grabbing his shirt, then wrapping her arms around his waist. "You came after me . . ." she cried against his chest.

He couldn't help it—he let go of Glory and wrapped his arms around her.

"Only so I could beat you senseless," he said against the top of her dark head.

"I deserve it. Oh, Zane, I'm such a fool. You should have left me out here to die."

"That's the first thing you've ever said that I agree with," he replied. He placed his hand under her chin and raised her face up so he could look into her deep brown eyes. The wind whipped her hair wildly into the air, and he pushed it away from her face.

For the first time in his life, his charm failed him. He felt like an absolute fool as he looked into her eyes and knew that if he hadn't found her, he would have spent the rest of his days looking for her.

"Mary . . ." He was surprised that he was able to speak. His mind and his body felt useless.

Yet his heart was pounding, and it spoke volumes. Her lips parted slightly, as if in surprise, as he lowered his mouth to hers and kissed her.

What was this feeling, this rush of blood, this strange heat in the pit of his stomach, this yearning? Was this love? Was this what his friends held on to with all their might and fought so bravely to keep?

Was this what he'd been missing all these years?

Her lips answered his. She wasn't innocent, but she wasn't used. She had loved once. Could she love again? Could she love him?

He desperately needed her to care for him. His lips burned on hers as he crushed her tighter against his chest, lifting her from her feet so she had to wrap her arms around his neck to keep from falling.

He was falling.

His head was spinning. He had to breathe yet he was afraid to, afraid that the feeling would go away. Lightning flashed and thunder rolled, but he didn't hear it. He didn't feel it. His world had centered on one thing.

"Zane." She pulled her lips away, and he went after them, clinging to them. "I can't breathe."

He stopped then, because he couldn't breathe either. Not without her.

His hand caressed her cheek as she looked up into his eyes.

She saw the doubt there and touched his cheek. "You were right. We can't find Marcus on our own. I'll do whatever you say."

He smiled then. Flashing white teeth and dimples. "Afraid I really will beat you?" he asked teasingly as he touched his forehead to hers.

"I'm afraid you'll realize how foolish I am."

"Mary. I promise that as soon as we get back, I'll do whatever I can to find Marcus. I swear. We won't give up until we find him."

"He's all I have, Zane." Her head found its way beneath his chin to rest against his chest. How could someone so small be so brave? And cause so much trouble.

"Not anymore." His arms tightened around her protectively. "You've got me."

"Ma-a-a-a." Lucifer butted his head against Zane's thigh.

Lightning flashed around them.

"Glory?" Zane looked around. The mare stood nearby, pawing the ground, trembling in fear.

"Oh, my," Mary said, drawn by something in the sky.

Zane looked over his shoulder.

It seemed as if God had reached down from the heavens and pulled the sky apart, leaving a long trail of swirling blackness that spun from the earth up into the sky.

"Twister!" Zane felt his stomach drop into his boots.

"What should we do?"

"We've got to find cover." The air roared as if a hundred trains were coming at them. "Fast."

Zane reached for Glory, but the mare was already dancing away in a panic. He grabbed the reins that trailed after her and swung onto her back, hauling Mary up after him.

"What about Lucifer?" she asked as she wrapped her arms around his waist.

"We can't." Zane dug his heels into Glory's sides. The mare didn't need any encouragement.

"Ma-a-a-a," Lucifer bellowed after them.

He couldn't look. He couldn't worry about the goat. Their lives were on the line.

Glory flattened out into a run that burned Zane's eyes as he leaned over her neck. He wrapped his legs around her, gripping with his thighs as Mary held on, clinging to his back.

The roar was louder, shaking the earth. He stole a glance over his shoulder and saw the spinning blackness. The twister had to be a mile wide.

He turned the mare southeast, and the funnel seemed to follow. He turned her east again, but the twister was so wide, there was no escaping. It was breathing down their necks.

Glory gathered herself for a leap, and then Zane realized they had jumped over a small crevice, no more than four feet down. He pulled on Glory's reins and to stop her, mare sat back on her haunches.

"Get off," he yelled to Mary. She slid off the horses back and ran for the embankment. Zane jumped off and pulled on the reins. If he could get Glory to the crevice, she'd be safe.

The mare fought him wildly. The twister was coming straight for them. Glory reared, and Zane fell back as her hoof struck his forehead. The reins slipped from his grasp, and he dove for them as the mare bolted away.

"Zane!" Mary was screaming, but he could barely hear her, the twister was so close. She grabbed him and pulled him toward the crevice. He felt blood trickling down his face but ignored it.

The sky had turned into a spinning hell. Zane pushed Mary toward the bank and covered her with his body just as the swirling mass of wind and debris poured over the land. With a roar that matched the wind, he scratched his hands into the dirt, seeking a purchase in the unrelenting earth as the sky threatened to suck them up and swallow them whole.

God save us. . . .

Chapter Twenty

"You're hurt," Zane exclaimed when the roar and the wind had stopped and he realized they were still alive. Mary tore a piece off her petticoat and wiped at the blood that covered the side of her face.

"It's your blood," she said, recalling how close they'd held each other, and then turned her attention to Zane's forehead.

Zane touched the cut that had come from Glory's hooves. "I guess that proves how hardheaded I am," he said. "I didn't even feel it."

"There were too many other things to think about it," Mary said as she wiped blood off his forehead. "How does it feel now?"

"Hurts, but considering that we're not dead, I can live with it."

Mary tore another piece from her petticoat and wiped off more blood. "It needs sewing."

"Help yourself," Zane said with his wry grin. "Got a needle and thread on you? Might need some for that petticoat, too. It looks like Lucifer's been chewing on it."

"My petticoat is none of your business," Mary said saucily. "And I just happen to be fresh out of sewing materials. Water would help."

Zane handed her the canteen, which was miraculously still hanging across his chest. Mary dampened her rag and wiped his forehead again.

"Be careful—we don't know when we'll find more water," Zane cautioned.

"Can't we just go back to the stream?"

"If we can find it. We came a long way on that run of Glory's, and I'm not really sure where we are."

"You'll find it," Mary said confidently. "Hold this. I've got to go."

Zane pressed the rag across his forehead as Mary moved away to a discreet distance. There wasn't any shelter beyond the crevice they had hidden in, and the grass was flattened by the passage of the twister. Zane turned away to give her privacy and grinned as he heard her ripping her petticoat. She was going to have to learn to adjust to just going and moving on or else she'd run out of clothes before they got back.

So what should he do next? Sitting down for a minute and catching his breath sounded like a wonderful idea except for the fact they were in the middle of nowhere and now without a horse.

"Do you think Glory survived?" Mary asked as she came back. "And Lucifer?"

Zane looked around at the miles of emptiness. The sky was clearing; the heavy clouds that had obscured the sun were now dragging along in the wake of the twister.

"I don't know. I hope so."

"Could Glory outrun that storm?"

"Possibly, without us to hold her back. We'll probably never know what happened to her."

"I guess I owe Jenny a horse."

"It's going to take a lot of teaching to pay for that one."

"Oh, my," Mary said.

"Maybe she'll let you clean out some stalls," Zane teased.

"I hope Lucifer's all right," Mary said as she shaded her eyes and looked off toward the west. "So what do we do now?"

"Start walking." Zane held out his hand and Mary took it as they climbed out of the crevice and looked at the path of destruction the twister had left behind.

"No mistaking this trail," Mary observed as they walked over the churned-up earth.

"Much more obvious than Marcus's, I must admit."

"I found it, Zane. I found his trail."

"So how come you weren't on it?"

"We ran into a rattlesnake. My horse threw me, and the thunder scared both of them off. I guess God was watching over me today. I can't believe I'm not dead or injured or spinning around in a twister right now," she said.

"You manage pretty well for a city girl," Zane said. "Part of the time, anyway," he added.

"I am not a city girl!"

"You are so touchy," Zane said. "You rile quicker than anyone I know."

"Oh, really? Tell me about the people you know. Tell me about your family."

"My family?" Zane gave her a sideways look. He knew she was trying to find out his secrets. But what difference did it make? She was going to meet his family very soon.

"There's Jenny and Chase, Cat and Ty—"

"Not that family. The people who raised you."

"There's nothing to tell. They're gone."

"Even your grandparents?"

"Nothing but a memory. Are you always this nosy?"

"Nosy? I'm not nosy, I'm just . . . curious."

"Curious is just a fancy word for nosy."

Mary jerked her hand away. "You are the most . . ."

"Mary," Zane said gently. "I've heard it all before." He looked pointedly at her right foot, which he knew was aching to let go with a swift kick. "Tell me about your husband. Did he have any trouble getting around in his wheelchair?"

"What do you mean, his wheelchair?"

"I figure if you kicked him as much as you kick me, he probably wasn't able to walk—or do much else, come to think of it. That was some blow you landed."

"Oh, my . . . I'm sorry about that, Zane. I didn't mean to, er, kick you there. It just kind of happened."

"What do you mean, it kind of happened? I thought I was going to die!"

"I reckon you survived it," Mary said with a smile.

Zane grabbed her hand and pulled her close.

"I reckon you're going to have to apologize for it, too," he said with a quick flash of his grin.

"I'll think about it," Mary said as she trailed a finger up his arm.

"You do that," he replied. He dipped his head then, suddenly serious as his lips found hers. Mary's arms twined around his neck.

What was he doing? Out here in the middle of nowhere kissing a . . . dang . . . schoolteacher, of all things. Yet somehow he felt he couldn't help himself. Even with the aggravation and the headache, he couldn't help it. He liked teasing her, the way she had a ready supply of sass to match his. And it wasn't as if she were an innocent playing silly games and setting boundaries that had to be tested. He had tried flirting with some proper young ladies when he first came to Laramie and had found the whores to be much easier. He didn't have to worry about making any commitment.

Commitment?

Now, where had that come from? Zane ended the kiss abruptly, and Mary looked up at him with a confused look on her face.

"We should get a move on," he said. "We've got to find a place to make camp."

"Did you ever find that hotel you were looking for last night?" she asked playfully as they started walking again.

"Yeah, I did, but it's not there anymore. I think I saw it fly off in the twister."

"Probably moving to a better location. I can't see as how they get much business out here."

"I heard they got too much and wanted a better class of customers," Zane said. "Have you ever seen what a buffalo does to a hotel room?"

"I don't think that will be a problem for them anymore," Mary said sadly.

"Don't worry, Mary. There are plenty of buffalo. More than you can count."

"There won't be forever. Not if what we saw keeps happening."

"Maybe you should tell Amanda about it when we get back."

"Amanda?"

"Amanda is the editor of our local newspaper. She's also married to a friend of mine, Caleb."

"A woman is a newspaper editor?"

"Yes. A darn good one, too. She's already run off a corrupt sheriff, and managed to break up a business that kidnapped young women off the streets and forced them into prostitution."

Mary suppressed a shiver. "That's horrible," she said. "How did she find out about it?"

"She was one of their victims."

"Oh, my."

"You're going to love the people at the ranch, Mary. They're like family."

"Sounds too good to be true."

"It's not paradise, if that's what you mean. There have been some bad times. Really bad. We lost some people that meant a lot."

"You mean Jamie?"

"Yeah, Jamie." Dang, she was easy to talk to when she wasn't fussing so much. "What do you remember about Jamie?"

"I remember his scars. I remember sitting out in an orchard with him when he told me how he was burned.

I couldn't have been much more than six years old. Then I showed him my scar."

"Your scar?"

"I have a scar on my leg from when I was a baby. I don't remember how it happened, but Marcus said I fell against the stove door and burned my leg. My uncle couldn't get me to quit crying and realized he didn't know how to care for a baby. That was when he took us to the orphanage. He just wanted to leave me there and keep Marcus, but Marcus wouldn't go with him."

"But your uncle came back for you later?"

"Yes, after he got married. We were in the orphanage in St. Joe around four years, I think."

"So tell me more about this scar," Zane teased. "Where is it exactly on your leg?"

"That is none of your concern," Mary said primly. Zane tugged on her skirt, and she slapped his hand away.

"You are incorrigible, you know," she said.

"Really? I'll put it on the list. The one you're keeping of all my faults."

"Anyway," Mary said, changing the subject. "I barely remember Jenny. I remember being in the orchard with her and throwing apples at some boys who were being mean—"

"Throwing apples? Is that how it starts? First you throw apples at boys, and that leads to kicking men, and before you know it, you're wounding and maiming them."

"Stop it," Mary laughed. "I'm trying to remember Jenny."

"Jenny is unforgettable."

"You have a crush on her."

"Had. For one brief moment before she wounded me in the same manner that you did."

"You are not wounded. You aren't even limping."

"I hide it well."

"Liar."

"Should I put that on the list, too?"

"Are you ever serious?" Mary asked.

"Yes. The problem is you didn't pay attention when I was. If you'd been paying attention, we wouldn't be where we are right now, would we?"

"Oh, my," Mary said. "That looks like Glory."

Zane turned to look and was amazed to see Glory running full out in their direction. "She acts like something's chasing her," he said.

"Maybe something is," Mary observed.

"Several somethings," Zane said, spotting riders chasing the mare. "We need to find cover."

Mary looked around. "What do you suggest?" The prairie surrounding them was flat, with not even a ridge or knoll in sight.

Zane sighed and pulled out his gun. "Are your feet loaded?" he asked. "I might need you to kick something."

Mary moved behind Zane's solid back. "Should I be frightened?"

"Probably," he said. "At this point in time I'm just trying to figure out what else can happen to us out here."

"At least we've got Glory back," Mary said.

Zane let out a sharp whistle to let the mare know he was there. "Maybe we can even keep her," he said more to himself than to Mary.

Glory heard his call and turned, still running flat out. Jenny sure had bought one heck of a horse. She had spirit to spare. The group behind her loomed larger.

"It's Indians," Mary said. "Maybe they're the same ones who took Marcus."

"Maybe they're not," Zane said. "Don't do anything foolish." He looked over his shoulder. "Please."

Mary nodded as she chewed on her lip.

Glory came straight to them, tossing her head as she snorted and blew. The mare was frightened, and Zane couldn't say he blamed her. She'd come a long way from her luxurious stable in the countryside of New York State.

"Grab her halter," Zane instructed Mary. "And get behind me."

Mary grabbed the mare and calmed her with soothing tones. Glory, as usual, responded to Mary, who led her behind the doubtful safety of Zane's back just as five Indians rode up on them.

The one in the middle was the strangest-looking Indian Zane had ever seen. His hair was kinky, he was balding, his skin was pale and covered with freckles, and he had a large hooked nose. He had to be a half-breed, but unlike Chase, who seemed to have inherited the best qualities of both races, this man had inherited the worst. The other four riders seemed normal enough, although they were raggedly dressed. The clothes they were wearing looked like castoffs.

Or something they had picked up off a battlefield.

The rifles looked as if they were standard cavalry issue.

Zane knew these Indians were in trouble.

The group of five fanned out, forming a circle around Zane, Mary and Glory.

If only Chase were here.

The strange-looking one pointed to Glory and then touched his chest.

"Sunka waken," he said.

Zane turned to look at Glory. One of the Indians had ridden behind her.

"No, she's mine," Zane said as he looked back at the homely Indian.

"Nitu we he?"

"Do you understand him?" Mary asked.

"Not a word," Zane replied, keeping his eyes and his gun leveled on the speaker. "But it's not hard to figure out what he wants." The Indian was smiling at him. Zane was pretty sure he didn't mean them goodwill.

"Yanchin wikhoshkalaka," the one behind Mary said. The others laughed.

"Zane?"

"Give them Glory. Give her to him," Zane said. "Maybe they'll be satisfied and leave us be."

Mary led Glory around Zane, and immediately the Indian behind him moved his horse up close. Mary handed the reins up to the homely Indian, who took it without a word. Mary backed up until she was standing next to Zane. The homely Indian backed his horse away while the other four moved theirs in closer with their rifles raised.

"What else can we give them?" Mary asked.

"Us," Zane said. He pulled Mary to him with one arm while keeping his gun leveled with the other.

"Doctor?" Mary said hopefully.

The Indians laughed, pointing at Mary as if she'd told a joke.

"What are you doing?" Zane hissed.

"Maybe they're the ones who took Marcus."

"I'm pretty sure they're not."

The rifle barrels were in his chest now and one was pressed into his back. Zane surrendered his gun with a sigh. What could he do against four mounted men with rifles?

"Zane?" Mary said as the one behind them dismounted. He ripped Mary from Zane's side and with a quick jerk ripped the front of her shirt. Mary slapped his hands away as he reached for the gold chain around her neck, but the Indians kept coming at her.

"Leave her be!" Zane yelled as another one grabbed his hands. Zane jerked away and made a dive toward the Indian that Mary was fighting off.

A rifle butt to the back of his head stopped his attack, and he landed face first in the dirt with stars exploding in his head.

What will they do to her? What will they do to us?
I'm sorry, Mary. . . .

Chapter Twenty-one

"Zane." Mary shook him as best she could considering her hands were tied. "You've got to wake up." She swiped the tears across her dirt-streaked face. "Please wake up. I'm afraid they'll kill you if you don't."

The Indian who had knocked Zane out nudged him in the side with the toe of his moccasin.

"Kokipi," he said, and the others laughed.

The canteen was still looped over Zane's chest. Mary managed to get the lid off and poured some water on his face.

Zane sputtered as the water entered his nose and mouth; he turned on his side. His eyes focused on Mary.

Her dark hair had been pulled out of its braid and curled wildly about her face. Her cheeks were streaked with dirt, blood and tears, and her jacket and blouse were gone, leaving her shoulders and back bared to the sun; she was wearing nothing but her undergarments and the torn remnants of her skirt and petticoat.

"Mary!" Zane rolled to his feet and swayed as the pain in the back of his head exploded.

Mary quickly caught him with her bound hands.

"What happened? What did they do to you?" Zane asked.

"Nothing." Mary held on to his shirt front with her bound hands. "They stopped." She looked down at his boots. "It's my time," she said in a whisper.

Zane wrapped his arms around her and pulled her tight against his chest.

"Leave us be," he said to the Indians, who were watching the two of them with amused looks.

"Gla," the homely one said from his horse. He kept a tight hold on Glory as he motioned his companions into action.

Hands grabbed Mary and pulled her away from Zane. Three Indians pulled off Zane's jacket and ripped off his shirt as the one holding Mary inspected the canteen.

Zane's hands were tied before him with a length of rawhide, and a noose was placed around his neck. Then he and Mary were led to the horses.

"You're going to have to keep up, Mary," Zane said as the rope around his neck was pulled taut. Zane grabbed it with his hands to keep it away from his throat. "If you don't, they'll drag you."

"I'm so sorry, Zane," Mary said as she was jerked along. "This is all my fault."

Zane staggered after the horse that was leading him. His head was still swimming with pain.

"We'll figure out whose fault it is later, Mary. Just don't fall."

The sun was already burning his back, but he was used to it. A quick glance at Mary showed her shoulders already beet red in the sun. She kept her head down, shielding her face as well as she could with her hair. She was doing her best to keep up.

"Are you still with me, Mary?" Zane asked. He had to keep his hands at the noose around his neck or he'd choke.

"Yes."

As soon as she spoke, the Indian who was leading her jerked on the rope attached to her hands. Mary stumbled forward, and Zane tried to grab her. The Indian who was leading him jerked him away from her, and he had to fight to keep his feet.

"Zane?"

"I'm all right."

"What are they going to do to us?"

"I don't know. Just concentrate on walking right now. Don't worry about the rest of it."

I don't know . . . But he did know. Their captors weren't dragging them along because they planned on treating them to a meal and a bath. This was just the beginning of the torment the Indians had in store for them.

But why? Did this band think them responsible for the death of the buffalo? Were they planning on punishing him and Mary for the sins of someone else?

Who were these Indians? They couldn't be part of the group that had taken Marcus. They seemed more like renegades.

Chase had told him that the Indians were people trying to survive in this world just like whites. They had homes, they had families, and they all wanted the same things that anyone wanted: to be happy, to be healthy, and just to be left alone to live their lives. The Indians who had taken Marcus were desperate to save a loved one's life.

These Indians just looked desperate. Their garments were a hodgepodge of Western clothing and Indian gear; their weapons looked equally disreputable.

What should he do? What could he do? He couldn't have fought four men with rifles pressed into his chest—no one could. They both would have died instantly, or worse yet, he would have died and Mary would have been left to her fate.

And what fate was that?

Maybe he should have fought them. Maybe they'd both be dead now, and at least it would all be over. Then they wouldn't have to deal with the pain that was coming.

There was no doubt in his mind that pain was coming. His captors were enjoying the ride too much. They were hoping their captives would fall so they could drag them and cause them more pain and suffering.

Zane wouldn't give them that satisfaction.

They were starting to climb a bit. The ground had changed from rolling plains to more rocky terrain. Maybe they were getting close to the Indians' camp.

Was that a good thing? Close to the camp just meant closer to the torment that awaited them.

"How you holding up, Mary?"

She didn't answer.

"Just pretend you're taking a stroll in Central Park," Zane said.

"Look how my last one turned out," Mary said.

He couldn't help it. In spite of the dire circumstances, in spite of the fact that they were probably facing imminent death, he had to grin at her.

"Are you hoping to charm your way out of this one?" Mary asked when she saw the look on his face.

"It's the only weapon I have left." The Indian jerked on Zane's lead. "Unfortunately."

"I guess we're in trouble, then."

The Indians turned around to look at them. They seemed frustrated that their victims hadn't fallen yet.

Zane resisted the urge to flash them his cheeky grin. He knew what the end result would be if he did.

They moved up a slope into a small canyon on the edge of more rocky ground. The Indian ponies scrambled up with bunched muscles. Mary and the men had to lean forward to climb. Zane kept putting his hands down to keep from falling. Mary's skirts tangled around her legs, and she stumbled forward.

"Mary!" Zane tried to get to her but couldn't. The Indian holding his lead deliberately pulled him the other way.

Zane grabbed the rope around his neck and jerked on it. The Indian was caught by surprise and fell backward off his horse.

Zane ran to Mary, who was being dragged through the rocks and scrub. He yanked the rope away from the Indian leading her and pulled her up.

She was covered with dirt. Her skin was scraped.

The front of her undergarment was ripped and torn, leaving most of her skin embarrassingly exposed. Zane made a circle with his arms around her just as his captor tugged on his rope.

"Let me carry her," Zane said. "I'll carry her."

Mary trembled within his arms, her face pressed against his chest.

"You can't, Zane. You can't do it."

"*Shkan,*" the homely one said. He looked at Zane down his hooked nose as the others waited.

Zane put his bound hands under Mary and with a good deal of awkward effort lifted her over his shoulder.

"I'll carry her," he said firmly.

The homely one shrugged his indifference and turned his horse back up the trail. The rest grinned broadly at the sight of the upended woman and followed their leader, who kept a tight hold on Glory.

"Hold on," Zane said.

"Put me down."

"Shut up, Mary."

It was easier this way. He didn't have to worry about her falling. All he had to do was put one foot in front of the other and do it fast enough so he didn't fall forward when the Indian yanked on the rope around his neck.

At least Mary was helping to keep the sun off him. The skin on his neck had been chafed raw from the rope.

I wonder where my hat is. . . .

It had been a good hat, shaped just the way he liked it, but it was long gone, blown away in their flight from the twister.

Not that he'd ever need a hat again.

Mary must be badly burned from the sun. At least he

was used to it. He'd been working with his shirt off since March, repairing fences and helping Chase haul rock for the house he was building by the lake. The lake. . . . what he wouldn't give for a dip in the lake right now. And a long, cool glass of water, or even better, some of Cleo's lemonade with shaved ice.

His mouth was dry but his body was wringing wet with sweat.

How much further?

Why, are you anxious to die?

What are they going to do to us?

I should have let them kill us, but I was afraid for Mary. I couldn't leave her alone with them.

I should have let them kill us.

"I'm sorry, Mary."

He hadn't meant to say it out loud.

"I'm sorry, too, Zane."

Was she crying?

I wish I knew what to do. . . .

Chapter Twenty-two

When they arrived at the camp, Zane and Mary were led down into a small clearing next to a rocky stream. The clearing was sheltered by high ridges covered with scrubby trees that had been beaten down by the wind.

It was a desolate place to live, Zane realized as he lowered Mary to her feet. Three tepees were set up around a central fire. A woman looked up from a hide stretched between two poles. Her face seemed strange, almost flat. Zane realized she was missing most of her nose.

The sound of the stream tumbling over the rocks was tantalizing. Zane swallowed hard at the dry, dusty lump in his throat.

There was no hope here. None at all.

"Mary?" he whispered. He was too dry to speak aloud.

Her head remained bent. He knew that being carried

must have been uncomfortable, but it was better than being dragged.

They would have dragged her until she was raw. She practically was anyway. Her shoulders were already blistered from the merciless sun.

Had it just been yesterday that it had been cloudy and so cool?

It seemed the men had forgotten them for the moment. Their ropes had been dropped as the Indians turned their attention to Glory, who had been led down to the stream along with the Indian ponies.

"Let's get a drink," Zane said, taking her arm. She made no response, but she followed him.

Slowly, almost casually, he led her behind the horses to the stream. Surely the Indians knew what they were doing, but for the most part their captors ignored them, except for the woman, who kept her eyes on them the entire time. A baby cried. The woman ducked into a tepee.

Zane dropped to his knees and scooped up some water in his bound hands. He checked on Mary, who was quickly drinking water from her own hands.

He brought his hands to his parched lips. The cool water trickled down his throat.

Someone grabbed him from behind, jerking the noose tight around his neck.

He choked the water down as he grabbed at the noose to keep it from cutting off his air. The hands dragged him back, and he landed on the ground, struggling to take a breath.

"Stop!" Mary shrieked. "You're killing him!" She kicked the shins of the Indian who was holding on to Zane.

Another one grabbed her from behind and held her.

Zane was hauled to his feet and dragged to a post by the camp. They tied his neck to the post, then stretched his arms over his head and tied them to the top. His legs were tied to the bottom.

God, I don't want to die.

The Indians laughed when Mary broke away and grabbed on to Zane. They laughed when she cried. Then they took her by the hair and pulled her away. She fought and she kicked, she bit and she screamed until she was flung inside one of the tepees.

Mary. . . .

Mary fell into a pile of furs. Her bonds had been cut before she was shoved into the tepee. Outside, she could hear laughter, guttural sounds she didn't understand.

What was happening? What were they going to do to Zane?

She clutched a fur to her breast and let the tears come. No need to be brave anymore. No one was watching. What did it matter if she cried? They were going to die. Zane was gong to die horribly.

Why? Why? Why?

It's all my fault. If only I'd listened. If only I wasn't so foolish and impetuous. Why didn't I listen to Zane? Why didn't I listen to Marcus? Why? Why? Why?

Zane is going to die because of me.

What can I do? What should I do?

Someone is coming . . .

Mary dashed at her eyes and moved as far back as she could, still clutching the fur to her breast. The flap opened, and the woman came in with a basket under her arm.

Mary couldn't help it—she gasped in horror at the woman's face.

The fleshy part of her nose was gone, as if cut away. There was nothing left but a hump above two holes in her face.

The most horrible thing was that, once upon a time, she had been pretty. Her eyes were big and bright with an upward tilt at the corners, and her mouth was full and lush. Her hair was also beautiful, thick and shiny and arranged in a neat braid.

She knelt before Mary and handed her a small clay pot from her basket.

"For skin," she said.

"You speak English?" Mary asked in amazement.

"Some," the woman said. "I am Wapka. It is river in your tongue."

"River?"

"Always moves. I want to leave this place."

"Wapka." Mary tried the name as she sniffed at the pot.

"Make skin not burn."

Mary nodded. "What will they do to us? What do they want?"

Wapka shrugged her shoulders. "My brother is bad. He likes the screams."

"Your brother?"

Wapka twirled her hand over her hair.

Mary nodded. Her brother was the homely one with the kinky hair.

"Two Bulls," Wapka said. "Same mother. Different father. His father was white."

"We didn't do anything," Mary said desperately. "We gave him Glory." She looked earnestly at Wapka. "We gave him our horse."

"He would take it from you. He hates all whites. He hates all Lakota. He hates all the tribes."

"What's going to happen to us?"

"They will kill your man, slow. You, they will keep. After your moon flow, they will use you, and when they tire of you, they will kill you."

"No" Mary said.

"It will start tonight with the fire." Wapka took the pot from Mary. She placed a gob of grease on her hand and rubbed it on Mary's shoulder. "Your man looks strong. It will take him long to die."

"God, please don't do this."

"Two Bulls is God here."

"Why are you here? Did he do that to you?" Mary asked, looking at the woman's nose.

Wapka shook her head. "My husband did this. He did not like me sharing my blankets with other men. Other men liked to look at me, so he made me ugly. I killed him and came to my brother."

She handed the pot to Mary and left as quickly as she had come in.

What is this place? Even the woman had killed someone.

And Two Bulls liked to hear people scream.

What would they do to Zane?

Mary flung the pot against the side of the tepee and watched as it slid to the ground.

"God help us!" she cried out.

Two Bulls is God here. . . .

Only the woman went in. Only the woman came out. Mary was safe for now.

His muscles were cramped. He was stretched to his limit and he couldn't move his head. The rawhide around his neck was loose enough now so he could breathe. He knew it had left a mark.

Zane almost laughed at the irony of it. A mark on his neck. As if that were all he had to worry about.

What were they planning?

What difference does it make? It's going to be horrible. Don't think about it . . .

I don't want to die.

Who does? Who wants to be cut down in the prime of life? Who wants to leave before they've really lived and loved and accomplished . . . something?

So what have you accomplished?

Nothing. A big fat nothing.

Jamie had died on his wedding day with his bride and his sister at his side while he gasped for life as the blood leaked out of his body.

At least Jamie had left behind a son.

What do you have to show for your time on this earth? Have you made the world a better place? Have you made it worse?

If only he could know that Mary was safe. If only he could know that she'd be taken care of, that they wouldn't hurt her. If only she could go free . . .

He had nothing to bargain with. He had nothing to offer. They were going to take his life.

God, I never thought I'd wind up like this . . .

They were watching him. They were making their plans.

If only he knew what they were saying. If only he could communicate with them.

Would it matter?

What should he do when the time came?

He'd never been to war. He'd never killed a man. Sure, he'd fired at a few, but he was a lousy shot and was pretty sure he'd missed every time.

He was okay in a fight. But he was much better at starting them than finishing them, and always liked to make sure that Jake, Ty or Chase was around to back him up.

He'd probably blubber like a baby when they started torturing him. He'd piss his pants and beg them to kill him.

No, he couldn't do that. He had to be strong. He had to hang on for Mary. He should have been stronger. He shouldn't have played with her. He should have been a man.

It's time to grow up, Zane.

It's too bad you waited so long to do it. . . .

Chapter Twenty-three

"Maarr . . . eeey."

Someone was calling her. Was it Marcus?

Where was she? She couldn't see. It was dark, and something was covering her.

"Mary. Come on!"

Was it Zane? Why couldn't she see?

It was dirt. She was covered with dirt. She couldn't breathe. She scratched at the dirt that covered her face, tickling her nose.

There was a baby crying. Where was the baby? Why was it here?

Zane!

Mary sat up with a start, sucking in air as the furs fell away from her.

She had fallen asleep. How could she fall asleep when she didn't know if she was going to live or die?

How could she fall asleep when she didn't know what they were going to do . . . had done . . . to Zane?

The tepee flap opened, revealing that night had come. Wapka stood in the opening. She handed Mary a buckskin roll. In her other arm she held a cradle board with a baby secured inside.

"Put on," she instructed Mary. "Wash."

They wanted her clean. Why should she bother to please them?

Mary unrolled the garment and found several essentials inside, among them a brush for her hair and a strap for her to wear to contain her flow. Maybe the men hadn't sent the garments. Maybe Wapka had brought them to her out of kindness.

"Thank you," Mary said.

Wapka stepped back and lifted the flap, gesturing to Mary to follow her.

When Mary emerged, she saw Zane on the other side of the fire. His eyes glittered, caught by the dancing light. His gaze followed Mary as she trailed Wapka down to the stream.

"What will they do?" Mary asked her.

Wapka shrugged her shoulders in a casual way. "What they always do."

She was so thirsty. She realized Zane's thirst must be even worse. He had carried her. She felt guilty drinking, but her thirst overcame her guilt, and she took great gulps of water.

"Wash," Wapka said. She removed what was left of Mary's bodice.

It was no protection anyway. Mary dropped what

was left of her skirt and petticoat in the dirt and waded into the stream.

The water chilled her. No wonder it had felt so good on her parched throat. It must come up from underground somewhere, born in the mountains that seemed ages away to the north. Where did the stream go? Did it feed into the Platte? Could she just float off in the water and let it carry her away from this awful place?

Could she leave Zane?

She couldn't. No more than she could leave Marcus.

Yet she had been ready to leave Marcus when Zane found her this morning. She had been ready to go back with him. She had realized some things about Zane: Under that charm and sass was a strong and brave man, a man she loved.

If only he'd left her alone. . . . If only she had gone with him this morning instead of taking off again. . . . If only the twister had sucked them up into heaven. . . . If only . . .

The water cooled her parched shoulders and back, soothed the scratches and scrapes on her arms and chest. Not that any of her pain or comfort mattered. It was all inconsequential when she looked at the big picture.

What did any of it matter? She had killed both Zane and herself.

"Wash," Wapka commanded.

Mary went under completely and scrubbed her hands across her body. She tingled, her skin came alive. She could feel.

I don't want to feel.

"Come," Wapka said when Mary finally surfaced for air.

Her teeth chattered as she walked out of the stream. Yet the air was warm.

Mary stared at the light from the fire as Wapka dropped the dress over her upstretched arms and combed out the tangles in her hair. The baby chewed on a toy with tiny pearl-like teeth. Mary looked at the child curiously.

"Zintkayla," her mother said. "Little Bird."

"So she can fly away?"

"Yes. Someday."

Mary looked closer at the child. She was of mixed blood. A half-breed. A pretty child with bright eyes and a thick swirl of hair. Who was her father? It couldn't be Two Bulls, could it? He was Wapka's brother.

"Her father was a white trader," Wapka said. "Very pretty man."

She had said that she'd shared her blankets with various men.

"You mean handsome," Mary said while Wapka braided her hair. "Men are handsome."

"Handsome. Like your man."

How could Wapka be so casual? They were going to kill Zane and she was talking about his looks. No wonder Wapka was here. She belonged with this group of renegades. Was she just used to their ways? Did torture and death happen so often that she had become immune to them?

This woman who was braiding her hair had killed her husband after he disfigured her face.

Yet she was kind.

Kind enough to help them?

"We go now," Wapka said and led Mary to the fire.

It won't be long now.

Was dreading it the worst part?

Zane didn't think so.

His arms were numb. He tried to wiggle his fingers to get the blood flowing again.

What did it matter?

Mary. At least she was covered now. She was wearing a buckskin dress and her hair was neatly braided.

She's so pretty in the firelight. Maybe if he just looked at Mary it wouldn't be so bad. He could think about what it would be like to be with Mary.

Only Mary.

I've wasted so much time. . . .

"Mary," he called out.

Mary jumped up, but Wapka pulled her down by her arm. The men by the fire watched her, their eyes probing.

"Zane?"

"Don't watch, Mary. I don't want you to see."

"Zane—"

"I wish . . ." There was a flash of his roguish smile beneath the dirt and the sweat and the shadow of his beard. "You know what I wish."

Mary bowed her head.

"You must be brave for your man," Wapka said.

"Hey, curly," Zane yelled. "You're the ugliest bastard I have ever seen."

The men rose from the fire.

Glory, tied with the Indian ponies, shifted and pawed the earth.

Two Bulls pulled a knife from a sheath at his side and laid it in the fire.

"Why didn't your mama do the world a favor and drown you the day you were born?" Zane yelled.

They spoke to each other then, the men who were waiting. Two Bulls grinned widely and shook his head. The rest put their knives in the fire as Two Bulls pulled his out.

"It's about time, you son of a bitch," Zane said as Two Bulls approached him with his blade glowing red. "Let's get this over with."

Two Bulls took his blade and laid it on Zane's abdomen. The skin sizzled as he pressed it in. The smell of burned flesh rose and hung over the fire, trapped in the muggy air.

Zane gritted his teeth.

I will not scream. I will not scream. I will not scream.

Little battles. Small victories.

I will not scream.

God, that hurts.

"Is that all you've got?" Zane said when he could finally speak.

Two Bulls smiled at him. An evil smile.

He wanted the challenge.

It was going to be a long night.

"Your man is brave," Wapka said.

Mary kept her head down. Why was her dress wet? Dark tracks stained the buckskin.

Was it tears?

How could Zane stand it? He never cried out. Sometimes he groaned, but it was an angry sound.

And he kept yelling at them to give him more.

She just wanted it to stop.

His chest and stomach were covered with burned flesh and trails of blood. His neck, his upper arms, even his cheek had been seared.

The smell was sickening, nauseating. She must not give in. She must not throw up.

How much longer could he last? How many hours had it been? Had it even been one hour?

Time had ceased to exist. There was nothing but the men and the fire and Zane strapped to the post so tight he couldn't move, couldn't do anything but grit his teeth and curse his captors.

Oh, God . . .

"They will tire soon," Wapka said. "They will want to rest so they can have their pleasure again tomorrow night." She nursed the baby girl, who had not made a sound the entire time.

Would Zane still be living tomorrow night? How could he? How could he survive this?

"Can I help him?" Mary asked.

Help him what? Get better so they could hurt him again?

What could she do?

"When they sleep, you may talk to him. Give him water."

The men were bored. Mary could tell. They weren't even paying attention to Zane. Perhaps because he hadn't given in. He hadn't screamed once.

How could he not scream?

Two Bulls stretched and yawned. He wiped his knife on a piece of something—was that her blue skirt? Then he flung the fabric in the fire.

The burning patch of wool created a dense smoke, and the smell mingled with that of burned flesh. Of sweat. Of despair.

Two Bulls paused in front of Mary and spoke to her. She didn't understand. She looked at him in confusion.

"He says tomorrow your man will scream and they will laugh at him. They were just"—Wapka searched for words—"play tonight. With him."

Two Bulls passed on and went into a tepee.

One of the Indians pulled on Wapka's arm and she went with him, taking the cradle board and the baby with her. All the others filed into their tents, leaving Mary alone by the dying fire.

With Zane.

Chapter Twenty-four

The camp quieted. Zane and Mary could have been alone in the world except for the quiet rustling in the tepee that Wapka had gone into.

The stream tumbled over the rocks. The horses shifted restlessly. The creatures of the night began their evening chorus as thin clouds drifted across the waning moon. Far off in the distance the howl of a wolf could be heard.

Nature teaches beasts to know their friends . . .

How could she think of Shakespeare at a time like this?

Mary sat, still as death . . . waiting. What was she waiting for?

She was terrified. She had seen what they had done to Zane from a distance. Could she look at it up close?

Help him, Mary.

What should I do?

Do something.

A bowl sat on the ground by the fire. Mary grabbed it up, looking around cautiously, wondering if someone was going to take it from her. She ran to the stream, filled the bowl with water and went to him.

"Zane?"

Mary held the bowl up to his mouth.

He opened his eyes.

"Please drink, Zane."

He wearily accepted the offer as she tipped the bowl so the water would run down his throat.

"Can you untie my neck?" he asked with a hoarse voice.

Mary's fingers fought the knot on the back of the post. Finally she was able to loosen it. Zane's head fell forward and he took a deep gasp of air.

"I can't reach your hands," she said with a trembling voice.

"It doesn't matter."

"Zane."

"Mary," he interrupted. "Take Glory and go. They'll never catch you on her. Do it now while they're not watching."

"I can't leave you." Her hand reached up and stroked his cheek. That side had been spared the wrath of the blade.

He leaned his face into her hand. "There's no hope for me. But you've got a chance. You've got to go."

"Zane," she pleaded.

"Don't you see? I can tolerate it if I know you're going to live. It makes my death mean something."

"We can both go."

"Mary, look at me."

She couldn't. It was too painful. How was he even able to talk to her? Why wasn't he screaming in agony?

"I won't make it. I'll hold you back. Glory can't carry both of us for a long distance." He swallowed hard, fighting the burning pain. "You've got to go."

Wapka stepped out of her tepee. She stood in front of it, watching them.

"Too late." Zane knocked his head on the post. "You should have gone."

"There are a lot of things I should have done. And shouldn't have."

"I don't want you to blame yourself for this."

"I just wish there was something I could do to help you."

"With what—this?" Zane looked down at his burned chest. He tried to grin, but it turned into a grimace of pain. "It takes my mind off my other problems."

"Other problems?"

"I really need to take a piss."

"Oh, my."

"I don't figure it can get any worse for me now, unless I piss on myself."

"What should I do?'

"Take it out. Hopefully it will do the rest on its own."

Mary unbuttoned his pants with shaking hands.

"This wasn't exactly what I had in mind when I met you," Zane said. His head was bent, watching her hands tremble. What did it matter now?

"Well, it was, but—" he continued.

"How can you joke at a time like this?" Mary stopped what she was doing to look up at his face. His dear, sweet, incredibly handsome face with the dancing eyes beneath thick dark lashes and the horrible burn that marred one cheek.

"It's all I've got left, Mary. A little bit of sass. It shouldn't take them long to finish me off. At least I hope it doesn't."

Mary went back to her chore, unsure of what to say. How could he speak so casually of his impending death?'

"Best move out of the way, unless you're planning on getting wet," Zane said when she freed him.

Mary turned her head discreetly to the side as the sound of water hitting the ground filled the air.

Zane sighed as he felt the pressure inside him give way. If only the cure for his outside could be as easy.

"As you know from this morning, he's not a bit shy," Zane said as Mary refastened his pants.

"Was that this morning?" Mary asked. "It felt like it happened a lifetime ago."

"It was a lifetime."

How could he smile at her, even if it was fleeting, gone as quickly as it came?

"I lived more with you today than in my entire life," he said, trying to ignore his pain. "Today was the day I realized what I'd been hiding from all these years."

Mary touched her fingers to his lips, quieting his confession. She didn't want to cry at the moment. It hurt too much. She was afraid she wouldn't be able to stop.

"I love you, Zane," she said.

Zane squeezed his eyes shut and bowed his head.

"It's worth dying, I guess, to hear that." He opened

his eyes and looked down at her. "Especially since no one's said it to me since my mother died."

Her heart shattered into a million pieces at his words. "I mean it, Zane. With all my heart." Mary bent her head. "If only I had realized it sooner instead of fighting my feelings, we might not be in this predicament." Tears fell unbidden beneath her lashes and trickled down her cheeks. She wrapped her arms around herself, wishing she could hold Zane, but she was afraid to touch him. She was afraid it would cause him more pain.

"What should I do?" she asked when she could speak again.

"You've got to survive this, Mary. You've got to live."

Survive. How could she survive when her heart had just been ripped out of her chest? How could she survive when just breathing was a struggle?

Something touched her arm. Something feathery light, something gentle. Wapka.

"Come. Sleep," Wapka said.

"Go with her, Mary," Zane said wearily. "My charm's about to wear out."

Mary stumbled after Wapka. She paused at the entrance to a tepee and looked back at Zane. He was watching her. How much longer could he hang there? Mary cursed his strength, his stamina, the rippling muscles that were pulled taut by the ropes. . . . Perhaps she should release him from his agony.

"You cannot kill him," Wapka said. "They will hurt him more if you try. You have not the strength to do it."

Had the woman read her mind?

"The sun will be bright tomorrow," the woman said as she pushed Mary into the darkness. "Perhaps the sun will be his friend."

Mary cursed the sun in her mind. She cursed the darkness. She cursed the circumstances that had brought them here. And as she fell into the pile of furs, she cursed herself for being foolish.

The price of her foolishness was too high.

As she cried into the furs, what scared her more than anything was the thought that she might just survive. Without Zane.

While Mary stared wide-eyed into the darkness of her future, Zane wearily closed his eyes.

The pain was everywhere. His skin screamed voiceless agony at the burns and cuts that had been inflicted on it. His muscles cramped in rebellion at their paralysis.

He had made it. He hadn't cried and he hadn't screamed and he hadn't given in. Yet he felt no victory. He knew that the evening just past was nothing compared to what the morrow would bring.

Remember this—that there is a proper dignity and proportion to be observed in the performance of every act of life.

Why was it he could quote Shakespeare now, but hadn't been able to recall it a bit when he'd been tested in school?

If only he could die tonight by some miracle. With dignity.

He tried to shake his head at his foolish wish but

then realized that as long as he was wishing, he might as well wish big.

Mary loved him. Even before she'd said it, he had known. He had known it this morning, when she had come running to him on the prairie. He had known it the moment he kissed her and she kissed him back.

All these years he'd spent running and hiding, and when he finally realized what it was he wanted, when he finally held it in his hands, it was torn away. Just as his mother had been torn from him all those years ago.

One could die of a broken heart, he realized. Just like his father had. For years he had scoffed at the idea and used it as an excuse to be frivolous, when in reality the thought of love had scared him more than anything.

Love was a powerful weapon. It could bring people back from the brink of death, and it could kill you if you let it.

If only he could die from it, right now, this instant.

God, let me die.

Was the terror worse than the torture?

At the present, he couldn't decide.

Maybe by tomorrow he'd know.

At least Lucifer had escaped capture.

Lucky goat. Or maybe this was his final revenge on Zane.

"Devil's git," that woman had called the goat a lifetime ago.

Maybe she was right.

Chapter Twenty-five

"Two households, both alike in dignity . . ."

Mary heard the words but could scarce believe her ears. The dawn had come, quietly, peacefully, creeping up on her even though she had prayed through the night that it would not come. She might as well have prayed that the world would end and the angels would come down from heaven and carry them home.

Zane was quoting *Romeo and Juliet.*

Why?

His voice sounded strong.

"I will bite my thumb at them . . ."

As if their captors would understand that.

But he was biting his thumb at them, in his own way.

Only Zane would see the humor in that.

The morning was warm. Wapka was gone from the tepee, but Mary was sure she was close. She could hear the cooing sounds made by the baby girl.

"Little Bird," Mary said. "If only I could fly away as you will someday."

If only. Her life had become an "if only." She had nothing to look forward to but the torture and degradation that was sure to come.

Zane wanted her to run away. He still wanted to save her. Her flight would give his death meaning.

But wouldn't her flight be taking the coward's way out? Shouldn't she face this trial with the same courage that he was showing? It was, after all, her fault. She should suffer the same fate.

"Why such is love's transgressions," Zane quoted Romeo. "Griefs of mine own lie heavy in my breast."

Mine, too, Zane.

She had to do something. How could she help him?

Could she run away? Should she? If she could get to Glory, they could make it. The mare was fast.

But if the Indians caught her, would they make it worse for Zane?

Could the torture get any worse?

Would the sun kill him before sundown? He must be weak from the experiences of the past few days, from the torment of the night before.

But he was also strong.

So strong.

He must be thirsty again.

Should she try to give him some water? Would that relieve his pain, or make it last longer?

If only she knew what to do.

If only. . . .

"Come," Wapka said from the entrance flap.

Let Wapka guide her. It was easier that way. No decisions to be made. Wash, eat, drink, sit, die.

If only . . .

Mary followed Wapka out into the morning sun.

"Oh, she doth teach the torches to burn bright!" Zane said from his post.

Had he been waiting for her to come out? His eyes were closed, or seemed closed. Maybe they were swollen shut. The flesh that had been burned looked horribly painful. Had the pain driven him insane during the night? Was all this just rambling?

Yet he spoke without hesitation.

Without thinking, her feet moved in his direction, but Wapka grabbed her arm and guided her to the fireside.

She handed Mary a ladle and pointed to the pot.

"Help cook," she said.

Why should I?

Rebellion might make their situation worse.

How could it be any worse?

It can. You know it can.

"Patience perforce with willful choler meaning . . ."

"What words he say?" Wapka asked.

"It's from a play." Mary kept her eyes on Zane.

Wapka shrugged her shoulders and went back to her cooking.

Two Bulls came out. He yawned, he stretched, and he scratched. He looked at Mary and then spoke to Wapka while tossing his chin in Zane's direction.

"Some sing, some cry," Wapka said. "Your man talk too much."

"It's part of his charm," Mary said.

"Have not saints and holy palmers, too?" Zane said.

Mary shook her head in disbelief.

"Ma-a-a-a."

The sound echoed around the small canyon.

"Aye, pilgrim, lips that they must use in prayer," Zane shouted.

"Ma-a-a-a."

Glory neighed in response.

Two Bulls looked toward the trail in confusion as Wapka picked up her daughter.

"The devil has come to save us," Mary said. She laughed.

"Oh, thy dear saint, let lips do what hands do, They pray."

Lucifer charged down the trail, straight toward Zane.

Two Bulls shouted, ran into his tepee and came out with his rifle. The rest of his band stumbled forth, one from the stream, the others from their beds. They all looked in confusion at Lucifer, who was butting his head against the post that held Zane.

Two Bulls raised his rifle.

Mary threw her shoulder into his midsection just as he pulled the trigger. Two Bulls fell back against the side of a tepee and the poles collapsed. The structure fell on top of him.

Lucifer charged at the sound of the shot.

"Now, Mary! Run!" Zane yelled.

The other Indians dove away in a panic from the hell-bent fury headed their way. Lucifer knocked over a skinning rack. He knocked over the pots by the fire. He knocked over a post on a tepee. The camp became a place of confusion. Mary watched as the Indians found what shelter they could.

Apparently, they had never seen a goat.

"Mary!" Zane yelled. His voice broke.

Had time stopped? Mary saw all the confusion, but it seemed as if everyone and everything were moving in slow motion. She heard Zane call out her name. She knew what he wanted her to do. Could she do it? It was now or never.

Mary yanked up her dress and ran to Glory. The sharp stones on the ground cut into her bare feet, but she kept going. The mare had already pulled free of the tether that held her. Mary jumped on a rock and flung herself onto Glory's back. She wrapped her hands in her mane and kicked her heels into her sides.

"Run!" Zane screamed. "Run!"

The mare flew down the trail with her ears laid back. Her mane stung Mary's face as she leaned over her neck, holding on for all she was worth.

She heard Zane's yell of victory as the camp faded behind her.

Mary didn't stop, and Glory wouldn't have halted if she'd tried to make her. The thoroughbred's powerful legs pounded the earth as the trail descended from the canyon into the plains.

The mare ran as if in a panic, as if the twister were on her heels again. Mary had no idea which direction they were headed in, nor did she care. She had to put the evil behind her. She had to get far enough away that Two Bulls and his men couldn't catch her.

It seemed as if they had run forever. But would they ever be far enough away? Glory slowed, blew, and eventually fell into a walk.

Mary looked behind her. There was nothing, not even a puff of dust, to show any sign of pursuit.

They had gotten away.

Oh, God, what have I done?

She was gone.

So was Lucifer. Gone just as quick as he had come. Almost as if he had never been there, except for the mess he'd left behind.

Thank you, God.

Zane's prayers had been answered.

Some of them, at least.

He was so thirsty. His tongue felt swollen in his mouth. His flesh was agony. He couldn't remember what it was like without the pain. The sun, only just risen, added to his anguish.

And yet Mary had gotten away. He felt like celebrating. Some Indians were just now mounting their horses to go after her. There was no way they could catch her on Glory.

I will love thee, O Lord, my strength. The Lord is my rock and my fortress, and my deliverer; my God, my strength, in whom I will trust; my buckler, and the horn of my salvation, and my high tower.

I will call upon the Lord, who is worthy to be praised: so shall I . . . shall she be saved from mine enemies.

Mary was saved. All that was left to do was the dying.

Lord, give me dignity. Give me strength. Give me faith. Give me death . . .

And if you don't mind, Lord . . .

The sooner, the better.

* * *

It didn't matter now what happened to her, Mary thought. Zane had wanted to escape her so she wouldn't see what happened, so she wouldn't have to watch him die. So he would know that she wouldn't share the same fate.

What did it matter? She was dead anyway. At least, inside she was.

The heartbreak she had felt when Marcus had been taken was nothing compared to this. She had thought herself alone before. But before, she had Zane.

Now there was nothing.

Nothing but endless prairie and blue sky and a bright sun that she knew was shining mercilessly on Zane.

To go back would be suicide. Remaining free was the only way she could help him. This was all she could do to show him that she loved him.

She loved him so.

Why had she fought it? From the first time he had swept her off her feet in Central Park, she'd recognized the attraction. And even while she had protested at his manner, she had sought him out, encouraged him even.

Her heart had known better than her mind.

Maybe she had thought it was an insult to Michael's memory to love another man.

But hadn't she already made the decision that it was time to move on? Wasn't that why she had left New York ? To start a new life? To start over again?

If only . . .

She was going nowhere. But she had been going nowhere for a long time.

"I'm sorry, Marcus," she cried out loud. "I'm sorry that you won't know what happened to me. I'm sorry that Zane's friends won't know that he died a hero. That he saved me."

She wrapped her fingers in Glory's mane and let the mare wander where she wanted.

It didn't matter anymore.

It didn't matter at all when an Indian on a painted pony rode up beside her and took Glory's dragging reins.

She didn't bat an eye as he led her to a group of riders who nodded in agreement before taking her away.

It just didn't matter.

Chapter Twenty-six

Dr. Marcus Brown leaned back in satisfaction after checking the progress of his patient, the Lakota Indian known as Gray Horse. The trepanation had been successful. The swelling on the man's brain had been relieved, and he was responding to those around him.

Marcus nodded and smiled at Rachel, or White Feather as the Lakota called her. She was Gray Horse's wife. His third wife, she explained. He had already survived two, and she was determined that he would survive her also.

"He should be fine," Marcus said to the woman, who smiled gratefully in return. "Just make sure he gets plenty to eat and see if you can get him up and walking."

"I'm certain he'll agree to that," she said. Her English had been rusty at first after not speaking it for over five years, but she had soon picked it up again while conversing with Marcus.

"Thank you," Gray Horse said.

"You speak English?" Marcus asked.

"Yes," he replied. "When necessary."

"Only when he wants to," Rachel said. "He makes me speak Lakota all the time."

"So you may speak well with the people," Gray Horse grunted.

"Yet some of the people speak English," she replied with affection.

"Is it not good that we know the language of our enemies?" Gray Horse asked.

"How about the language of your friends?" Marcus asked in return.

"I had a friend once, long ago, who was white," Gray Horse said.

"See, we're not all bad," Marcus said.

"Not all good. My friend was killed by whites."

"And my parents were killed by Indians," Marcus said. "Many years ago."

"There are good and bad in both worlds," Rachel said.

"That is true," Marcus agreed. "And I think this conversation tells me that you are well recovered from your wound. Just give yourself some time to get your strength back."

"You will return to your world now?" Gray Horse asked.

"If you let me."

Gray Horse looked questioningly at his wife.

"We took the doctor from a train," she confessed.

Gray Horse uttered something that sounded like a curse in any language.

"We were afraid you would die!" she said, trying to justify the abduction.

"My sons are as foolish as my wife," Gray Horse said. "Were any killed?"

"No," Marcus said. "Some wounded but not seriously. Of course, my sister might have done some damage after I left."

"Is she as stubborn as my wife?"

Marcus smiled and nodded.

"A strong woman makes life interesting," Gray Horse said. "We will get you back to your sister."

"Thank you," Marcus replied. "I'm sure she's worried about me. She's probably imagining all kinds of horrible things."

"Women worry too much," Gray Horse said.

"I was right to worry over you," Rachel said. "And I won't say I'm sorry for what we did, even if I do have to put up with your complaining."

Marcus left them then. He knew the banter was harmless and necessary for the couple. Rachel had been afraid she was going to lose her husband. She must love him very much. She had lain down in front of a train to save him.

How had she come to be here? he wondered as he looked around the village.

It was a peaceful place along the banks of a wide river. He didn't have a clue as to where he was and didn't really care. If he didn't know the location of the Lakota village, then he couldn't tell anyone about it. He was certain there would be questions when he returned. Knowing Mary, she would probably have the entire United States Army out looking for him.

Children played while the women went around their daily business of homemaking. One of the men waved at him from his place by a fire. He had been wounded in the attack on the train, but the bullet had not done much damage.

Marcus realized he really wasn't in such a big hurry to leave. He had learned a tremendous amount about the benefits offered by plants in healing. He was hard-pressed to remember it all and had made several entries in his journal. The information was priceless. The Lakota's knowledge was immeasurable.

And yet the people had been amazed when he drilled a hole in Gray Horse's head to relieve the pressure on his brain.

He hoped they wouldn't try it themselves. At least not without the proper equipment.

All in all, his time with the Lakota had been an interesting one. He had no regrets, though Mary would probably kill him for the decision he'd made.

The thought of his willful sister brought a smile to his face. Marcus was confident that she was well on her way to Wyoming now.

With Zane.

And they were probably either at each other's throats or . . .

Maybe he shouldn't think about that. Mary was, after all, his sister.

A shout rang out through the camp. Everyone looked up. The hunting party that had gone out earlier this morning was returning.

With a strange horse.

Marcus felt the blood drain from his face as he recognized the leggy thoroughbred and the dazed rider on her back.

"Mary!" he yelled as he moved through the children who had gathered around to admire the mare.

"We found her," Gray Horse's son, Roan Eagle, said. "She is the woman from the train."

Mary looked around the camp in confusion.

"Mary?" Marcus said. Her eyes settled on him. They showed terror, anguish, fear.

She toppled off Glory in a dead faint and landed in his arms.

"She's my sister," Marcus said to the surprised crowd. "How did she get here?"

Marcus lowered Mary to the ground. Someone handed him a bowl of water and he trickled it down Mary's throat.

She blinked.

"Am I dead?" she asked.

"No," Marcus said with a huge grin. "But I might have to kill you for coming after me," he said teasingly.

Mary burst into tears.

"I'm sorry, Mary," Marcus said. "I just can't believe you're here."

"Oh, Ma . . . Ma . . . Marcus, they've got Zane. They're going to kill him."

"What?" Marcus said, trying to understand her words.

"Two Bulls," she sobbed. "Zane."

"Two Bulls witko, sica," Roan Eagle said.

Marcus was confused.

"Evil," Roan Eagle clarified.

"He has Zane," Mary sobbed. "They're torturing him."

"Two Bulls will skin him," Roan Eagle said. "Slow."

Mary's eyes widened, and she grabbed Marcus's shirt. "We've got to help Zane."

"This man is your friend?" Roan Eagle asked.

"Yes," Marcus said. "Our friend."

"Please help him," Mary begged. "Please."

Roan Eagle turned away and the band of hunters followed him.

"Will they save him?" Mary asked tearfully.

"I don't know," Marcus said. "Can you tell me what happened?"

"It's all my fault. Oh, Marcus, I am such a fool."

Marcus smiled ruefully as his sister clutched at his chest and sobbed her heart out. He caught a few words, and managed to figure out most of it, although the mention of a twister was a shock.

"I love him," she finally said. "We can't let him die this way."

"Are you sure he's not . . . dead already?" Marcus had to ask.

"No. He's not. He's too strong. They want him to die slowly. We've got to get to him before the sun sets. That's when they'll start . . . again."

"Come," Roan Eagle said.

Marcus helped Mary to her feet.

"Mary, your feet—they're bleeding," Marcus said. "Let me look at them."

"Not now," Mary said. "Later."

Marcus recognized the look on her face as she followed the warrior to the fire.

"Tell us of the camp," Roan Eagle said.

Mary's heart soared at the prospect that the warriors were going to help Zane. "There are five men and one woman," she began. She picked up a stick and sketched in the dirt. "A stream here, three tents here, a small cliff on the other side of the stream, the trail here, and Zane"—she marked an X in the dirt—"is here, tied to a post."

"You must lead us."

Mary's heart sank as quickly as it had soared. "I don't know if I can. I think I can recognize the trail, if I saw it, but I don't know which direction . . ." Her voice trailed off as she saw the reaction on the warriors' faces when Roan Eagle translated her words to them.

"Can't you track the mare she rode in on?" Marcus asked. "Her feet are shod and your ponies aren't."

Roan Eagle nodded in agreement, and as he translated, one of the warriors pounded on his chest. He would track the mare back to Two Bulls's camp.

"Who is the woman?" Roan Eagle asked.

"Wapka, his half-sister," Mary answered.

"She is there? She killed her husband. She must be punished."

"She killed him after he cut off her nose," Mary said.

"He what?" Marcus asked.

"She is whore," Roan Eagle said as if that explained it all. "Two Bulls is evil, he has bad spirits inside him. His village sent him away."

"It sounds as if he's started his own."

"With his evil friends," Mary added.

Roan Eagle stood. "We will try to help your friend. But it may be too late. Two Bulls will be angry that you escaped."

"How did you escape, Mary?" Marcus asked.

"Lucifer."

"The goat?"

Mary nodded. "He attacked the camp, and I got away."

"Who is this Lucifer?" Roan Eagle asked.

"A friend," Mary said.

"A very small, very gallant friend," Marcus added. "A goat."

"Perhaps he can help us when we need him," Roan Eagle said with a smile.

Horses were brought around. The decision had been made.

"Are you sure you can do this?" Marcus asked Mary.

"I have to."

"We may be too late."

"I know." Mary leaned her face against the side of Glory, who had been brought for her, drawing comfort from the horse's soft hide. "I have to do what I can."

Marcus lifted her onto Glory's back. "I'm going, too," he told Roan Eagle.

"The man is your friend," Roan Eagle said. "Your heart is full for him."

There were ten of them, including Mary and Marcus.

Mary looked at the group before her, strangers who had risked their lives to save someone they loved and were now risking their lives to save someone they didn't even know. She looked at Marcus. She hadn't even asked him about his experiences. But she knew from what she had seen that these men respected him. They liked him. They were going because Marcus had said Zane was his friend. "My heart is full for these new friends," Mary murmured.

God protect us.

Please, God, let him be alive. Let us save him. . . .

Chapter Twenty-seven

"Take me out of the oven, Cat," Zane said as the door popped open and Cat peered into his face.

Cat ladled gravy over his chest. "You're not done yet, Zane. When you're cooked to perfection, I'll take you out."

Zane turned his head to look at the table. All his friends were sitting around it, licking their lips as they held their knives and forks.

At the head of the table he saw his grandfather. He held a huge carving knife in his hand. "At least you'll make a good meal," the old man said with an evil leer. "That's all you've amounted to."

"It shouldn't be too much longer," Cat said. She stuck an apple in his mouth. "Now don't make a sound."

She shoved him into the oven and slammed the door. Don't leave me.

The door opened again. It was Jenny. Her golden braid shone gloriously as it hung over her shoulder, and her eyes were as bright as the sky.

Thank you, God. Jenny will get me out of here.

"Zane," she said, yanking the apple from his mouth. "Where's my thoroughbred mare?"

"I'm sorry, Jenny. I'm sorry."

She popped the apple back in. "I guess I'm going to have to fire you."

Fire me. . . . I'm on fire.

He was so hot. So thirsty. Why didn't someone help him? Zane blinked his eyes against the sun that beat mercilessly down upon him.

His friends couldn't help him. No one knew where he was.

How much longer?

If only he could move his arms or legs. Stretch his cramped muscles. Put some salve on his burns.

Lie in the snow. Jenny had packed him with snow to get his fever down when he'd been sick. Snow. What a wonderful thing snow was. So cool. So soothing. He'd never complain about snow again.

You're never going to see snow again, Zane. Or have anyone to complain to, except for these bastards, and they want to hear you complain. They want to hear you scream. And they won't stop until they hear it, loud and long.

He knew what they were doing. His body longed for the sun to set, but his mind knew that with the setting of the sun, the torture would start again.

So which was worse? The waiting or the torture?

The torture. There was no doubt in his mind. None at all.

How much longer?

How many more minutes to live?

How many more minutes to live without screaming his head off?

As if he could. His throat was so dry, he would be surprised if he could do any more than croak.

One look through swollen eyes at the group lounging around the fire let him know that the torture would begin again soon.

They were just waiting.

Waiting for the sun to set.

This is it. The summation of your life. What have you done? What have you accomplished?

A whole lot of nothing. Nothing to record that Zane Brody ever walked this earth except a few silly stories that his friends would tell at special times of the year.

"Too bad Zane isn't here."

"We sure do miss him."

"Remember when he. . . ."

Mary had gotten away. He had that much to comfort him when he reached the pearly gates.

I hope it's enough.

What would it have been like to lie with Mary? To know what the heart felt as the body gave way to physical release. To have that one memory to take with him. To know what it was really like to love.

Oh, fortune, fortune! all men call thee fickle.

She would never read Shakespeare again without thinking about him.

Who knew that all that stuff he'd been forced to memorize would come in handy someday.

Yeah, he could die happy knowing that.

He tried to smile, but it hurt his cheek too bad.

Jamie had been burned on his cheek. A lot worse than this. Jamie had survived it. He had gone on with his life, fallen in love. Had a son before he died.

He'd had a doctor to take care of him. And a sister who loved him. He had a reason to live.

Mary. Mary's a reason to live.

But they weren't going to let him live.

So how much longer would he have to wait for death?

Mary waited with Marcus and the horses at the mouth of a small canyon. It seemed familiar to her. The sun was flirting with the mountains to the west, deliberately teasing her.

What would Two Bulls do once the sun went down?

This was taking too long. Zane was suffering.

One of the warriors came back. He was just a boy, maybe sixteen. His name was Smiling Bear. He was proud that he knew some English.

"Roan Eagle says come."

Marcus and Mary dropped the reins of their horses—the animals were trained to stay. They followed Smiling Bear up a rocky path to a high point in the canyon.

The sun dipped lower, casting long shadows over the rocks that they ducked behind as they tried to move quietly along, following in the silent tracks of Smiling Bear. The smell of a fire filled the air.

Mary's stomach turned as she remembered the smell from the night before. Burned flesh. She'd never forget it.

Smiling Bear dropped to his belly and crawled toward Roan Eagle and the other warriors.

"Stay here," Marcus said as he crept after Smiling Bear.

Mary nodded in agreement. She was afraid to look. She was afraid to smell. She was afraid to see.

What about Zane?

The men talked. A few cautiously looked over the rocks that sheltered the camp below. Marcus looked also, and then made his way back to Mary.

"Is he alive?"

"I think so," Marcus said. "He's tied to the post, just like you said."

"How . . . how does he look?" Mary asked.

Marcus shook his head. "Belligerent?"

Mary smiled tearfully and nodded.

"What are Roan Eagle and his men waiting for?" she asked.

"Darkness."

"So is Two Bulls."

"You've got to trust them, Mary," Marcus said. "They don't have to do this."

"I know." Mary looked at the warriors, who were moving off in the darkness. "I know."

Smiling Bear appeared again.

"Come," he said. "I take you to horses."

"Go, Mary," Marcus urged as Smiling Bear handed him a rifle.

The realization that Marcus could be hurt in the raid hit Mary as she followed Smiling Bear down the trail.

Was it worth it? Trading one life for another?

Yet Zane had gladly traded his for hers.

God, protect us as you protect all fools and children.

So foolish . . .

The sun was gone. Her eyes were caught in the half-world of twilight, where objects looked strange and dim.

Or maybe that was just her future she was looking at.

Smiling Bear seemed sure of his feet on the trail, and she followed quickly after him.

What are you afraid of?

She should be doing something, but what? Hadn't she done all that she could?

You left him.

He wanted me to leave.

He's all alone.

Zane . . .

Light from a huge fire danced against the rocks. Smiling Bear grabbed Mary's arm and pulled her to the ground.

"Shadows," he said, pointing toward the light.

Zane . . .

Night was here. A man couldn't stop the passage of the sun any more than he could stop the foolish turns of his heart.

So much time wasted. Even waiting to die. He should have just gotten it over with, out there on the plains when four rifles had been stuck in his chest.

But Mary would have died, too.

This way, she was alive.

But she wouldn't have to hear his screams.

He was going to scream tonight. He was going to scream loud and long.

Whether he wanted to or not.

Zane looked at Two Bulls as he casually stretched by the fire. He shared a joke with his friends. The woman picked up her baby and made her way to one of the tepees.

Even she didn't want to watch it.

Must be a real treat coming.

His lips were dry, his throat closed.

He had to continue his recitation. It was his only link with civilization. He couldn't remember where he'd left off. But he knew where he was going.

"What here? A cup closed in my true love's hand."

The words were slurred, but he could see them as clearly as if they were on a page. He saw them as he had back in his classroom when he was a boy.

Now, *that* had been torture . . .

Two Bulls walked up. His knife reflected the firelight as he showed it to Zane and smiled his evil smile.

"Oh, happy dagger," Zane said, looking directly at Two Bulls. "This is thy sheath."

Two Bulls placed his dagger under Zane's right pectoral muscle. He pushed on the tip until it pierced the skin, and with one clean motion he shaved off a strip of skin.

Zane opened his mouth and yelled as loud and as long as he was able.

"Oh, God," Mary gasped. She covered her ears as Zane's cries echoed through the canyon.

"Roan Eagle will kill him to end his suffering," Smiling Bear said.

"He'll what?" Mary gasped. *"No!"* She wrenched her arm away. "He can't."

Mary shook her head. The boy didn't understand. They couldn't kill Zane. They had to save him.

Smiling Bear reached for her. "Come. We wait."

Mary kicked him in the shin and took off running toward the fire.

Chapter Twenty-eight

Rifle shots sounded. Mary ran, ignoring the pain as her bare feet came into contact with sharp stones and scrubby brush. Her pain was nothing . . . nothing.

She heard the battle cries of the Lakota as they raced down the hill. She heard Marcus yelling at her. She ignored all of it.

Zane . . .

"Ma-a-a-a."

"Lucifer?"

The goat was on her heels. Where had he come from?

Two Bulls's men were diving for cover and searching for their weapons. Roan Eagle's band kept firing, but the darkness had become a friend to Two Bulls.

It was also Mary's friend. It was as if no one saw her in the confusion, or else maybe they thought she was Wapka.

Mary saw a knife glistening in the firelight. She grabbed it and ran to Zane.

"What are you doing?" he gasped. His chest was covered with blood, and a large piece of skin hung from his body, dangling like a piece of torn fabric.

"Rescuing you."

Mary cut the bonds around his feet. His hands were almost beyond her reach. She stood on tiptoe and began to saw at the bonds.

"Hurry, Mary."

She looked around. Two Bulls was running toward them. Behind him she saw Wapka running from her tepee with the baby in her arms.

"I can't reach."

"Get out of here."

Lucifer charged toward Two Bulls with his head down. The warrior jumped out of the way and swung his knife in an arc, hitting the flesh by the goat's spine.

Lucifer went down with a cry.

"Lucifer!" Mary screamed.

"Get out of here, Mary!"

"I've almost got it."

The rawhide frayed and gave way.

Pain shot through Zane's arms as he lowered them. Pain from the restored blood-flow, pain from his burns, pain from cramped muscles screamed through his body. He wanted to collapse on the ground and scream his pain.

But Two Bulls was coming toward them with his knife raised.

"Run," he said to Mary.

She grabbed his hand and placed the knife in it. "I won't leave you."

Two Bulls screamed his battle cry, and Zane answered with one of his own.

Where did he find the strength? The two bodies clashed. Two Bulls was healthy and whole, Zane close to death.

Once again, time slowed for Mary. She looked around, hoping for a weapon.

Lucifer's hooves flailed against the ground as he struggled to stand. Marcus ran past the goat, coming toward her. Two men were locked in a death struggle by the fire. Wapka was attempting to mount a horse with the baby in her arms. She fell as a bullet struck her.

Zane and Two Bulls continued to battle, but Zane was losing ground. He was covered with blood, with sweat, with dirt. He was weak. How could he hold on?

Mary picked up a rock and struck Two Bulls on the head.

He shook his head as if dazed.

Zane's knife slid between the Indian's ribs and up, piercing his heart.

Blood gushed as Two Bulls looked at Zane, his face shocked. The ground below them grew slick as the blood pumped. Two Bulls clawed at Zane, his fingers digging into damaged flesh.

Zane screamed in pain and fell forward, crashing into Two Bulls and Mary. They all went down to the ground.

"Mary!" Marcus yelled. He pushed the two men away from his sister.

"Zane! Help Zane," she cried as she scratched her way to him.

Zane lay across Two Bulls's chest. The Indian's hands were sunk into Zane's flesh in a death grip.

Marcus pulled Zane away and rolled him onto his back.

"Am I alive?" Zane asked weakly.

Mary wiped at the blood that covered his face.

"Yes," she said, smiling down at him.

"Good," he said, flashing a hint of his grin. "I think." His hazel eyes closed and he went still.

"Zane?" Mary shook him. "Zane!"

Marcus dropped his ear to Zane's chest.

"Is he alive?"

"Barely," Marcus said. He leaned back. "I don't know how."

"You've got to save him."

Marcus looked at the man lying on the ground, then at the tearful face of his sister.

"I don't know if I can, Mary."

Smiling Bear walked up. He was carrying the baby.

"Her mother is dead," he said.

Roan Eagle came up behind him, followed by the others. One was wounded. They stopped by Lucifer, who lay panting in the dirt.

One man placed his rifle at the goat's head.

"No!" Mary yelled. She ran to the goat. "He saved us. He saved me."

"Does your friend live?" Roan Eagle asked.

"Yes," Marcus said. "But we must get him back to your village."

Roan Eagle spoke to his warriors. Some went to the

fire; others went down the trail to get the horses. They quickly fashioned a sled from one of the tepees and brought it to Marcus.

"There's not much I can do here," Marcus said. The Indians had also made quick work of scavenging the camp. Zane's shirt appeared, and Marcus cut it apart to make a bandage for his chest. "I need to sew this back before it dries," he said as he looked at the flap of skin.

Wapka's sewing kit was found. Roan Eagle held a torch while Marcus worked.

"There's not much I can do for the burns," Marcus said, more to himself than to anyone else. "I think he's got some broken ribs, too. And that cut on his head isn't good, either."

"They beat him when we got here, before they tied him," Mary explained.

"He must be strong," Marcus said. "And stubborn."

"He is."

"He's going to need every bit of it." Marcus said. "Find something to cover him with."

"Won't it hurt him?" Mary asked.

"He's going to be dragged on that sled, Mary, and it's going to stir up dust. He's already got a lot of dirt in those burns. I need to clean them. I can't do it here. I don't have the supplies I'd need. We've got to protect the wounds as best we can."

Lucifer bleated weakly from where he lay forgotten once again.

"Let me see what I can do for Lucifer," Marcus said. "You do what you can to make Zane comfortable on the sled."

Lucifer's cries as Marcus stitched him up were a happy sound, as far as Mary was concerned. Marcus wouldn't bother with him if he didn't have a chance of making it.

Mary packed the sled with skins to cushion Zane's ride. He hadn't made a sound since he'd passed into unconsciousness, not even when Marcus had sewn the skin flap on his chest. Only the shallow movement of his bloody chest let her know that he was alive. She nodded to Roan Eagle, and he and his friends lifted Zane onto the sled.

She covered Zane with a blanket and was relieved to see a grimace of pain flash across his face.

"I'm sorry, Zane," she said gently. Thank goodness he was unconscious. Otherwise the trip would be excruciating for him.

Marcus carried Lucifer to the sled. "Think there's room for him?" he asked.

"How is he?"

"He's lost some blood, but I think he'll survive."

"Put him next to Zane."

They found room for the goat between Zane's legs, which were the only parts of him that remained undamaged. Lucifer laid his head on Zane's thigh and let out a sigh as Mary tucked a blanket around him.

"You're a hero, you know," she said to the goat. "I promise to always take care of you."

The goat closed his gold-rimmed eyes.

Smiling Bear seemed to be waiting for her. He handed her the baby as she stood.

"What am I supposed to do with her?" Mary asked. Miraculously, the child was sleeping.

"You woman."

"But I'm not a mother."

"You woman," he said again as he backed away.

"What did you do . . . with Wapka?" Mary asked Roan Eagle.

He pointed to the fire. They were going to burn the bodies.

Burned flesh.

Mary turned her head and emptied her stomach on the ground.

Chapter Twenty-nine

Pain.

Darkness.

Pain.

Movement.

Pain.

Hot? Or cold? He couldn't tell.

Pain.

Thirst. He couldn't recall what it was like not to thirst.

Pain.

"Is this hell?"

"Stop!" a voice cried. Not him crying. Someone else.

A jerk. More movement. Restless horses. A voice, soft, soothing, along with a hand on his forehead. Moisture on his lips and then a cool trickle teasing his tongue.

"Drink," she said.

A shadow above him.

"Mary?" Was that his own voice?

"I'm here. You're safe."

Safe? He must be dead. Thank God he'd missed dying. The worst part. He couldn't remember it. But the pain was there. The constant, mind-numbing, screaming pain.

Water trickled down his throat. So cool, so comforting. He needed more. His hand reached for the skin that held it.

"Not too much," a voice from above said. "A little at a time or he'll lose it."

"Who? Where?" He couldn't see. Had they taken his eyes?

Shadows. Darkness. Night.

Mary . . .

"He's out again," Mary said.

"It's the best thing for him," Marcus said, doing a quick check on Zane. "That way he can't feel the pain."

"Do you have any morphine?" Mary asked.

"I used all I had on Gray Horse when I performed the surgery. Everything else is in my trunk on the train."

"That all seems so far away," Mary said, looking off into the darkness. Roan Eagle and his friends were waiting for them. Little Bird, snug in her cradle board tied onto Mary's horse, sucked on her fingers, making a smacking sound that echoed loudly in the night air.

"We'd better ride before she gets hungry," Marcus said.

"I think Smiling Bear thought I would be able to feed her just because I'm a woman."

"I think Smiling Bear has a lot to learn about women," Marcus said as he helped Mary onto her horse.

"They are good people," Mary said as they rode.

"They've been good to me," Marcus replied. "Roan Eagle said that Two Bulls should have been stopped years ago, but he was always too smart to get caught."

"I wonder why he was so cruel. We didn't do anything to him. We were lost and alone. We were harmless. We gave him Glory, and yet he still wanted to harm us."

"That was probably all he wanted, Mary. Some people are like that."

Smiling Bear interrupted them by handing Mary a thick piece of rawhide. "For baby," he said.

Mary put the piece in Little Bird's hand, and the child promptly put it in her mouth.

"And some people are wonderfully kind and generous." Marcus watched Little Bird as he moved his horse back into line. "She's probably teething."

"I wouldn't know," Mary said. "I usually get them after they're walking and talking. I can't remember being around a baby this small."

"I wonder how old she is," Marcus said.

"I don't think she's walking yet. But she's not an infant, either. She has some teeth."

"So we've got it narrowed down to somewhere between birth and going off to school?"

"Marcus," Mary said as she managed a smile.

"Why did you follow me, Mary?" He was suddenly angry with her. Justifiably so. "If I had thought for a minute that you would follow me, I would have just told the Lakota to bring you, too."

"I don't know," she said. "No, I do know. I was afraid of being alone."

"But Zane was there."

"I was afraid of being alone with Zane. Or maybe I was afraid he wouldn't follow me. I didn't think, I know that much. I just got on Glory and took off. I figured it would be easy to catch you on such a fast horse."

"No, wait. Let's go back to what you said about being afraid Zane wouldn't follow you. What are you talking about?"

"I love him, Marcus. That entire time on the train I was just fighting it."

"I figured as much," Marcus said. "So you took off after me just to see if he'd follow you."

"Maybe that was part of it, but I was also terrified something would happen to you, that I'd lose you."

"You had no way of knowing that Gray Horse and his people wouldn't harm me," Marcus said gently. "But you should have thought things through before you took off," he continued firmly.

Mary looked back at the sled. Even in the dim light, she could see the sheen of sweat on Zane's face. "At first it was easy to follow your tracks. But then I came to the buffalo."

"The buffalo?"

"Hundreds of them. All dead. Just killed for the sport of it. Zane said it had to be white hunters. He said Indians would never be so . . . wasteful."

"That was why we rode in an arc. I thought they were just trying to confuse me. Rachel said we were avoiding an evil place."

"Rachel?"

"Rachel White Feather. She's the woman from the train. Her husband, Gray Horse, was the one who was hurt. His horse had gone down beneath him and he struck his head. The swelling had put him in a coma. I had to drill a hole in his head to relieve the pressure."

Mary held out her hand to stop him. "Marcus, you know I hate hearing the gory details of your work."

"You're going to have to get used to it, Mary. It's going to take a lot of gory work to bring Zane back."

"That's different."

"Why?"

"Because I love him. I'll do whatever's necessary to save him."

"That reminds me, why did you take off running like a crazy woman when we attacked?"

"Smiling Bear said that Roan Eagle was going to stop Zane's suffering. I was afraid he was going to shoot him."

"The plan was for Roan Eagle to shoot Two Bulls. Apparently, he's been causing trouble ever since he was a small boy. They thought he suffered from bad spirits."

"Oh. I guess I didn't understand."

"So you ran off foolishly without giving it any thought?"

Mary blinked as Marcus's words sank in.

"Sound familiar?" Marcus teased.

"Do you ever quit being such a . . . doctor?" she snapped at him.

"I can't help it, Mary. Besides, you're so easy to rile."

"I guess I'd better work on that, too."

Pain.

Movement.

Pain.

Burning pain.

"We're here," Mary's voice said.

Where was here? Where was he? What had happened?

Shadows. Smoke. A dim light. He was inside, some-where, someplace.

God, it hurts.

"We'll take care of you," she said.

"Drink this," a man said. Who? Marcus?

Coolness on his throat again. If only it could be cool on the outside. *Make it stop. Please. It hurts.*

Shadows.

Mary.

"What do we do now?" Mary asked Marcus as Zane faded back into blessed unconsciousness.

Their arrival in the village had been announced by the hungry wailing of Little Bird. A woman took the child to nurse. Mary barely noticed that she, herself, was no longer crying. All her attention was centered on Zane. Lucifer, once moved from the sled, shook himself as if embarrassed at being caught sleeping on the job and trotted off to find something to eat. The first thing he found was a skin curing on a rack, and the woman working on it chased him off with a screeching threat.

"Ma-a-a-a," he protested as he moved on to a tasty patch of thimbleberry.

Gentle hands had carried Zane into a tepee and laid him on a soft bed of furs. He had stirred at the movement, and they had given him water.

"I need to clean the wounds," Marcus said. "And you look exhausted. Why don't you go with Rachel and let her take care of you."

"Show me how to care for him," Mary said as she knelt by Zane's side.

"We will help you clean his wounds," Rachel said, her eyes sending a private message to Marcus. *Let me help your sister as you helped my husband.* "We have medicines that will help him."

"Mary, are you sure you can do this?" Marcus had not forgotten how squeamish his sister was when it came to medical emergencies. He also didn't like the way she looked. Her face and neck were sunburned, yet she seemed pale, with great circles under her eyes. Her hair was a tangled mess, and her feet and legs were covered with scratches and bruises. Beneath her ill-fitting dress, he could see scrapes and scratches on her shoulder.

"I can do this," she said without blinking. She was determined, if nothing else. Impetuous and stubborn to the end.

Marcus lifted the blanket from Zane's body. His torso had turned a violent red from the sun. The burns and slices from the hot knives were yellow and oozing.

Mary swallowed the bile that rose in her throat.

A woman came in with a basket under her arm. She made a tsking sound as she knelt on the other side of Zane and began chattering in Lakota.

"She says he is a very brave man to have killed Two Bulls. Braver still because he was in great pain when he did so," Rachel translated.

The woman was all business. She pulled off Zane's boots and socks and then used a knife to slice away his pants as she continued with a chanting song.

"She's praying for his recovery," Rachel said. "Tonight we will celebrate the victory over Two Bulls's evil spirits and offer up prayers for your man."

"Thank you," Mary said.

Zane's lower torso came into view as his clothing was pulled away. The contrast of color between the skin that had been protected and the skin that was burned by the sun only made his condition seem even worse.

Rachel laughed with the other woman.

"She says he is a fine specimen of a man and it would be a great waste for women if he dies," Rachel said to Mary with a smile.

Mary felt a flush creep up her neck as Marcus grinned at her.

Another woman carried in a kettle filled with tepid water. A smattering of herbs floated on top.

"This will help with the cleansing," Rachel explained. She handed Mary a cloth wrung in the water.

Mary looked at Marcus as she hesitated.

"You're going to have to pull the dead skin away," Marcus explained.

Mary touched the cloth to the burn on Zane's cheek.

He flinched.

"If you can't do it, then leave, Mary," Marcus said firmly. Rachel and the other woman had already started on his chest.

Mary stroked the cloth over his cheek, gently but firmly. Dead skin rolled away, leaving a yellow ooze in the wound.

She wrung out the cloth and wiped the raw wound.

Zane moved his head and murmured in discomfort.

"We're taking care of you," Mary said in soothing tones. "Everything is going to be fine," she continued. "You're safe."

The other women were quicker, more businesslike in their motions. The woman with the basket brought out salve in a small pot and performed some sort of prayer over it before rubbing it on Zane's burns.

"Medicine Woman has asked the animals and plants that went into this potion to share their magic with us," Rachel explained. "It's more complicated than that," she said. "That's just the simple explanation."

Mary arched an eyebrow at Marcus, who shrugged. "They know a lot about the medicinal qualities of plants and animals that I can't begin to explain," he said.

"Do you think it's safe?" Mary whispered.

"I think it can't hurt, and it's better than what I have to offer right now, which is nothing."

"Marcus?" Mary asked as fear shot through her.

"Mary, he's got serious burns over quite a bit of his body, and he's dehydrated. It's hard for the body to recover from such abuse. He's strong, but he's been through a terrible ordeal. I've seen stronger men die from less."

"*No*," Mary said as she chewed on her lip to keep from crying. "I won't let him die."

"I just want you to be prepared for the worst," Marcus said. He took her hand. "It's not going to be easy. He will probably get a fever."

Mary nodded.

The woman who had brought the water came back carrying a tin mug with what looked like tea inside.

"This will help him sleep," Rachel explained. "And it will help him fight the sickness."

Medicine Woman lifted Zane's head and poured the drink down his throat. Zane sputtered, his eyes open but unfocused. Then he succumbed to the pain and drifted back to the netherland where he had taken refuge.

"Come," Rachel said to Mary. "You will need your strength to care for him."

"I can't leave him."

"Medicine Woman will stay," Rachel explained. She motioned to the younger woman who had carried in the tea. "Let Dove care for you."

Mary watched as Medicine Woman placed a blanket over Zane, pulling it up only to his waist.

"Go, Mary. He'll be fine for now," Marcus said.

Mary nodded as exhaustion crept over the stress that had kept her moving. She followed Dove.

"I hope," Marcus added as she left the tepee.

Chapter Thirty

How long had it been? How many days had passed since she'd left New York? How many days since she'd jumped off the train? How many days since they had carried Zane to this place? How many days had he lain in the tepee, near death?

Mary couldn't remember.

High summer was upon them, yet the village was cooled by a constant breeze that washed over the plains, tossing the white blossoms of the yarrow that grew in the meadow across the river. Mary watched the plants as they danced beneath the wind before she went back to her task of washing out the cloths she was using for compresses.

Yarrow was what Medicine Woman used to help Zane. A tea had been made from the fern-like leaves. She had been pouring it down his throat and also using it as a compress on his burns.

Marcus had explained it all to her. He was learning all he could from Medicine Woman, in spite of the language barrier.

And yet nothing had changed since they had come to this place. Or maybe it had. Zane's skin had blistered and peeled, and then blistered again. The deep burns from the knives had started to crust, but his constant tossing and turning tore off the outer layer, and then the bleeding and oozing would start again.

He was going to be horribly scarred on his chest.

If he survived.

At least his face was looking better, although it was hard to tell beneath the growth of beard that covered the burn. Medicine Woman planned on shaving him today. Maybe because he was finally lying still, so she wouldn't be in jeopardy of cutting his throat as he fought the fever. Maybe she thought he'd want to look his best when he met his Maker.

Mary was terrified. At least when he was tossing and turning and mumbling in his fever, she knew he was alive, that he was fighting for his life.

"Ma-a-a-a," Lucifer cried as he trotted to her side. The goat had quickly recovered from his wound and had integrated himself into the life of the village. He had become a novelty of a sort. The children played with him, and the women spoiled him with treats. The goat butted Mary's hand with his knobby horns, and she rubbed the space between the horns absentmindedly as she watched river water wash over the flat stones along the shore.

How long had it been?

It was easy to lose track of time in this peaceful

place. As she watched the loving and kind way the people of this village lived their lives, it was easy to forget the violence she had seen.

And yet the violence had been real. Zane was proof of it.

Why did it have to happen?

Mary knew Two Bulls was not from this village. Yet he had to have come from a place similar to this. The people of this village had known him, or known of him. How had he grown so evil? Had he truly been full of evil spirits, as Roan Eagle had said?

And what about Wapka? Apparently, she had been a whore, willing to share her blankets with either Indian or white man. Her husband must have known what she was like. And she must have known what the consequences would be when she was caught. What kind of man would cut off his wife's nose? What kind of people would allow it?

The same people who had treated her and Marcus and Zane with such kindness. The young mother who had taken Little Bird to nurse waved at Mary as she came out of some brush downstream. Mary usually forgot that the child even existed until she saw the woman. How many other mothers would do the same for an orphaned child? Only someone with a kind and generous heart.

And yet these same people had produced a monster like Two Bulls.

No wonder there was so much misunderstanding between the whites and the Indians. Yet Rachel had managed to cross those boundaries. She seemed happy. It was obvious that she was in love with her husband, who was now managing short walks around the camp, accompanied by Marcus, who was soaking up all the knowledge that Gray Horse had to offer him.

Rachel had chosen this life.

"It's so beautiful here," Mary said to Lucifer, who was busy tasting the beadwork on her buckskin leggings. "I can see why she was tempted to stay."

Mary shoved the goat away from her clothing. She had adapted quickly to the Lakota style of dress.

"Of course, giving up corsets would make the decision easier," she added as she gathered up her cloths and placed them in a basket.

Lucifer followed Mary as she made her way through the village to the tepee that had become her home. The goat plopped down in his familiar place next to Zane and laid his head on the still thigh.

Medicine Woman had shaved Zane. She greeted Mary with a smile and said something in Lakota as Mary ran her hand over Zane's cheek. There, at least, he looked pretty much the same. That wound would fade, given time. Did he have that much time ahead of him?

"Thank you," Mary said. She had given up trying to understand what Medicine Woman said, having discovered long ago that she had no gift for language. She just hoped that the woman felt her gratitude.

Medicine Woman nodded and left Zane to Mary's care.

Mary went through the now familiar routine that occupied the major portion of her days. A pot of water that she had heated earlier was now cool enough to wash his body. She dropped a cloth into the pot, wrung it out and then went about the task.

Every day it seemed that there was less to wash. The

muscles of his abdomen, which had once been well-defined ridges, were now nothing but ribs and hollows. His chest, once thick, was now shallow and covered with oozing scabs.

How long had it been?

His hands, once so strong and yet gentle—Mary remembered how firmly he'd held her when he pulled her into the alleyway back in St. Louis.

She wiped the sweat from his brow and the hollows of his cheeks. Her fingers lingered, longing to dip into the dimples that showed when he smiled.

"Zane," she began. Marcus had told her to talk to him to keep him connected with this world. "Remember, Zane? This was how we met. Well, officially anyway. Remember on the train? When I was bathing you?" He had to have a reason to stay here. "And you thought I was a prostitute?" She smiled at the memory.

I remember, he dimly thought through a haze.

She wanted to be the reason he stayed.

I want to stay. I don't know how.

"We miss you, Zane. Me and Lucifer. Come back to us. Please. It's so pretty here, nice and peaceful. You'd like it. I promise."

I'm trying. I'm lost.

Mary knew she was rambling, but what else could she say?

"I love you," she said. "I know you know that. I told you . . . before . . . but I want to tell you again."

I love you, too. I never told you. I was so afraid . . . before . . .

"Love found under these circumstances might not be enough," Rachel said.

When had she come in? Mary looked at her, confusion in her brown eyes.

Rachel knelt beside Mary and ran her hand over Lucifer's ratty hide. The goat needed a bath.

"Love created out of gratitude is not true love," Rachel said. "It's just gratitude."

"I loved him before," Mary said. "I was just too stubborn to admit it."

"Why did you fall in love with him?" Rachel asked.

Mary wrung out the cloth and wiped Zane's neck. Always before, there had been some sign that he was alive, some movement, but now there was nothing but the shallow sound of his breathing.

"Probably because he infuriated me the first time I met him. It was the first time I felt truly alive since my husband died," Mary said. "And he was such a flirt, so cocky, so sure of himself. I just wanted to knock him down a peg or two. And he had such a spark in his eyes." Mary dashed at the tears that had welled in her eyes. "You've never seen his eyes. They are so beautiful— they have a fire in them, a glow, as if he has a great secret. And he's so funny, but he's also gallant."

Rachel smiled encouragingly as Mary's words tumbled out in a rush.

"He carried me. When they captured us and were making us walk behind their horses. I fell and they dragged me. Zane carried me after that."

Mary touched the side of his face.

"I told him I love him, but he never said it back. He never got the chance. But I don't care. As long as he survives, I don't care. I just want him to live."

"Where love is great, the littlest doubts are fear;

when little fears grow great, great love grows there," Rachel said.

"Hamlet?" Mary asked.

"Yes."

Hamlet . . .

"You two would have a lot in common. He's been quoting Shakespeare ever since we met."

"This is not exactly the place you'd expect to hear it," Rachel said with a sweet smile.

"No. But this has been nothing if not a learning experience. I've learned that people and places are not always what they appear to be."

"I learned that lesson also," Rachel said. "Five years ago."

Who was talking to Mary?

Zane wandered through the fog that had shrouded him for longer than he could remember. He heard the voices through the haze. He'd heard Mary calling out to him and he thought he had answered, but then there was another voice, a voice he didn't recognize. The voice took Mary away.

He was alone.

He was so tired of being alone. He had always been alone. Even when surrounded by his friends, laughing and playing, he had been alone.

Zane wandered through the fog. Something was there. He could see the movement, darkness against the light. A quick flash of something red, bright in the dim light that surrounded him. He followed it.

The fog cleared as if the air had been cleaned by the wind. There was a large stone before him, an ancient

*stone that looked as if it had been hewn from the earth
in a time long ago. A man sat on it. He had his back to
Zane and was chanting in what should have been a
strange tongue, but the words were oddly familiar.*
Hamlet?

*Zane felt himself move around the stone, even
though he knew his body was not moving. His body
was lying in a strange place, being cared for by Mary.
The man on the stone was dressed in a strange outfit
that consisted of a high-necked ruffled shirt and a
loincloth. It was Two Bulls. Two Bulls dressed like
Shakespeare, except that his face looked like a skull,
the skin stretched tight, the teeth revealed in a frightening, evil leer. He pointed toward the fog that was coming in again, and Zane walked in that direction,
cautiously, afraid of what else he would meet along the
way. But afraid also to stay because of Two Bulls.*

*He saw the flash of red again, skimming along the
ground as if leading him along. Zane followed it. It
was the only thing to focus on, and he was afraid of
getting lost.*

*He was lost. The flash of red was gone, as quick as it
came. Zane stood in the fog. He couldn't move. It was
if he were tied to a post.*

But he wasn't, was he?

It was over, wasn't it?

*Had he been saved, or had his mind, gone mad from
the sun and the torture, just imagined it?*

He had to know.

Mary?

He had seen Mary. She had come to him. She had

cut him down. She had put the knife in his hands so he could kill Two Bulls. She had poured cool water down his parched throat and carefully tended his wounds.

He could hear her. She was talking. Where was she? Mary?

Zane wandered on through the fog. There it was. The flash of red again. He hurried then; he didn't want to lose it.

Once again the fog cleared. How had he gotten inside? The room where he found himself was as dark and dreary as the fog.

His grandfather. Why was he not a bit surprised to see him? The man had tormented him in life; why not torment him in death also?

"You're worthless, boy. Trash just like your father. I was right about you. I was right!"

The old man cackled in glee as Zane pressed his hands over his ears. He didn't need to hear his grandfather's condemnation. He already knew it. He had wasted so much time. He had wasted his life. He had become just what his grandfather had predicted all those years ago. He had run away to prove his grandfather wrong. Instead, he had proved him right.

Zane ran back into the fog once again. If only he could find Mary. He needed to find her. He needed to tell her so many things.

So many secrets . . .

Mary . . .

The flash of red came again. It was practically twirling around his ankles, teasing him to follow, so he did. It was becoming harder to move, as if the fog were *taking on a solid form. His lungs burned and his legs worked as he chased after the patch of red.*

Zane knew he was going uphill. The red was above him. Maybe if he got high enough, he would be above the fog and the clouds. Maybe if he got high enough, he could make it to heaven.

You're fooling yourself there, Zane.

Whatever my hell is, Lord, I'll take it. Just let me see Mary one last time. One last time. . . .

The fog cleared once again. Zane found himself on a grassy knoll. The flash of red disappeared over the other side.

He realized it was a fox's tail. A wide grin split his face as he followed the fox. He had seen the creature before, a few years back, when he almost died from the chicken pox.

Zane saw a house below. A small sod hut with one window.

"Mama?" he said. Suddenly he couldn't walk anymore. Zane dropped to his knees in the long grass in front of the hut.

A woman came out of the hut. A woman with golden brown hair and laughing hazel eyes.

"There you are," she said. "I've been waiting for you." She cupped her hand under his chin and smiled at him.

"Am I dead?" Zane asked.

"Not yet. Not if you don't want to be."

"It hurts, Mama."

"Life does that to you, son. And it hurts some more than others. How you deal with the hurt is what sets you *apart. Do you give up or do you push through to find out what's waiting for you when you're over the pain. You get to choose."*

"Pa chose to die."

"We all have our strengths and our weaknesses. You've got some of both of us inside you."

"Is he here?"

"He is." His mother pointed to the cabin. "See? With your sister." He was there. Zane felt as if he were look-ing in a mirror as he saw the man with the little girl on his lap. His father looked up at him and smiled. He put Zane's sister's hand in his own and waved it at him.

"Can I talk to him?"

"You can. But you must choose. You can stay here, or you can go on. It's up to you."

Mary . . .

"I'm going on," he said.

"Be happy, Zane," his mother said. "I'll see you again. Someday."

"Mama?"

"Go, Zane. She's waiting for you."

Zane looked ahead. The fox was sitting on the oppo-site side of the rise. It smiled at him with its tongue hanging out to one side before it turned, and with a fi-nal look, disappeared over the rise.

Zane ran after the fox. He felt weak and he ached all over. His skin screamed in agony at the stretching caused by his movement. He couldn't stop. He ran. His lungs protested as they gasped for air, and still he ran. Straight uphill. He felt something dragging at his heels, something holding him back. He ran harder. He had to make it. He could see the fox now, leaping ahead of him through the tall grass of the plains. He had almost reached the top.

She was there. Mary was waiting for him. She was calling his name.

"Zane. Come back. Please. I love you. Zane. . . ."

His lungs were going to burst. He had to make it. He reached out his hand.

"Zane!"

His eyes blinked against the light that poured in through the opening in the tepee.

"Mary?" *he said hoarsely.*

She nodded with tears streaming down her face. His hand was clasped between both of hers, and she kissed it.

"You're back," *she said finally, smiling through the tears.*

"I'm back," *he said. A grin split his mouth and dimples creased his cheeks.* "I love you."

Chapter Thirty-one

Who would have thought that watching a river roll by would be so exhausting? Zane wearily closed his eyes as he leaned against the brace that someone—Smiling Bear—had put up for him.

He was still unable to do the simplest task for himself—even walking was a chore—but he was making progress. He had made it to the river without hanging on to Mary and Marcus. That in itself should be worthy of celebration.

He was too exhausted to consider it.

Marcus had told him it would take a while to get his strength back. He had almost died of an infection. His chest was still sore to the touch, although the scabs were finally healing and crusting off. Even the faded calico shirt he was wearing aggravated his skin.

He couldn't stand to look at his chest. He could still feel the torture, as if it were still happening.

The last day of his captivity was a blur in his mind. He couldn't remember what was real and what was not. Mary had told him that he'd killed Two Bulls, but he didn't really remember it. It seemed as if the fight were part of the dreams he'd had while trapped in the fever.

Some of the warriors had commented on his victory over Two Bulls. Songs had been sung, he had been told. Zane didn't care. It was over. He couldn't believe it was over and he had survived. He couldn't believe he was alive.

The aches and pain that he still felt confirmed his existence. It was hard to believe that he used to put in a full day's work. How long ago had that been? Forever? A lifetime? Summer had just begun when he had left, now it was fading. There was a slight touch of color on the trees, and the night air was beginning to have a nip. How long had he been gone? Weeks? Months? Years?

And he still had a job to do: Get Glory home. The thought of climbing on a horse was scary. All he wanted to do was sleep.

Wyoming seemed so far away.

Lucifer trotted up to his side and folded his legs to join Zane in his contemplation of the river.

"What are you thinking?" Mary asked as she knelt beside the goat.

"I was wondering if I could fall into the river and let it carry me home," Zane said. He shielded his eyes from the morning sun as he looked at her. Even the feel of the sun on his face was painful.

"Funny, I had the same thought that first night in Two Bulls's camp."

"Really?" Zane asked, confused. He couldn't remember a river.

"There was a stream. Wapka made me wash and put on a dress. I remember just wishing the water would carry me away."

"Wapka," Zane said. "I had forgotten about her. What happened to her face?"

"Her husband cut her nose off because she slept with another man. She's dead, killed in the attack. She had a daughter. Little Bird. Her father was white."

"Daughter?" Zane closed his eyes. "There was a baby. I remember hearing her cry. What happened to her?"

"She's here. We brought her back. There's a woman who's caring for her, and she's even been weaned. Rachel says no one wants to adopt her because they're afraid of the spirits that surround her."

"Two Bulls's spirits?"

"Yes. Apparently, he had quite a reputation."

"Well deserved," Zane added.

"Yes," Mary said. "Killing him was a good thing."

Zane shook his head. "I don't want to think about it. If I think about any part of that time, I'm afraid I'll remember other things. Things I don't want to remember."

"Zane. You have nothing to be ashamed of. You were incredibly brave, incredibly strong. I don't know how you did it. How you survived."

"You're just saying that because you adore me," Zane said teasingly.

"Don't," Mary said. "Don't do that."

"What?"

"Hide what you're really feeling. Don't do that with me."

Zane looked at her. Her hair was in two braids, and her face had turned as brown as some of the Lakota who passed by in the distance. She was wearing a buckskin dress with fringed leggings and moccasins. She had come a long way from the prim and proper lady he had met in the park.

"Remember the hat you were wearing when we met?" he asked.

"The one with the daisies?"

"Yes. Daisies. I remember that several hours after we met, I was still thinking about you and that hat."

"So that's what made you pay attention to me? My hat?"

"Actually, it was your backside that caught my attention."

"Zane!" Mary said, blushing beneath her tan. "You're incorrigible."

"Mary, since we've met I've been thrown off a train by a goat, beaten up by horse thieves, thrown around by a twister and sliced and burned by a crazy Indian. I have no pride left and I have nothing to hide. But I do have some things to tell you about myself. About who I am and where I came from. Not that any of it really matters. But I want you to know because I love you."

Mary shoved Lucifer away from Zane and curled into his spot.

"Ma-a-a-a," the goat protested and trotted away to a tasty patch of clover.

"I've been waiting to hear that again," she said as she leaned against Zane.

"Ow," he said. "Hear what?"

"That you love me."

"I do." Zane lifted a tender arm and placed it around her. Mary's cheek found an unharmed place on his shoulder and settled there. "That's what saved me, Mary. Knowing you were here waiting for me. I came back because of you. I've been searching for you my entire life. I wasn't about to let you go when I had just found you."

"Zane, when I told you I loved you the first time, you said that since your mother died, no one has said that to you. I can't believe that no one has loved you. What about your friends in Wyoming?"

"I've never let anyone love me, Mary. I've always kept those walls up. You know which ones I'm talking about."

"Yes, I do."

"I was afraid of what love could do to me."

"Why?"

"Because I saw what it did to my father, and my grandfather."

"Tell me."

"It killed my father, and it made my grandfather bitter and mean."

"How?"

"My mother was an only child. Her father was very controlling and never let her alone for a moment. But one day, there was an accident and her escort was late picking her up and she met my father."

"And he swept her off her feet."

"Yes." Zane looked at the river rolling by, at the sparse blossoms of the yarrow, now spent, and at the mountains in the distance. Everything seemed so far away. He was weary, but he needed to tell it as it had been told to him. Funny how he had heard his mother's story from the cook, who had been there when it happened, instead of from his mother herself.

"Not hard to imagine, if he was anything like you."

"He was, or I am." The dimples flashed. "Whichever."

"Go on."

"My father wasn't acceptable to my grandfather. I wonder if anyone would have been. She managed to sneak out to see him, and then they ran off when my grandfather threatened to send her away to Europe."

"Europe? Her family must have been rich."

Zane let that comment slide. "So they ran off to Missouri and started a homestead,"

"And then you came along."

"Yes. I came along. We were happy. And when I was eight, she died in childbirth."

Mary placed her arm, gently, gingerly across his chest. He sounded so tired; maybe she should have him stop and finish the tale later.

Maybe not. Maybe he needed to tell this story.

"My father wrote to my grandparents and my grandfather sent some men to get me. And my father let them take me. I cried and I begged him to let me stay, but my father just shoved me to them and slammed the door. They took me to my grandparents, and I found out about six months later that my father had died. Drank himself to death, my grandfather said during one of his tirades. He was always telling me how worthless I was. How I was responsible for my mother dying. How I was just like my father, and my mother should have been a whore instead of his darling Emily."

"You were only a boy!" Mary exclaimed as she raised herself to look at him. A little boy who'd lost his mother, and whose father had shoved him away because his heart was breaking. Had he seen Zane's mother's face whenever he looked at her son? Mary's heart broke for the little boy he had been. And for the lonely man he had become.

"Yes, I was. And I got tired of hearing how worthless I was. So I finally left."

"But it wasn't your fault."

"No, it wasn't."

"How old were you when you ran away?"

"Just short of fifteen. I was lucky, too. I made my way to Chicago, and that's where Jason Lynch found me. He took me in and gave me a job, and I've been at the Lynch ranch ever since. But lately I've started to think I'm just wasting time."

"What do you mean, wasting time?"

"Mary, I am not this brave, strong man you keep saying I am. I'm a big coward. All I do is hang around the ranch and cause trouble, just for laughs, and chase whores. I puked my guts up the first time I saw a man get killed. I'm lucky I didn't piss my pants when Two Bulls took us."

"But you didn't."

"Only because you saved me from doing it."

"Zane, there are not many who could have done what you did. There are not many who could have survived it. Marcus didn't think you had a chance when we brought you here. The man I watched Two Bulls torture was brave and strong and was willing to fight to the end just to give me a chance to survive."

"And just look at me now, Mary. I'm a mess. There's nothing left. I'm weak as a kitten."

Mary gently traced her hand over his chest. "These scars are your badge of courage, Zane. You went through hell and came out the other side. You'll get your strength back."

"Mary, I don't want you to love me because you think I'm a brave, strong man, like Michael was. I'm not the type to run into a burning building. I'm more the type to go get my friend to run into the burning building."

"I know better than that, Zane, and you do too. And I fell in love with you the first time I saw you. I was just too stubborn to admit it."

"At least we have that in common."

"I plan on having more than that in common with you."

"What do you mean?"

"Zane—"

"Are you talking about forever?"

"If you want . . ." Mary chewed on her lip, unsure suddenly. He had revealed so much about himself.

"Mary, when I was sick, I had dreams, or visions, I don't know. I saw people."

"Rachel calls it a spirit journey."

"Funny, Chase calls it that, too," Zane said. "I saw my mother and she told me I had a choice. She said I could stay there with her—"

"You mean die?"

"Or I could go on. I guess she meant go toward my future. And that's what I did. I wanted a future. I ran toward it as hard as I could. And then I saw it. I saw you.

I didn't come back for one time. I came back for forever." Zane touched Mary's cheek. "If you'll have me."

Mary's arms stretched around his neck. "Are you proposing marriage?"

Zane made a face. "Yes." He swallowed hard. "Will you marry me?"

"You act as if it's painful," Mary teased.

"It is. You're leaning on a scab."

"Zane!"

Zane wrapped his arms around her and kissed her. "I love you, Mary. I want to say it every day, every time I look at you, every time I think of you. For the first time in my life, I'm in love."

"It's not my first time, Zane, but I hope it's the last. I hope we have a long time together, but if we don't, then I want to make sure that the time we have is good and unforgettable." Her lips touched his. "I love you."

"Good," he groaned. "Now get off, you're killing me." He couldn't believe he was saying it. Things had changed. He couldn't even remember the last time he'd had a poke, and here he was with a woman who actually loved him and he was pushing her away. But only because he knew he wasn't ready. Physically, anyway.

"You are such a baby," Mary said as she rolled off his chest.

"Oh, really? How about I skin you alive and we'll see how you feel."

"Zane, you're milking it. That was weeks ago."

"Really? It feels like yesterday. Help me up."

"Are you always going to be this helpless and demanding?" Mary said as she stood and held out her hand. "Am I going to have to hire a nurse to take care of you when you're old and gray?"

Zane slowly rose and gave her his most devilish grin. "I'll be demanding—you can count on that."

"Promises, promises," Mary said over her shoulder. "Once upon a time I would have believed you," she said, deliberately looking down at the front of his buckskins.

"Count on it," Zane said, dimples flashing.

When I get my strength back.

Chapter Thirty-two

It felt good to ride again, even without a saddle. Zane rubbed the neck of the horse that Roan Eagle had loaned him. It was a fine animal with fine lines. Somewhere along the way, this group of Lakota had gotten lucky with a stud.

Roan Eagle had taken Zane to get Glory. The mare had been running with Roan Eagle's herd since his rescue. Zane prayed that the mare had not come into season while running wild. Jenny had plans for her, and they didn't include dropping a random foal.

"Take ten," Roan Eagle said as they crested the rise above his herd.

"Ten?" Zane asked.

"Ten horses for one," Roan Eagle said.

Zane looked at the herd of horses in the hollow below. The thought of ten horses was tempting. How easy it would be just to accept them, take Mary and go.

Disappear. His friends probably thought he was dead anyway. And when the letter didn't arrive in New York this Christmas, his grandfather would think so, too.

Then he wouldn't have to face anything, or anyone. Hiding who he was, where he came from, had been easy. Facing up to what he had become, or not become, was a bit more difficult.

One thing hadn't changed, though. He still had a job to do.

"I keep telling you, she's not mine," Zane said. Roan Eagle had been trying to trade him for Glory ever since he'd first stuck his head out of the tepee. "She belongs to my boss. I have to take her back."

"Twelve?"

"No."

Roan Eagle shook his head in disgust. "Your life for my father's was a good trade for all of us," he said. "But I am looking for a bride, and your mare would help."

"Just use your charm," Zane said. "You won't have to part with your horses."

"What is this charm?"

Zane grinned and waggled his eyebrows. Roan Eagle nodded and laughed as Zane put his heels to his horse and went flying down to cut Glory from the herd.

The feel of the rope in his hands was as natural as putting his gun belt back on. He had lost his clothes, except for his jacket, but he still had his boots and the money stashed inside. Except for the clothes he was wearing and the lack of a saddle, he could be back in Wyoming working the ranch.

It felt good to be himself again. They were leaving

tomorrow. Going home. Marcus was busy packing and labeling seeds and making notes in his journal while Rachel was helping Mary prepare food for them to eat along the way. In just a few short weeks, he should be home again.

Glory didn't give him any trouble.

"I guess she wants to go back to being a pampered lady," Zane said as the mare willingly followed along.

Roan Eagle shrugged. He had no idea what kind of life Glory had led before coming to this place. He just knew she was fast and would have added a lot to his herd.

"I think I'm going to miss this place," Zane said as they rode back toward the village.

"It is good in the summer," Roan Eagle said. "We will move soon for winter. Too much snow here."

Zane nodded. He knew the Lakota moved with the seasons. They moved so they couldn't be found. They survived.

"Too bad you won't be here for the hunt," Roan Eagle added.

"I hope you do well," Zane said. Was there anything left to hunt after the devastation to the buffalo herd he had seen?

The women of the village were already preparing for the hunt and the move. They worked so hard, they made life on the ranch seem like a holiday.

Medicine Woman walked up to him as he dismounted. She placed her hand on his cheek and said something. Zane had long ago given up on trying to figure out what she said. He had picked up a few common Lakota words but never found a trace of them in her speech. He looked at Roan Eagle in confusion as she went on.

"She say you were lucky she was here to save your pretty face," Roan Eagle translated with a smile. "She say that many years ago another was here, one with fire in his hair and on his face. His face was scarred. She might have saved his pretty face if she had been there when it was burned."

"Sounds like Jamie," Zane said. "Fire in his hair and his face."

Medicine Woman smiled and nodded.

"Yes, Jamie Duncan," Roan Eagle said. "His father and my father were friends. When I was a boy, we would visit and play with Jamie and Jenny with the hair like sunshine."

"Dang it all!" Zane exclaimed. "You know Jenny! Why am I not surprised?"

Roan Eagle was confused. "I know Jenny. She was here after her brother. She lived with us one winter. My father wanted me to marry her, but she would not stay. She had to find her brother."

"Jenny is my boss. Jenny owns Glory. Dang if the world isn't a small place."

Roan Eagle nodded in agreement. "We must tell my father this news."

"I have often wondered about my old friend's children," Gray Horse said later that evening. They were all sitting around the fire, talking about Jenny, Jamie and Chase. The ones who knew Jamie had been saddened to hear of his death, but were glad to know he

had a son, who looked just like him, according to
Zane. Marcus added his part in the story while Mary
and Rachel sat and listened.

Mary watched Zane as he told the stories of his
friends. They had been more of a family to him than
the grandparents he had left behind when he was a boy.
That took courage—to leave the security of home and
strike out on one's own.

But he had made himself a new home on the Lynch
ranch. He loved his friends. Mary saw it all as she
watched and listened. His eyes held that secret glow
again. It warmed her when his gaze landed on her. She
knew the secrets now.

Mary also knew there was a sadness there, one that
had not been in his gaze before. She longed to make
that sadness go away. Zane had been through so much,
it wouldn't be easy. Even now, after weeks in this
peaceful place while they waited for him to grow
strong enough to travel, he had nightmares. Night after
night their sleep was interrupted in the tepee she
shared with Zane and Marcus. She longed to go to
Zane and soothe the torment away, but it was difficult
with Marcus in the tepee, too.

Mary knew in her heart that Zane would probably
always have nightmares. She smiled at the thought of
easing them. Someday.

They had not spoken of the future since that day a
few weeks back when he had proposed. He had revealed so much to her that day. At least she now knew
why he acted the way he did. And she had realized that
she loved the way he was. He was a combination of
mischievous boy and hardworking man. He acted as if

he didn't have a care in the world, but he cared deeply for everyone around him.

Mary knew he hadn't told her everything: whether his grandparents were still alive, where he had gotten his education, or why he had kept these things hidden from his friends. He hadn't even told her that he had kept his past secret from his friends, but she knew in her heart that he had.

Zane still had some thinking to do. He had demons he had to put to rest. She understood that he needed time.

His eyes were on her again, their secrets glowing in the firelight.

Mary felt herself grow warm as his gaze touched her, caressed her. She looked down at the fire. She knew without looking that he was grinning at her, that his dimples were showing.

She was in trouble. If he could make her feel this way with just a look, what was going to happen when their relationship became more physical?

So what was wrong with being swept off one's feet? What was wrong with feeling this way? Zane loved her. She loved him.

Oh how she loved him. Every passing day, she knew it more and more.

She loved his determination to get his strength back, trying just a little bit harder each day.

She loved his humility, the way he admitted his weaknesses, not realizing his own strengths.

She loved his gentleness with the children of the village, even while pretending they were a bother.

She loved the way he worried over Lucifer, while still vowing to put him in the cook pot their first night

out on the trail. He knew the goat had helped to save
his life. And the goat followed him like a dog. Even
now, Lucifer was curled up behind Zane as he sat by
the fire. Every now and again he would peer around
Zane's broad back to see what was causing the com-
panionable laughter around the circle.

It was different for Mary this time. She had always
thought that love was just love, plain and simple. She
was wiser now. What she had felt for Michael had been
new and sweet and exciting. They had been nothing
more than children, although life had made them mature faster than others. Mary had been orphaned;
Michael had fought in the war.

Would their love have lasted once the charm wore off?
Mary hoped it would have, but that was all in the past.

With Zane it was different. He made promises just
by looking at her. He needed her. She had opened a
door for him.

There was plenty of time to figure it all out. They
had a lifetime. They hadn't even made plans yet. She
hadn't even told Marcus that Zane had asked her to
marry him.

But Marcus knew. He'd been worried about her
while Zane was so sick. And he'd rejoiced for her
when Zane recovered.

As the days passed, Marcus had watched her as she
watched Zane.

*Brother, you need to quit worrying about me and find
yourself a wife,* Mary thought as Marcus laughed with
Zane over a story.

Had he heard her? Marcus looked at her with his
own sly grin.

Tomorrow they were leaving. Back to the real world. But hadn't what they'd faced been more real than the lives they'd been living?

Mary realized she hadn't been living at all, not for a long while, not until a carriage had practically run over her in Central Park and Zane had swept her off her feet.

In more ways than one.

When she looked at him, she knew her grin had to be a mile wide. And his was, too.

Tomorrow they were leaving. They would spend days on the trail, camping out at night, and then civilization: baths and real beds. That was something to look forward to. But it would also mean people and work and things like corsets. Was she ready for that?

Tomorrow they were leaving this place of peace and contentment.

The fire became too hot for her. With a quick word to Rachel, Mary left the heat and the camaraderie and made her way along the familiar path to the river. It was easy to follow, lit as it was by the moon. Lucifer saw her go and followed behind her, occasionally stopping to sample the banquet of plants that grew in abundance by the trail.

She had known he would follow. Just as she had known he would follow her off the train.

"I'm going to miss this place," Zane said as he came up behind Mary and wrapped his arms around her waist. He placed his chin on top of her head, and they both soaked in the peaceful sound of the river flowing by.

Since when had just being with someone felt so right? Zane wondered. That was easy. Since Mary.

"Me too," Mary said. She leaned against him, pressing her back against his chest, tentatively. A few weeks past, just that gentle pressure would have knocked him flat. Now he bore it. His legs were planted firmly; his strength was returning. He was solid once again, but it would take a while longer for his endurance to come back. The long days on the trail back to Wyoming would build it up.

"I didn't know riding again would make me so sore," Zane said as he felt her relax against him.

"Better get used to it," Mary said. "I know I'm not looking forward to this trip."

"One thing I *am* looking forward to is a hot bath," Zane said.

"I've been dreaming about that."

"And some of Grace's cooking," he added. "She fixes the food on the ranch, and she's the best cook in the world."

"You'd better wait to make that judgment," Mary said playfully. "You have yet to taste my cooking."

"You can cook?" Zane teased at her ear. "I didn't know city girls could cook."

Mary twisted in his arms. "I want to show you all the things I can do," she said softly, seductively, her eyes veiled as she looked shyly down and away, as if shocked at her own boldness.

Her words hit him like a punch deep in his gut. He had wanted her for a long time—since the first time he saw her stomping away from him in Central Park. But he wanted her in the right way. He wanted it to be good and proper, the way it should be between a man and a woman. The way God had meant it to be.

He didn't deserve her.

"Zane?" Mary looked up at him, surprised by his slow response.

His hand traced the side of her face, and he smiled at the braids she still wore. Where had the prim and proper schoolteacher gone? Would she return once they reached Wyoming?

"I want it to be right for us, Mary. Always right. Sometimes when I look at you, I wonder why you love me."

"I love you because you're you. And you're all I need. All I want. And I want you now, Zane, in this beautiful place."

There it was again. The punch in the gut. The twisting that could bring him to his knees if he let it.

She looked up at him with the moonlight shining on her face, and he recognized it. The look. The one he had been wanting and wishing for without even knowing it. He had seen it hundreds of times on the faces of his friends. And he never knew what it really meant until this exact moment.

Her lips were waiting, and his were eager. It had all been worth it, he realized as they kissed. Every bit of pain and torture, just to get to this moment in his life. He wouldn't have appreciated it otherwise. He might have treated her callously and never realized what he had lost until it was too late.

The realization of what he could have lost made Zane hang on all the tighter as they sank to their knees in the long grass by the river.

Lucifer, curious as usual, stuck his nose between their necks, and Zane shoved him away with a growl.

"Ma-a-a-a," the goat said indignantly as Mary dissolved into a fit of giggles.

"What's so funny?" Zane asked as she clung to him, weak from laughter.

"You and Lucifer," she gasped. "Everything."

"Come on," he said, pulling her to her feet.

"Where are we going?"

"A nice hotel that I happened to find," he said, grinning and flashing his dimples.

They hurried then. They had waited so long that they couldn't wait any longer. Back down the path and through the village to the tepee with Lucifer on their heels.

And when they arrived, Zane firmly shut the flap in Lucifer's face. Mary opened it a moment later to put Marcus's belongings outside where he couldn't avoid finding them.

"Do you think he'll get the message?" Zane asked Mary as they found each other once again in the dim moonlight filtering through the smoke hole.

"It's time for Marcus to take care of Marcus," Mary said.

"And let me take care of you?"

Mary's hands moved under his shirt and skimmed over the ridges and scabs there, drawing a gasp from Zane. "Let me take care of you," she said.

She took his hand and led him to the pile of furs that had been his bed for so many weeks. She pulled back the blanket and knelt, pulling him down beside her.

Zane followed, willing but hesitant. He wasn't sure how he should act. He knew the mechanics without a doubt, but the rest was a mystery. Yet he was anxious for the discovery. Chills ran up his spine and down his arms as Mary lifted the tail of his shirt and pulled it over his head. Her hands settled on his shoulders, and she leaned in shyly for another kiss.

Mary pulled back with a smile and slid the ties from her braids, then slowly combed her fingers through her hair.

Zane had to help—he couldn't resist. His fingers joined hers and he ran them through the long curls, combing them into one thick mass that flowed like a river down her back.

Another kiss and Mary stood. She lifted the hem of her dress and undid the leggings, slipping out of her moccasins as the leggings fell and she kicked them away.

Ties at her shoulders held up her dress, and it soon fell to join the leggings. Zane's hands touched her knees as he looked up at her body, illuminated by the moonlight. She had an ethereal glow about her that took his breath away; he had to touch her to make sure she was real. His hands touched her knees and then skimmed up her thighs, pausing as they touched the crescent-shaped scar on the outside of one.

He grinned when he touched it.

"What?" Mary asked, puzzled by the look on his face.

"Isn't it funny how something as simple as this"—he traced the scar—"tied our lives together?"

Mary came down to his level as his hands moved up her sides. "I don't want to question fate, Zane. I just want to give thanks for the way it turned out."

"I've been a fool most of my life, Mary. But I promise, from now on, I will do the best I can for you."

"I know," she said. She pushed him back onto the furs and moved over him, stretching her body over his.

"Ow, wait, that . . . hurts . . . ow," he said as he adjusted to her weight, her feel, against the raw skin of his chest.

"Shhh," she said, lowering her lips to quiet his.

His arms wrapped around her as she kissed the fading redness on his cheek and then the mark on his neck, and the long ridge on his chest where Marcus had stitched him back together. Her lips touched the scars, and the pain magically went away as his veins filled with the warmth and tenderness she offered him.

Zane, who had always taken control and done it well, lay there and let her love him as she wanted. As he wanted.

Mary guided his hands to the places that she wanted him to touch, and he let her lead him so that he would learn.

He watched her face in the moonlight and realized he had never known what he'd been doing. He had just been going through the motions. He had been just as mechanical as the whores that he had paid through the years.

He knew it was good now, because she lost herself. He watched her face and her eyes grow unfocused with sweet bliss before he allowed himself to take the same pleasure.

It was good. It was the way it was supposed to be. It was the way it always should be.

The journey had all been worth it. He would gladly go through it again for Mary.

Chapter Thirty-three

Who knew that saying good-bye could be so hard? Maybe it was because Zane, Mary and Marcus knew in their hearts that they would never see the kind people of Gray Horse's village again.

But Mary's sentiments quickly changed when the woman who had taken Little Bird to nurse handed the baby to her, along with a pack.

"What am I supposed to do with her?" Mary gasped in astonishment.

Rachel laid a gentle hand upon her arm. "She will never be welcome here. She would never be more than a slave," she explained. "Find her a place where she will be loved. She deserves that much."

"I don't know how to care for a baby," Mary protested. But what choice did she have? She couldn't just leave Little Bird here. Not after Wapka had shown Mary kindness, in her own strange way.

Zane took a good look at the little girl who kicked against Mary in excitement when he took her tiny hand. A cherubic smile split her rosy cheeks as she looked up at him with deep brown eyes, all the darker because of her creamy white skin. His face fell into its familiar grin as something in the child's brown eyes caught his attention.

"I know someone who will take her," Zane said, "if you don't mind taking care of her for a while."

"We can all care for her," Marcus said.

"Besides, it will be a learning experience," Zane added. "After all, I'm planning on having at least half a dozen children. All boys."

"And who were you planning on having them with?" Mary asked, raising an eyebrow as she adjusted the baby in her arms. "Have you got a harem of women hidden somewhere that I should know about?"

"Is there something you two want to tell me?" Marcus interrupted.

They ignored him as Zane put his arms around Mary and Little Bird. "I have only one mother picked out for all my children," he said, kissing the top of Mary's head, and then adding one for Little Bird. The child squealed in delight as she squirmed around between them. "I also heard that she's an excellent teacher, so not only will my boys be handsome and charming, they will also be well educated."

"Just like their father?" Mary said.

"Just like their father."

"I'm pretty sure there's something going on," Marcus said with a knowing smile.

"There is," Zane said with a wide grin. "Your sister seduced me."

"What!" Mary exclaimed.

Zane pointed to her feet. "No kicking or you'll drop the baby."

"She's always been impetuous," Marcus said teasingly.

"Incorrigible also, if last night was any indication," Zane added.

"Oh, my," Mary said, blushing beneath her tanned skin. "I just might kill you."

"You'll have to do a better job of it than the last person who tried," Zane said.

"There's only one solution for this," Marcus said. "You're going to have to marry her."

"I plan on it," Zane said, and his eyes danced as he looked at Mary. "Just as soon as we get to Wyoming."

"Well, then, let's get going," Mary said. "Before you change your mind."

"Don't tempt me," Zane said.

Marcus took Little Bird and her cradle board and placed it on his back. Zane lifted Mary onto her horse and mounted his own. Gray Horse had provided a mount for each of them. The horses were to be gifts for Jenny, he had told them, and were descended from her father's horse, Storm. Zane knew Jenny would be thrilled to have them.

They waved their good-byes to the village.

"Come on, you dang goat," Zane yelled to Lucifer, who was being hugged by the children. "I'm looking forward to roasting you over a spit tonight."

"Ma-a-a-a," Lucifer replied as he trotted after the three riders and Glory.

Jake Anderson, sheriff of Laramie, looked at the envelope on his desk. The corners of it were well worn, as he had picked it up and put it back down at least a hundred times since its arrival nearly a month before. He looked up at his friend Caleb.

"When are you going to give in and open it?" Caleb asked. "Maybe it could tell us where Zane is." Caleb had made that suggestion nearly as many times as Jake had picked up the envelope.

"It's from New York City, Caleb. I'm pretty sure he's not there," Jake snapped.

Caleb ignored Jake's temper. He had grown used to it through the years.

"Maybe we should answer it," he suggested. "Tell whoever it is what's happened."

"We don't know what's happened," Jake said. "Do we tell them Zane just disappeared? His note didn't go into great detail. Shoot, we wouldn't even know what territory he was in if that conductor hadn't included a letter telling us about the raid on the train when he sent the trunks along."

"Zane has been gone for close to four months," Caleb said, looking at the calendar on the wall behind Jake's desk. "Maybe it's time we just accept the fact that he's gone, along with the doctor and his sister. We'll probably never find out what happened to them."

"Chase wants to go looking for him," Jake said. "Since Jenny's had her baby and everything is fine, he's been thinking about setting out. I think he's just waiting to make sure Cat gets through her delivery without any trouble."

"I hope she has as easy a time as Jenny had with Ryder." Caleb leaned back in his chair and braced his good leg against the desk. "Chase said he practically fell out."

"I'm glad it's the women that have them. After watching what Shannon went through to have Will . . ." Jake let his comment trail off awkwardly. He wished he hadn't mentioned his wife and son. He knew how badly Caleb and Amanda wanted children. But Amanda hadn't been able to conceive.

"Don't worry about it, Jake," Caleb said.

The sound of running footsteps on the sidewalk interrupted whatever Jake had been about to respond. Caleb's wife, Amanda, burst through the door, with Shannon behind her, holding Will in her arms.

"Cat's having her baby," Amanda announced. "Zeb said for me to come." Her face was white. She was terrified. There was still no doctor in town, and Amanda had minimal experience as a midwife, having only helped with the delivery of Jenny's daughter Faith and young Will.

Cat had already suffered several miscarriages. No one wanted to think about what it would do to her and Ty if they lost this child now.

"It's about time," Jake said. "I figured she was keeping it in until we got a doctor in town."

"She's waited long enough," Shannon said. "I asked Bill to fetch a buggy for us."

"Does this mean we're all going?" Caleb asked.

Jake nodded. "Bill can watch things for a while. It's

not like there's anything going on around here." He picked up the letter from his desk and stuffed it in his pocket. Caleb nodded. It was time to decide what to do about Zane. They might as well all have a say in it.

Everyone went outside. Caleb and Jake's horses were tied to the rail, and they waited there with the women for Jake's deputy Bill to return from the livery with a buggy.

"Was that a sheep I just heard?" Caleb asked as a strange noise came from the outskirts of town.

"Dang, I hope not," Jake said. "The last thing we need around here is another sheep herd."

"Ma-a-a-a."

"Sounds more like a goat to me," Shannon said. "My gran had a nanny goat. They give good milk."

"It is a goat," Caleb said as three riders and a black mare came into view with a goat trotting after them.

"That woman looks Indian," Jake said. "She's got a baby with her, too." The sun was behind him and shining full in the riders' faces. The men had their hats pulled down low, and the woman was wearing a hat, too, along with a buckskin dress and leggings.

"Poor child," Shannon commented. "Maybe I should have said 'poor mother' instead. It can't be easy traveling like that with a baby."

"Nice-looking horse," Caleb said as the black mare showed her form.

"I guess I'd better check them out," Jake said. "You go on and I'll catch up."

He stepped out into the street, and Caleb limped behind him.

"Think I can't handle it?" Jake groused.

"Look again," Caleb said.

One of the riders urged his horse into a quick canter as the two men stepped out into the street.

"Dang," Jake said.

"Did you miss me?" Zane asked with a wide grin as he pulled his horse to a stop in a cloud of dust.

"Thane!" Will laughed as if he had just seen him yesterday.

Caleb quickly grabbed Zane and gave him a bear hug. "We thought you were dead!"

"I nearly was!"

Caleb looked at his friend and noticed the fading marks on his cheek and forehead and then the brighter one on his neck. His sandy brown hair, usually neat and trim, hung down to his shoulders, and his face was covered with a growth of dark beard along with the grime of the trail. He looked great for someone who was supposed to be dead. "I guess you were," Caleb said. "What happened to you?"

"I only want to tell it once," Zane said, remembering similar words that Jake had once spoken when everyone had given him up for dead during the war.

Jake looked at Mary and Marcus, who had just ridden up.

"Does this mean your near-death experience turned out as well as mine?" Jake asked, gazing at Mary.

"Well, I'm not married," Zane said. "Yet. I thought I'd save that for when you guys were around."

Zane went to the riders. "This is Mary Dunleavy." He looked up at her with his familiar grin.

Shannon saw the look and goosed Jake in the side.

"And her brother, Marcus Brown," Zane added by way of introduction.

"You're the schoolteacher," Jake said. "Cat's going to love this."

Zane took the little girl down from Mary. "Caleb, Amanda, I brought you a present." Zane gave the child to Amanda. "Her name is Little Bird, but we've started calling her Robin. We thought it suited her better, and her new life."

Amanda looked at Zane as if he had lost his mind, but Caleb had his eyes on the baby.

"She's clean," Zane said, as if that explained it all. "We gave her a bath and fixed her up before we got here."

"Oh, my," Mary said, shaking her head at Zane's sudden stupidity. He had been so excited about finding a baby for Caleb and Amanda that he hadn't explained her situation to them at all.

"She's orphaned," Mary said. "Her mother helped us."

"When I looked into her eyes, I thought of you, Caleb," Zane said. "Her father was white and her mother was Lakota."

"We can't just keep her, can we?" Amanda asked Caleb, who had placed his hand on Robin's cheek. The little girl grabbed his finger.

"How did you get her?" Jake asked.

"The Lakota gave her to us," Zane said. "They thought she'd have a better life in our world."

"Where exactly have you been?" Jake asked.

"It's a long story."

"She must be starved," Shannon said as she leaned over Robin.

"We all are," Marcus said.

Amanda looked up at Marcus, who was still mounted. "Aren't you Dr. Brown?" she asked.

Marcus smiled. "You look well, Amanda. Zane told me about your life here."

Caleb placed his arm around Amanda. "Thank you for helping her," he said.

"You got me started in the right direction," Amanda added.

"A doctor," Shannon said. "Just what we need at the moment."

The rest looked at her in confusion.

"Remember?" Shannon said. "Cat?"

"Dang it," Jake said. "Where is Bill with that buggy?"

"Bill?" Zane asked.

"You remember Bill," Jake said, with his cool smile.

"You mean Maybelle's Bill?"

"Yes, he's my deputy now."

"What?"

"Things change, Zane," Caleb said. "You've been gone for a while. Maybelle's is closed."

"Closed?"

"Maybelle's?" Mary asked. "Someone I should know about?"

"Oh, I like her," Shannon said to Amanda.

Amanda nodded in agreement. She was still a bit overwhelmed to have Robin in her arms.

"Where's Missy?" Zane said out of the side of his mouth to Caleb.

Jake laughed as Caleb answered. "Married."

"Married?"

"Who is Missy?" Mary asked.

"She ran off with a miner who'd just struck it rich."

"And Missy is?" Mary asked again.

"Nobody," Zane replied. "At least, no one you need to worry about." All he felt was relief. He'd been worried that Missy would take one look at him with Mary and pitch another hissy fit. Probably bring down the house with her screams.

"Are you sure you want to marry him?" Jake asked Mary.

"Yes, she does," Zane answered for her.

"Oh, my," Mary said.

"What about Cat?" Marcus asked.

"She's in labor," Shannon said as Bill and the buggy made an appearance.

"We'd better get a move on," Marcus said.

"Howdy, Zane," Bill said as he got down from the buggy. "Haven't seen you around much."

Zane laughed. "Sorry you missed me, Bill." He tied Glory to the back of the buggy, and Caleb put his horse, Banner, beside the mare.

"Thank you, Zane," Caleb said. "You don't know what this means to us."

Zane looked into the warm brown eyes of his friend and then up at Mary. "I think I do," he said. "Now."

Jake helped the women into the buggy, and then Caleb climbed in, Jake watching as he always did to make sure his friend didn't have any trouble with his wooden leg.

"Wait a minute," Zane said as Caleb picked up the

reins. Zane picked up Lucifer and put him in the back of the buggy next to Shannon.

"What is this?" she asked.

"Dinner," Zane replied as he swung up on his horse.

"Ma-a-a-a," Lucifer mumbled as he tasted Shannon's shawl.

"I see what you mean," Mary said to Zane as they rode out of town. Jake and Marcus had taken off ahead of the rest of the party. Zane and Mary followed on horseback after the buggy.

"About what?" Zane asked.

"Family."

"Nice, isn't it? And this is only part of the gang."

"That was a good thing you did with Robin."

"I know it was hard, caring for her on the trail, but I knew how much they wanted a child of their own."

"I'm glad you brought her to them," Mary said as they looked at the two dark heads bent over the little girl. She had settled onto Amanda's lap in the buggy as if she belonged there.

"Isn't it amazing, after all she's seen, that she's always so content?" Mary observed.

"Maybe that's why she is," Zane said. "She had to learn to deal with trouble at an early age."

"I hope she doesn't remember any of it. I'd hate to think of the things she's seen in her short life."

"If anyone knows how to make bad memories go away, it's those two," Zane said. "They have both survived a lot."

"So have you," Mary said.

"It was easy"—Zane smiled—"since I knew you were on the other side."

"Don't ever say it was easy, Zane. It wasn't." He was still inclined to hide behind his charm. But now she could see through it.

"They don't need to know all of it, Mary."

"They'll figure it out, Zane. They'll see the scars eventually."

"Jake and Caleb have scars. Dang, Caleb lost his leg. Jake's back is a mess because his father beat him. Chase has got a couple of bullet holes in him and almost died of pneumonia, and Ty was in a prison camp during the war. I'm not about to get into a pissing contest with any of them."

"No one said you had to. But don't make light of what happened, either. You survived it, and that in itself shows how strong you are."

"I'm not sure I had anything to do with that." Zane looked off into the distance, toward the mountains to the north—ever-present, solid, welcoming. "I'm pretty sure that was in God's hands."

"And I give thanks everyday for the way it turned out," Mary said.

"Me too."

"One thing I've noticed, Zane," Mary said as they got closer to the ranch. "I haven't heard any Shakespeare out of you since it all happened."

"Do you miss it?"

"No, I was just wondering . . ."

"I think I used it before as a wall of sorts. That way I wouldn't have to say what I really felt. I just used someone else's words. I guess I just don't need to do that anymore."

"No more secrets?"

"Not exactly."

"What does that mean?"

"I've still got some things to tell you."

"Like about Missy?"

"Missy who?" Zane grinned. "I swear I forgot all about her when I met you."

"I guess it was lucky for me she forgot all about you, too," Mary said with her own grin.

"Me? I'm unforgettable."

"Only in your own mind," Mary said.

"So I guess I'll have to prove it to you," Zane said, turning on the charm.

Mary rolled her eyes. "Promises, promises."

The buggy turned down the drive to the ranch.

"This is it," Zane said.

"Glad to be home?" Mary asked.

Zane reached for her hand. "Home is wherever *you* are."

Chapter Thirty-four

Mary felt as if she were caught up in a whirlwind as they arrived at the big white house that was the center-piece of the Lynch ranch. Marcus was nowhere to be seen, having already been swept up the stairs in a rush of tears and hugs when Jenny saw him. A beautifully elegant older woman burst into tears when she saw Zane and hung onto him for dear life as a whole crowd of people gathered on the front porch and dogs barked at the excitement of the new arrivals, and at the nov-elty of Lucifer, who was delighted to find a patch of chrysanthemums by the front step.

Children were everywhere—Mary didn't even at-tempt to count them. There was a mixture of boys and girls, with hair that went from Will's pure white to a rich dark brown, including a toddler who must belong to the tall woman of color clapping her hands in glee at the celebration. They ranged in age from around seven down to a dark-haired infant that a tall, dark-haired man with eyes like flint held in his arms. The infant reminded Mary of Robin, who was also getting a lot of attention as everyone asked who she was.

"This is my daughter," Caleb explained. "I'll let Zane tell you the rest."

Zane finally disentangled himself from the older woman and pulled Mary up on the porch. She tripped on a step and suddenly became intensely self-conscious. She was still covered with dirt from the trail and wearing clothes from the Lakota village. Her hair was in need of a thorough washing, and she couldn't remember the last time she'd seen a brush.

"This is Mary," Zane said as he caught her before she fell flat on her face. "We're getting married."

That brought another eruption of tears and celebration as Zane was hugged and then Mary was hugged and passed around the porch in a whirl. She tried to put names with faces, which turned out to be easy when she had a moment to think about it. Zane had told her so much about his friends.

The older woman with the scars on her face was Grace, and the older man must be her husband, Cole. He had the same eyes as Amanda, which made sense since he was her uncle. There was a little girl with rich brown hair and the same gray eyes. That had to be their daughter Jacey.

The colored woman was easy: Cleo. Her husband was Zeb, who had quietly disappeared with Glory after exclaiming in excitement when he saw her. The older man watching shyly from the shadows of the front hall had to be Cleo's father, Pharaoh, and their little boy was Hector. Mary had done a good job of memorizing the names.

Jake and Shannon were easy, since Shannon had the flaming red hair Zane had mentioned, and Will looked just like his father. There was also a boy with hair close to Shannon's color, though his had more gold in it. He had to be Fox, Jamie's son. She recognized the blue eyes when she saw them. Jamie had had those same eyes. Then she saw those blue, blue eyes again, all the more startling in the face of a boy with long dark hair. Chance. And Chase was his father. Even though he had been mostly quiet throughout the commotion, Chase was an intimidating presence. Strangely so, since he was holding the infant, whose name she did not know and there was a tiny blond girl wrapped around his leg. That must be Faith. Zane had told her that Faith had a limp, like Caleb, though she had been born with hers.

Mary knew she'd recognize Jenny when she saw her. Which left just Cat and Ty, who were busy at the moment.

"Who is this?" Zane asked Chase when some of the commotion had died down.

"This is Ryder," Chase said. "Born a month ago."

"Looks like his daddy," Zane said. The child was the image of his father.

"How are you, Zane?" Chase asked, his eyes searching Zane's.

"I'm good, Chase," Zane said. "Finally."

"Yes, you are," Chase said. "Sometimes it takes a while to get there."

Zane reached for Mary's hand. She was behind him, talking to Amanda about Robin.

"It was worth the trip," Zane said. Mary leaned into him, resting under his arm as he brushed his lips against her brow. "But I'm also glad it's over."

"Me too," Mary said.

"So when is the wedding?" Grace asked.

"As soon as possible," Zane said. "After all, my wife-to-be is also our new schoolteacher. She's got work to do."

"And you don't?" Mary said with an arch of her eyebrow. "I recall someone promising me a hot bath as soon as we got here."

"I'll get the water started," Cleo said. "I've got pots of it boiling for Miss Cat."

"Your trunks are here, too," Grace said. "We stored everything when we got your note."

"Note?" Mary asked.

"That's all it was," Chase said and then quoted from memory: "The Indians took Dr. Brown. His sister took Jenny's horse. If I don't come back, you can fire me. Your friend, Zane. P.S. Cat's schoolteacher is Dr. Brown's sister."

"We've read it about a hundred times," Cole said. "Trying to figure out where you were."

"I didn't know where I was," Zane said. "But I did run into an old friend of yours," he added, turning to Chase.

"Of mine?" Chase asked.

"Gray Horse."

"Dang," Chase said. "I guess you only want to tell it once."

"Yes," Zane said. "I'm going to need lots of Grace's food to get me through the whole story." He gave Grace one of his grins.

"We'll have a feast tonight," Grace promised.

A scream from upstairs stopped the commotion. "Hopefully, we'll have a lot to celebrate."

"We will," Zane said. "I think the worst is behind us now."

"One thing, Zane," Jake asked as everyone settled down. "What about the goat?"

"I'm not so sure I want goat for dinner, Zane," Shannon added.

"Anyone touches that goat and they answer to me," Zane said. "That goat saved my life."

"Someone please tell Cat to hurry up with that baby," Cole said. "I can't wait to hear this one."

Mary looked at the tub of steaming water as if it were a banquet and she was starving. It had been a while since she'd had a good meal. Since the night in St. Louis, actually, and she had barely eaten that night, since she'd been so confused about Zane. But of the two choices, a bath was what she most longed for. And confusion over Zane was no longer inhibiting her appetite.

She felt a little guilty bathing while upstairs Cat was going through labor, but there was nothing she could do to help. And in the meanwhile, she desperately needed to get clean. Towels, soap and a bottle of shampoo for her hair, specially made by Cleo, sat on a stool by the tub. Her trunk was handy; the tub was in a storage room off the kitchen. Mary looked gratefully at the brush and mirror. She felt as if she were looking at a great treasure. Cleo had taken one of her dresses to press, and a set of underclothes lay on the stool, ready to wear after her bath.

Mary made a face at the corset. As skinny as she was now, she wouldn't need it. Maybe she should just stay that way. She had gotten used to going without the restricting garment, and she had a feeling the women she had met today weren't too fond of corsets, either.

Imagine showing up to teach school in New York City without a corset on. Mary tested the water. It was extremely hot, but she wanted it that way.

Of course, a lot of things weren't quite the way she'd imagined them. She stripped out of her clothes and kicked them to the side, wondering if she'd ever wear the Indian dress again.

Mary sank down into the tub until the water touched her earlobes. Her skin turned red from the heat, and she looked ruefully at the pale skin of her breasts and stomach compared to the darker skin of her arms.

How long before it all faded away? What they had been through, what Zane had suffered was just a memory now, but he would have the scars until the day he died.

And what they had found would last a lifetime.

Yet how close they had foolishly come to letting their love slip away.

"Mary!" Marcus pounded on the door and then burst through. Mary shrieked and slid deeper into the tub.

"Sorry. Jenny said my trunk was in here." He went straight to it, clearly distracted.

"How's Cat?" Mary asked. She covered herself the best she could with the washcloth, but Marcus wasn't looking in her direction.

"Tired. She needs some help. I've got forceps in here somewhere."

"No details, Marcus, please," Mary said.

Marcus looked up and grinned at her. "Are you planning on sleeping through the birth when you have your own?"

"What are you talking about?" Mary said. "And quit looking at me."

"Mary, I'm a doctor. I know what a woman's body looks like. And I'm talking about you having children. Remember, Zane mentioned something about six boys?"

"Go away, Marcus. Go do whatever it is you do and leave me in peace."

Marcus found the desired instrument and held it up for Mary to see. "You'll thank me someday," he said.

"Go!" Mary pointed toward the door with a splash of water.

"Save some water for me," he said on his way out.

Mary smiled at his back. She'd make sure he got his own fresh water, even if she had to carry and heat it herself. Too bad all the women around here were already married. He needed a good wife. But she'd have to be special, like he was.

She sank her head into the water to wet her hair and then came up sputtering when she realized that she had company once again.

"Isn't there a lock for that door?" she asked.

Zane just grinned at her. His hair was wet and pushed back behind his ears, his beard was gone, and he was wearing clean clothes that hung a bit loose upon his frame.

"Need some help?" he asked suggestively.

"Oh, my," Mary said. "What will your friends think?"

A scream sounded from upstairs.

"They're thinking about other things right now," Zane said. "And Lucifer found the kitchen garden."

"Poor Cleo," Mary said.

"Poor Cleo, nothing," Zane laughed. "She swatted him with a mop. I remember what that feels like."

"What?" Mary asked as she looked up at his laughing face.

"I think he's hiding in the barn with Glory." He picked up the bottle of shampoo and arched an eyebrow in her direction.

Mary obliged by leaning her head forward. Zane pulled the stool up to sit on and placed a bucket in a handy spot.

"So you got hit by a mop?"

"Jenny did it."

"Why?"

"I implied that she looked like a cow when she was carrying Chance."

"You are—"

"Shhhh."

His hands were gentle yet strong, as they had always been. She enjoyed the sensation as he massaged her scalp and temples, taking a moment to place some suds upon the tip of her nose, which made her sneeze.

Mary didn't give him the satisfaction of snapping at him. She knew he was doing it just to get a rise out of her. Besides, his hands in her hair felt wonderfully soothing. She felt all the stress of travel fade away as if she were melting into the warm water. There was no way she was going to do anything to make him stop.

"Remember the night we camped by the stream?" Zane asked. "And I rubbed your back?"

"Uh-huh." Mary felt too good to speak.

"Did your back hurt because of your time?"

Mary opened one eye and gave him a look.

Zane grinned down at her. "I was just thinking, most women call it a curse, but in your case it wasn't. At least not then."

"Is that the kind of thing you usually think about?" Mary asked, both eyes open now.

"I guess I have to start thinking about it now. Or at least every time you want a back rub."

Mary closed her eyes again. Let him think what he wanted, as long as his hands stayed busy.

Zane poured a pitcher of water over her hair and let the soapy residue flow into the bucket he'd placed below her bowed head. He then toweled off her hair and wrapped the towel around her head.

He became quiet then. Strangely so for someone who usually had a smart remark to make. Mary opened her eyes to see what he was up to.

"What are you looking at?" she asked when she saw his hazel eyes smiling down at her. She smiled back at him. "You look funny upside down," she said.

"You're the one who's upside down," he replied. "Is there anything else that needs to be washed?"

Mary arched a foot against the end of the tub. It was tempting. The water was still warm, and they were alone for the first time since they had left the village. Should they—

"Zane Brody!" someone called out.

"In here!" he yelled back.

"Zane!" Mary hissed as the door flew open.

It was Jenny. Jenny, all golden and as beautiful as Mary remembered her. She flew into Zane's arms with a squeal and a laugh.

Mary took advantage of the distraction of the reunion to grab a towel. In her excitement, Jenny had left the door open.

"It's a boy, Zane," Jenny said between her tears. "And you're back. You're alive. You're safe."

"I brought your horse, too," Zane said as he hugged her.

"I don't care about the horse. I just care about you." Jenny's blue eyes widened as she saw Mary. "And Mary—my goodness, you're all grown up."

Jenny grabbed Mary and hugged her, even though she was dripping wet and only wrapped in a towel.

"Didn't Cat tell you to stay away from her schoolteacher?" Jenny said to Zane with a laugh.

"What can I say, Jenny? I couldn't resist." Zane looked toward the stairs. "How is Cat?"

"Fine. Cat's fine, the baby is fine, Ty is floating on air. He has a son. Cameron Lynch Kincaid. Why don't you go up and say hello and let Cat wring your neck?"

"Mary?" Zane asked.

"Go on. I'll be fine."

Jenny wiped at a tear. "I can't remember the last time I was this happy," she said to Mary as Zane left the room.

Chapter Thirty-five

Later Jenny said the same thing again, when everyone was gathered in the parlor. Even Cat, finally released from the prison of her bedroom, came down, proudly carried in the arms of her husband and placed on the sofa with several blankets and pillows around her and her son sleeping safely in her arms.

Marcus had enjoyed the benefits of the tub and propped a chair in front of the door so Mary could not get revenge on him.

Robin had been bathed again by a nervous Amanda and Caleb and dressed in one of Jacey's dresses. They had tied a piece of ribbon in her hair, and she finally slept contentedly in her new papa's arms. Most of the other children slept also, except for Chance and Fox, who had stationed themselves before the fireplace on the Oriental rug and waited for Zane's story with blue eyes open wide.

"I swear you two have grown a foot since I was gone," Zane said to the two boys as he took a seat in the parlor.

"So what happened?" Jenny asked. She held her new baby, Ryder, over her shoulder and rocked him as he drifted off to sleep. The rocking chair was a new addition to the parlor, placed there when they finally realized that Cat was actually going to carry a baby to full term.

"Well, it all started with this goat," Zane said.

"It started before that," Mary said.

"It did?" Zane looked at Mary and broke into a grin. "It started in Central Park."

He told the story from the beginning then. They laughed when they heard about Lucifer. They laughed when Marcus told them that Zane thought he had the clap. Chase shook his head in anger when Mary told them about the buffalo, and they all shook their heads in disbelief when Zane told them about the twister.

"Then what happened?" Shannon asked, on the edge of her seat.

"We figured Glory was gone and we were pretty sure Lucifer was gone, too, so we started walking," Zane said. "Then from a distance we saw Glory and there was a group of Indians chasing her. We followed them, ran into Marcus and the bunch that he was with, and got her back and found Lucifer, too. I reckon he had followed Glory's trail."

"Zane," Mary said. "That's not what happened."

"Leave him be, Mary," Marcus said.

"No," Mary said. "The truth is that the Indians who were after Glory captured us. There were five of them, all with rifles pointed right at Zane's chest. He gave them Glory, hoping that would be enough, but they were evil, and they took us, too."

Zane shook his head, but Mary kept going, her eyes focused on Zane as she talked.

"He sacrificed himself to save me. When they were dragging me, he carried me, even though he had a noose around his neck and if he fell they would have dragged him to death. He took a beating so I could get a drink of water. And when they tortured him, he didn't make a sound." Her words came out in a rush, but she kept her eyes on Zane, even when they filled with tears and she had to wipe them away as they trickled down her cheeks.

"Then he almost died from the wounds and the infection. Gray Horse and his people helped us."

"Zane?" Jenny said. The room was deathly quiet. Zane kept his eyes on the carpet.

"What do you want me to say?" he finally responded when the quiet became enormous and the ticking of the tall clock was only silenced by the beating of his heart. "It happened. I surrendered. I took the coward's way out and just got lucky that we weren't both killed."

"Son of a bitch!" Jake jumped to his feet. "Don't you *ever* say that."

"Jake," Shannon said quietly. "The children."

Jake looked around the room and quieted his tone. "Dying is the easy way out, Zane."

"He's right," Chase said. "It takes courage to walk through fire. You have a mark on your face. I imagine there are several more on you that we can't see. I can't begin to imagine what they did to you. What it felt like. What you were thinking."

Zane looked up at the men in the room, all of them

looking at him with empathy. They had all faced their own failings at one time or another.

Chase had left Jenny when she needed him most to track down the man who murdered her brother and his best friend. He had nearly died in the process, and it had taken him a long time to recover from the guilt he felt at putting his need for revenge over the needs of his family.

Ty felt responsible for Caleb losing his leg and Jake nearly losing his life. He had taken them to fight in a war that he discovered too late he didn't believe in. There wasn't a day that he didn't look at Caleb and think "what if?"

Cole had failed to find Amanda after she'd been abducted and forced into prostitution. His sister, Amanda's mother, had died of grief while still blaming Cole for Amanda's disappearance. She died not knowing that her daughter would be found eventually and would one day lead a happy life.

Caleb had lost his leg. He would never be whole again, never be equal with his friends. Even though they'd accepted him, it had taken him a long time to accept his handicap himself.

And Jake, more than any of them, knew what Zane had gone through. He had suffered beatings at his father's hand for as long as he could remember, for no other reason than the fact that he was a boy, doing what boys normally do. His father claimed he had the devil in him and had scarred his back with a whip until Jake had run off, certain that he was the devil until he fell in love with Shannon and allowed the goodness that was inside of him to surface.

They had all been there. And the women had been

there with them. Patiently waiting and going through their own trials.

They understood. Zane nodded his head. There was no need to say anything else. They knew the rest of the story—she was sitting right beside him.

Mary's hand crept into Zane's. "They're your family," she said. "They understand."

"I haven't been entirely honest with all of you," Zane said. "About me, that is."

"What are you talking about?" Cat asked.

"When I came here, I told you I was an orphan." Zane looked around at the expectant faces. "My parents are dead, but my grandparents are still alive. I ran away from home because I couldn't stand my grandfather. He hated my father and blamed him for my mother's death in childbirth."

"Sounds like a good reason to run away," Grace said. "Why are you telling us this now?"

"My grandfather is Ezra Cunningham."

"Who is he?" Jenny asked.

"*The* Ezra Cunningham?" Ty asked.

Marcus started laughing. He recognized the name, too.

"Who is Ezra Cunningham?" Cat asked.

"One of the richest men in the country," Ty said.

"A big tightwad," Marcus added. "I treated him once, or tried to. There's no cure for meanness. He told me I was too young to be a doctor and he sent me packing. It's a good thing New York is full of doctors. He just kept going through us until he found one who would agree with everything he said."

"So you're rich?" Caleb asked Zane.

"No. Not me," Zane said. "He disowned me a long time ago. But I write my grandmother a letter every year at Christmas just to let her know I'm still alive. She'll never know how close she came to not getting one this year."

Jake pulled the letter out of his pocket. "Looks like she'll find out," he said. "This came for you around a month ago."

Zane looked in shock at the postmark. "It's from New York. It's got to be from one of them."

"Why didn't you ever tell us?" Cat demanded. "Did my father know? Why did you keep it a secret?"

"Caleb, Jake and I all got here at about the same time. We all know what Jake came from—all you had to do was look at his back; and Caleb was nearly starved to death. What would it have sounded like if I had said my grandpa was a rich, mean bastard so I ran away?"

"He's got a point," Cole said.

Zane looked at the envelope in his hand and then at Mary.

"Go in the study," Jenny suggested.

"I'm sorry for blurting it all out," Mary said when they were behind the closed door in Jason's study. "But then again, maybe I'm not."

"I always knew you were impetuous, Mary. I think I knew all along that you weren't going to keep quiet. Like I said, I'm a coward." He grinned sheepishly at her.

Mary wrapped her arms around his waist, and his arms came around her. "No using your charm on this one. They needed to know. They love you."

"I know. Why is it that those three words are the hardest to say to the people you love the most?"

"Because it means so much. And it makes us vulnerable. What if the people you love don't love you back?"

"I reckon I don't need to worry about that anymore."

"No. You are well loved by everyone who knows you."

"Not everyone," Zane said as he looked at the letter.

"Just open it and get it over with. You said he's disowned you. How bad can it be?"

With shaking hands, Zane tore the letter open. He felt a bit embarrassed to know that despite all the years and distance he had put between them, his grandfather could still intimidate him.

Dear Zane,

"It's from my grandmother," he said.

Dear Zane,
It is my sad duty to tell you that your grandfather departed this world on June 24, 1867. While clearing out some of his papers I happened upon a stack of letters, all unopened and all addressed to me. I was thrilled to see that you were alive and well and willing to reach out to me even though I failed you and your dear sweet mother. There are so many things I want to tell you. Would it be possible for you to make a trip to the city for a visit? If not, I would be happy to come visit with you and see the sights that Wyoming has to offer. As I have never ventured much farther than our front gate in all these years, I must admit that the thought of traveling such a great distance frightens me, but if that is the only way

*I can see you, then I will do it. Please telegraph
me as soon as possible and let me know. I anxiously await your reply.*

> Mrs. Rose Averitt Cunningham

"It came a month ago. I wonder if she's given up on
my answering her," Zane said after he read the letter
aloud to Mary.

"There's only one way to find out."

"Should we go to New York?"

"Don't you think you should go alone?"

"No. Never again. I want you by my side. I want her
to know you." Zane looked into her eyes. "Do you
mind leaving Marcus?"

"Marcus will be fine," Mary said. "Can we get married first?"

"As soon as possible. Ty can do it. He's a lawyer and
a justice of the peace. Or Jake can do it, since he's the
sheriff. We could even get the preacher to do it if you
want. Although he might drop dead when I ask him. I
don't think he held out much hope for me."

"I did," Mary said. "Even when I knew you were
incorrigible."

"Are you still keeping that list?"

"Always."

"Maybe I can add some good things to it," Zane said
as he wrapped his arms around her.

"Like what?"

"Husband, father, happily ever after?"

Mary looked up into his dancing hazel eyes. "That
will do for a start," she said.

"I love you, Mary."

"I love you, Zane. Forever." She looked up at him with a mischievous smile. "I just have one question."

"What is that?"

"Is Lucifer going with us?"

New York City, 1882

The four girls sat like stair steps on the sofa in a comfortably worn parlor of a mansion on Fifth Avenue. Bright summer sunshine poured through the window along with a soft breeze. The hustle and bustle of the street could be heard above the restless movement of feet that didn't quite reach the floor.

"How long does it take, Daddy?" the littlest one said. Her big brown eyes were wide with worry.

"It won't be here until it gets here," Mary Rose said. She was the eldest at fourteen and had, after all, been through this before.

"But what about Mamma?" Rachel asked again with trembling lips.

"Come here, sweetie," Zane said as he knelt on the floor. Three-year-old Rachel ran into his arms and immediately started playing with the buttons on his shirt.

"Mamas do this all the time," he said. "Mamas are used to having babies."

"Does it hurt?"

Zane looked over the dark curls at his oldest daughter, who had just blossomed in the past year into a beautiful young woman with gentle curves and a sudden maturity about her. She had the elegant poise of her grandmother and namesake.

Grandmother Rose had been thrilled at the birth of Mary Rose. Even more so when Emily came along, named after Zane's mother. Then there was Amy. Rose had died before Rachel came, died in her sleep with a gentle smile on her face.

She had made up for a lot of missed time in the ten years she had with her only grandson.

Zane had learned a lot also. He had found out that his mother had had a twin brother, Zachery, who died when just a small boy from the chicken pox.

As Zane had almost died of the same disease. It was one of his greatest fears that his daughters might catch the dreaded disease also.

But he knew he needed to let them live life, experience it. So instead of locking them behind doors and closed curtains as he and his mother had been imprisoned, he exposed them to the world. They spent their summers in Wyoming. And in return, the children of the Lynch ranch came to New York and went to school when they were old enough.

Chance and Fox were now grown men. Chance was back at the ranch, which he loved more than anything. Fox had gone on to tour Europe for a year.

Jacey and Faith had just left New York to go back home. They both had one more year of school left. They'd taken Will and Robin with them. They had just finished their first year.

Then Cameron and Ryder would be arriving.

Even though Zane and Mary now lived in New York, they had remained close to the people they'd left back in Wyoming. They were family.

Zane now ran the company left to him by his grandmother. He had been surprised to see how diversified the business was. He was involved in shipping, mining and railroads. He also owned a publishing house. It had been a learning experience.

This summer would be different, however. Their fifth child was coming. There was no way they could make a trip to Wyoming. They did own a house down by the shore. When the baby was old enough, they could go down there for a few weeks.

What was taking so long?

"Why don't you girls go out in the garden and play for a while?" he suggested. "Rosie, will you watch them?"

Rosie stuck out her lower lip. It was hard being trapped in the world between children and adults. She realized at the last minute that the mature thing to do would be to watch her sisters, so she herded them down the hall and out the door to the garden.

Zane followed along, because he really didn't know what else to do. He paused at the door and looked out at the marker that was the centerpiece of the garden.

Lucifer's grave.

Zane had no way of knowing how old Lucifer had been when he'd come into his life. Probably about the same age as Glory, who was still fat and sassy back on the ranch. The goat had died last year. Died in Zane's arms as he sobbed over his loss.

Zane later told Mary it was the hardest thing he had ever gone through. Crying over that dang goat.

"At least he got to die in your arms," Mary said. "That's where I'm planning on going."

Zane had dug the grave himself and then had the

marker made with Lucifer's name on it. The girls had even held a memorial service for him. He had been their pet also. Of course, everyone who came to the house thought it was strange that the family had a goat lying before their fireplace like a dog.

Maybe he should get a dog now.

The house was deathly quiet. He had given the servants the day off. No need to have them creeping around the house, trying to stay out of his way, yet wondering how the birth was going.

What was taking so long?

There was no noise coming from upstairs. Shouldn't there be? Why did the city doctors and midwives think it was a crime for a father to be present at his child's birth?

Zane recalled watching Chance being born and knew that Chase had been there for all his children's births. He had even delivered Jacey, and Cole had been there for that. Jake had stayed in the room with Shannon. Ty had been there for Cat.

"Dang it!" he said and took the stairs two at a time.

"Mr. Brody!" the midwife exclaimed as he walked through the door.

Zane ignored her and went straight to the bed.

"How are you?" he asked.

Mary was soaking wet with sweat. "Hot," she said. "Thirsty."

"She must not drink anything," the midwife insisted.

Zane looked at the doctor, who just shrugged. He left most of the work up to the midwife.

"I wish we were in Wyoming," Mary said as she tossed against the sheets and pillows. "There's probably a cool breeze blowing there."

"There's one blowing here, too," Zane said. He went to the window and opened it wide. The curtains instantly billowed as a cool breeze blew into the room.

"Mr. Brody, the air is dangerous," the midwife protested.

"If fresh air is so dangerous to babies, then how is it that we have so many grown-up Indians?" he asked the woman.

She clamped her mouth shut, and Mary managed a smile as he sat down on the edge of the bed and took her hand.

"Problems?" he asked.

"Just one so far," Mary said, looking at the midwife. "I really wish Marcus was here."

"You know he would be if he could. If he knew."

"I know." A spasm silenced her for a moment. "It just seems like this one is taking too long."

"You mean she's not impetuous like her mother?"

"It's a boy this time. It has to be," Mary panted.

"Boy or girl, I don't care."

"Yes, you do," Mary argued. "Oh, my!"

"Is it bad?" Zane asked, helpless to do anything about her pain.

"Remember Two Bulls?"

"Every time I look in the mirror."

"Well, just imagine he's inside." She was panting hard. "Cutting his way out with his knife."

"Ouch!"

"Oh, my. It's coming!"

"You're in the way, Mr. Brody," the midwife said.

"Stay here," Mary commanded. She hung on to his hand as her gown was shoved up. "I need to push."

"I can see the head," the doctor said. "Go ahead and push."

Mary bore down. She had done this before. Zane watched in amazement as a head appeared, followed by a shoulder and then a torso.

"It's a girl," the doctor announced.

"Oh, my," Mary said as she fell back. "I'm sorry."

"She's perfect," Zane announced as he looked at the tiny girl before she was snatched away by the midwife.

"Why does it still hurt?" Mary gasped. "I still need to push."

The doctor looked again. "There's another one."

"Twins?" Zane asked.

"Oh, my," Mary said.

"Push!" the doctor commanded.

"Mary?" Zane held on to her hand as she bore down again.

"This one is a boy!" the doctor announced as a wail hit their ears.

"Finally!" Mary said as she relaxed once again against the pillows.

"Mary, just look at him," Zane exclaimed. He took the child from the doctor and held him up. The tiny boy was perfect in every way as he squirmed around in his father's gentle hands, his eyes blinking and searching for life.

Mary reached out her hands and Zane placed him in her arms.

"I need to clean him up," the midwife said.

"In a moment," Zane replied. "So what should we call them?" He sat down next to Mary on the bed.

"I don't know. I think in my heart I was afraid to pick out a boy's name. Afraid I would jinx it."

"We could call him Lucifer," Zane said with his grin.

"Don't even say that," Mary scolded. "Naming our son after a goat."

"You are so easy to rile."

"How about Zachery?" Mary suggested, ignoring his comment. "I think it would have pleased your grandmother to know that we used his name."

"Zachery Marcus?"

Mary nodded in agreement.

"And what's your name to be, little one?" Zane looked down at the precious tiny girl.

"I've run out of people to name her after," Mary said. "Unless you want to start using our friends' names."

"You mean something like Jenny Cat Shannon Amanda Grace?" Zane grinned at his joke. The little girl broke into a wail. "I don't think she likes it. Besides, we used all those as middle names already."

"These are going to be the last names we pick out. Make it a good one," Mary commanded.

"Alice is nice," the midwife suggested. She took Zachery from Mary for his bath. The baby boy howled as soon as she picked him up.

"Isn't that her name?" Zane whispered to Mary who broke into a fit of giggles.

"Since she's the last and her brother's name starts with a Z, let's give her one, too," Mary said when she realized laughing was painful. "How about Zoe?"

"Zoe is nice. Miss Zoe Brody." Zane kissed the forehead of his youngest daughter and then placed her in her mother's arms. "I never thought I'd wind up like this, Mary. Stinking rich, living in New York City with five daughters and a son."

"If I recall, you said you wanted six sons. All like you."

"Dang, I'd kill myself if I had to raise six of me. I was just saying that because I wanted an excuse to—"

Mary tilted her head toward the doctor and midwife, who could hear everything they said.

Zane leaned forward and whispered in her ear. "Make love with you."

"Oh, my," Mary said.

He kissed her lips.

"I love you," he said.

Three words that he probably said a thousand times a day to the women in his life. Now he would get to say it thousands of times more.

Funny how it had gotten so much easier with practice.

Forgive the Wind
CINDY HOLBY

Caleb Conners returned from battle a changed man, uncertain whether he could still meet the rugged demands of ranching in Wyoming, unwilling to take up the drawing that had once been his life. With only half a leg, can he really perform as a whole man?

Amanda Myers knows what it means to live without hope, without dreams. For years she has been forced to do the will of others, but now she's landed in a safe haven on Lynch Ranch, bolstered by smiling faces, the laughter of children, and Caleb. When she looks upon his portrait of her, she sees a new vision of herself. Through his eyes she rediscovers her own purity and strength of purpose, and in him she finds the enduring love she's prayed for.

A Texan's Honor
Leigh Greenwood

Bret Nolan has never gotten used to the confines of the city. He'll always be a cowboy at heart, and his restless blood still longs for the open range. And he's on his way back to the boundless plains of Texas to escort a reluctant heiress to Boston—on his way to pick up a woman destined to be a dutiful wife. But Emily Abercrombie isn't about to just up and leave her ranch in Texas to move to an unknown city. And the more time Bret spends with the determined beauty, the more he realizes he wants to be the man in Emily's life. Now he just has to show her the true honor found in the heart of a cowboy.